This is for you, my dear niece, Terri Lee Piel. I was able to tap into your knowledge of coexisting with your wolf, Face, and Jake the parrot. I drew heavily on the fact that your wolf was intimidated by the parrot. And so, too, was my leopard intimidated by the hawk.

LORD OF THE NILE

LORD OF THE NILE

CONSTANCE O'BANYON

THORNDIKE
CHIVERS

This Large Print edition is published by Thorndike Press, Waterville, Maine, USA and by BBC Audiobooks Ltd, Bath, England.

Thorndike Press is an imprint of The Gale Group

Thorndike is a trademark and used herein under license.

LIBRARY OF CONGRESS CATALOGING-IN-PUBLICATION DATA

O'Banyon, Constance.
  Lord of the Nile / by Constance O'Banyon.
    p. cm. — (Thorndike press large print romance)
  ISBN-13: 978-0-7862-9880-8 (alk. paper)
  ISBN-10: 0-7862-9880-4 (alk. paper)
  1. Egypt — History — 332–30 B.C. — Fiction. 2. Romans — Egypt —
Fiction. 3. Large type books. I. Title.
PS3615.B36L67 2007
813'.6—dc22   2007026373

BRITISH LIBRARY CATALOGUING-IN-PUBLICATION DATA AVAILABLE

Published in 2007 in the U.S. by arrangement with Leisure Books,
a division of Dorchester Publishing Co., Inc.
Published in 2007 in the U.K. by arrangement with Leisure Books,
a division of Dorchester Publishing Co., Inc.

U.K. Hardcover: 978 1 405 64262 0 (Chivers Large Print)
U.K. Softcover: 978 1 405 64263 7 (Camden Large Print)

Printed in the United States of America on permanent paper
10 9 8 7 6 5 4 3 2 1

Prologue

Greece — Pharsalus Battlefield, 47 B.C.

General Tausret, otherwise known as Lord Ramtat, of the house of Tausret, emerged from Caesar's tent and paused for a moment to survey the devastation the Roman army had left upon the land. He was immediately assailed by the stench of the dead bodies that littered the battlefield, and he frowned as his gaze swept upward to the huge black scavenger birds that circled the skies. Smoke rose into the air as the corpses of friends, as well as foes, were tossed into huge bonfires, depriving the vultures of their prey.

Where only the day before the noise of war had been deafening, there was now a deep and heavy stillness. In this place two mighty warring forces had come together in a struggle of life and death, leading finally to triumph for Gaius Julius Caesar and defeat for Magnus Pompey. An eerie quiet fell across the encampment.

Caesar had been victorious, and the vanquished Pompey had fled to Egypt with what remained of his troops.

Ramtat flexed his hand, feeling pain shoot up his arm to the wound on his left shoulder. His shield had been battered and his sword bloodied, but he'd come away from battle with only minor injuries.

He turned his gaze in the direction of Egypt and drew in a long, steady breath.

Home — at last, he would be going home.

CHAPTER ONE

Egypt

Lady Danaë paced the corridor outside her father's bedchamber, as restless as the wild cats she trained. She had never known fear until now, and that fear was not for herself, but for the health of her beloved father. He had always been such a robust man, but in the past few days his health had failed; he'd stopped eating, and she was watching him waste away to a frail shadow of the man who had guided her life.

When the physician finally emerged from her father's room, her heart sank when she saw the concerned frown on his face. Tall and reedlike, Tobolt had bushy eyebrows that arched above intelligent eyes. Danaë had known Tobalt all her life; he was like a member of the family. She could tell by the grim expression in his dark eyes that the news he had to tell her was not good.

"Your father will see you now," Tobolt said

gravely. "Don't let him know that you are worried."

"Tobolt, be honest with me. What is his condition?"

The physician's gaze hit the floor so he wouldn't have to look into the young woman's eyes. "It grieves me to tell you your father's life can only be measured in days, perhaps hours." He patted her hand. "But you have known for some time this time would come. You have seen his health failing daily."

Danaë dropped down onto a stool and hung her head. Until now she had not allowed herself to admit how ill her father had become. Feeling immeasurable sorrow, she raised her head and searched the physician's eyes. "Only yesterday Father roused a bit and took some broth and a few sips of wine. Is that not a good —"

"Lady Danaë, do not cling to idle hope. You know in your heart your father is passing out of this world — into the next."

Her eyes filled with scalding tears, and she could hardly speak. "Is there naught you can do for him?"

Tobolt looked at her sadly. "The sickness that eats at his entrails has spread to other organs of his body. I have no skill to heal him and can only make his passing as painless as possible." He shook his head regret-fully. "He refuses to take the medicine that will help ease his pain until he has spoken to you. Go to him now, and try not to tire him."

Not wanting her father to suffer need-lessly, Danaë rose and gathered her strength to face what she must. When she entered the bedchamber, the air was heavy with the aroma of incense and healing herbs. Her heart was breaking as she gazed at the shrunken figure on the bed. His eyes were closed, and she dropped down onto a stool beside him, not wanting to disturb him if he was sleeping. She lowered her head and silently asked Isis to send peace to her father on his journey to the afterlife.

"My dearest child," her father said, lightly touching her hair. "Do not grieve for me. I go to tame animals for the gods, and I will be happy there — can you not think of my leaving in that way?"

She raised her head, her fingers trembling as they closed around his frail hand. "For your sake, I shall try."

He gave her a weak smile and then glanced away from her as if something weighed heavily on his mind. "I have much to relate, and I fear I have selfishly put it off for too long."

"There is no need to talk," she urged gently. "Please save your strength, Father."

"Danaë, this must be said — pay heed to me — listen well, for the rest of your life may depend on what you do after I am gone."

"I shall carry on as if you were still guiding my steps and giving me counsel," she said in a choked voice.

"Nay!" Lord Mycerinus's voice came out more harshly than he had intended, and he attempted to raise his head, but dropped back weakly against his headrest, gasping to catch his breath.

"Please don't distress yourself on my account, Father," she pleaded, fighting tears. "I would not have you be concerned about my future."

"Danaë, I wonder if you can forgive me after I tell you what I have kept hidden from you all these years. Keeping your mother's secret seemed the right thing to do at the time." He spread his hands in despair. "But now —"

She frowned. "You don't need to tell me that my mother was not of Egyptian blood — I already know that. I once overheard you and Minuhe talking — you were telling her that my mother had named me after her own Greek mother. I have also noticed that my skin is not dark like that of an Egyptian of full blood."

"That much is true," he admitted reluctantly, "but that is not what I have to tell you. Go to the big chest in the corner and bring me the small jeweled box you find inside."

She did as he bid, then dropped back onto the stool, running her fingers over the green silk box inset with rare green turquoise. "I have not seen this before, Father."

He closed his eyes, waiting for a bout of dizziness to pass. "Open it and remove what you find inside."

Danaë raised the lid and gasped as she lifted out a pendant in the shape of a coiled cobra. Never before had she seen an emerald as large as the one in the cobra's sunken eye. She met her father's gaze. "The cobra is a royal symbol. Was this given to you by the king when he made you Royal Animal Trainer?"

" 'Tis not mine — it belonged to your mother, and now to you. Place it around your neck and never take it off — but take precautions . . . keep it hidden from all prying eyes."

Puzzled, Danaë fastened the chain about her neck, the weight of the cobra falling between her breasts. She looked into her father's troubled eyes while a voice inside her head warned her he was about to divulge something she would rather not know. "You need not say anything more."

Lord Mycerinus gripped her hand as another pain hit him. Gasping, he waited until it passed before he spoke. "I've allowed you to look upon me as your father, and in this I have misled you."

Unease was growing in Danaë's mind. "You are my father."

After a long pause, Lord Mycerinus slowly shook his head. "No, you are not the child of my body, but you have always been the child of my heart. Keep that thought with you and try not to judge me too harshly."

It took Danaë a moment to find her voice, and when she did, it was hardly above a whisper. "I'm not your daughter?"

"Listen well, and try to forgive me. The year my own father died and left me lord of this household and lands, I was but a young man of nineteen years — two years older than you are now. It became prudent for me to make a journey down the Nile to Alexandria to purchase field slaves for the upcoming harvest. I'd never been so far from home without my father, and the sights and sounds of the city were like nectar to me."

Danaë felt like a brittle piece of papyrus that had been left too long in the sun to dry. She was ready to collapse from the anguish that cut through her. Her father blinked his eyes, and she saw tears in their shimmering depths. "You don't have to tell me this if it grieves you so."

Lord Mycerinus weakly raised his hand as if to silence her. "The crowd was sparse because it was two days before market day. I bought five slaves and was about to leave when I spied the figure of a woman huddled in the shadows. I asked the slave master to bring her into the light so I could better see her. When he led her forward and jerked off her soiled headdress, I stared at the loveliest woman I'd ever beheld — and the most frightened. I soon discovered why the slave master had been hesitant to bring her to the block — she was heavy with child. As you know, not many would buy a woman who is about to give birth, because the cost would be for the slave and the unborn child — the price of two. And many slaves die in childbirth, as happened to my beautiful Eilana."

Danaë felt as if some unseen force squeezed her heart; it took a moment to catch her breath. Everything she had believed in was a lie — the man she had loved like a father was, in fact, not her father at all. And her mother had been a slave!

Lord Mycerinus's eyes suddenly became clear as if his pain had subsided a bit. "The moment your mother raised her head to me that day and I gazed into her sad eyes, I was hit by a love so strong I had to drop back against the wall to remain standing. If only the slave master had known I would not have left there without Eilana, he could have asked any price and I would have paid it. I brought her home with me and took her as my beloved wife. Although she was loving to me, I always knew her heart belonged to another. But this I did not mind, for I loved her, and wanted only her happiness.

"All too soon, I held her in my arms as she lay dying." He turned his full attention on Danaë. "But I always had a part of my Eilana with me because I had you. You have been my most precious gift, and I have often thanked the gods for such a daughter."

Tears gathered behind Danaë's eyes, but she struggled to prevent them from falling. "If you are not my father, then who is?"

"Eilana told me naught about her past life, and I didn't press her. She did beg me to guard you well and keep you safe. I know that she had greatness somewhere in her lineage, perhaps even royalty, but the tomb holds its secrets, and you will most probably never know your mother's true identity. Perhaps that is for the best."

Lord Mycerinus nodded at the pendant. "You have already guessed that is no trinket, and it probably holds the key to unlock your heritage. But I caution you to leave it alone. Your mother was terrified of something, or someone, from her past, and there must have been a reason for her concern."

Danaë was confused, hurt, devastated. "Father," she cried in agony, going down on her knees and clutching his hand. "No daughter of your blood could love you more than I."

He gently touched her hand. "Promise me you will always think of me as your father. Promise!"

She tried to smile but could not. "That is a promise easy to keep."

From his expression and the way he avoided her gaze, Danaë knew he had more to tell her. "I have kept my promise to your mother, but I must go further and explain to you why I cannot leave you my land and possessions."

"I beg you, don't speak of such things, Father. It is of little matter to me."

"You must know that if you remain here you will be in danger. I see you can guess of whom I speak."

Danaë nodded. "My cousin, Harique." She shuddered; just invoking the name brought to mind the image of the man she despised above all others. "Harique is your nephew — your true blood. It is only right that he should inherit from you."

"Nay, that is not the reason," Lord Mycerinus said, taking a deep breath. "He knows the circumstances of your birth and that you are not my true daughter. If you are named my heir, Harique has threatened to expose your background and claim you as his slave. I can no longer protect you when I have gone to the afterlife."

Danaë well remembered how repulsed she had been whenever Harique turned his lustful gaze upon her. She shuddered with disgust just thinking about him. Harique had been blessed by the gods with a handsome face and a strong body — but inside he was malevolent and lecherous. Danaë had always taken great care to avoid being alone with him on the occasions he'd visited the villa. "You think he will force me to marry him."

"As bad as that would be, it will never happen," Lord Mycerinus said with conviction. "He already has a wife, and should he put her aside, he would lose her wealth. And

I know Tila well enough to guess she would never allow Harique to have a second wife."

Fear and sorrow battled for control of Danaë's battered emotions. "What, then, must I do?"

"I have made arrangements so your future will be secure," Mycerinus told her. "I would have done all this sooner, but my nephew was in the north with Ptolemy's legions. May I be forgiven for praying the gods would strike him down in battle. For had he died, you would have gone through life believing I was your true father. As it is, Harique has already heard of my illness, and my informant tells me he and his entourage are within days of the villa. You must be gone before he arrives."

"I'll not leave you, Father," Danaë said with a stubborn tilt to her chin. "Don't ask it of me."

"Heed me well. You are to go to Uriah in Alexandria — he is the only person I trust with your safety. You will leave before first light on the morrow."

Uriah was a Jew who had been Danaë's teacher for many years, and she loved him almost as much as her father. Uriah now handled her father's affairs in Alexandria, as well as other parts of Egypt. Under his skillful management, Mycerinus's holdings had

19

doubled. But even the joy of being reunited with her beloved teacher failed to lessen her pain. "Father . . ." A tightness in Danaë's throat kept her from speaking. She swallowed several times and buried her head against his shoulder. Finally she raised her head and looked into his eyes. "I cannot go from you at this time — you need me."

Lord Mycerinus's voice suddenly became stern. "As you love me, Daughter, you will do what I say. I have given Uriah instructions concerning your future. Faraji, my most trusted guard, will stay at your side. Have no fear — all has been arranged."

Looking at Danaë, Lord Mycerinus saw so much of her mother in her. She had the same black hair and delicate bone structure — the same brilliant green eyes. Her features, so unlike those of Egyptian women, had caused Danaë a great deal of embarrassment because people often stared at her when she ventured outside her home. She was so innocent, she had never realized it was her unusual beauty that drew attention.

She looked at the old man sadly. He had always been a wonderful father to her — patient and understanding, never raising his voice in anger even when she made mistakes. He had seen that she was well educated and had inspired her with love for the written word. They had shared a passion for the animals they'd trained together, and she wondered what she would do without him in her life.

"I will do as you say, Father," she assured him. "But know that my heart is breaking."

"As is mine."

She saw his jaw tighten and knew the matter was causing him undue distress. Calling on all her fortitude, she vowed to herself she would make it through their last moments together without crying. "I'll go to Uriah in Alexandria as you wish. But what about Obsidian and Tyi — I cannot leave them behind."

"The leopard and your falcon would both die of grief if they were separated from you." He paused as pain ripped through him. After a moment, he said, "Their transport has been arranged."

"I am afraid, Father," Danaë admitted.

"Overcome your fear and uncertainty, my daughter — put your sadness aside for now. Trust that I am doing what is best. I've seen great strength in you, and you will need it for what lies ahead. There are tasks you must undertake for me when you reach Alexandria."

"Anything, Father."

"Jabatus, the cheetah, you are to deliver to

21

the palace. Seven days ago a dispatch arrived from young King Ptolemy — he requested an exotic cat, and Jabatus is worthy of a king. When you give the cat to King Ptolemy, you must take no payment, but present him as a gift."

"If that is your wish."

His fingers gently drifted down her cheek. "My child, I've been laying down good will for your future. It is my hope that King Ptolemy will take you under his protection." He grimaced in pain. "Should Harique cause you trouble, I am counting on the king to remember your generosity and stand as your friend." He blinked his eyes as if trying to recall what he wanted to say. "In your name, I have sent to Kheleel, the high priest of Isis, the albino tiger skin. Kheleel can be a very powerful ally and will look on you with favor as the donor of a rare and valuable gift."

Danaë knew that both the cheetah and the albino skin were worth a king's ransom. "I understand."

Lord Mycerinus attempted to smile, but it came out as a pained grimace. "I'm hoping the king will bestow my title on you. Although the title has never gone to a female, I have told him about your talent each time I stood before him. There is not a wild creature you cannot tame if it has never been corrupted by eating uncooked flesh." He sighed, looking into her eyes. "Be cautious of those who stand beside the young king — they are cunning and conniving."

"You are saying I should not trust them."

"Never. I cannot say why, but I've always believed you have some connection with the royal house. Take care when you are among them."

They were far removed from the intrigues of Alexandria, but Danaë had been tutored well on the policies of Egypt, and she had her own opinions. "I don't believe the royal family will pay much notice to me."

"At the moment, King Ptolemy has the greater force of Egyptians fighting for him, while Cleopatra has no more than a ragtag army. Although King Ptolemy is but a figurehead surrounded by a corrupt council, it is my hope that he will rise above those men and become the king we need him to be." He closed his eyes briefly, and then focused on her once more. "My body fails me, but I must not fail you. And it is my hope you find a friend in the king."

Dread and unrest stirred inside her because she knew naught about court life, or even how to approach a royal. But her father was a wise man, and she trusted his guidance in all things. Seeing that he was tiring, and the lines on his face were deeply etched, she leaned over and kissed his forehead. "Thank you for the wonderful life you've given me."

He touched her cheek, and she almost cried out when she saw the tears in his eyes. "Farewell, daughter of my heart." Then he reached for her hand and gripped it. "Trust very few with what I have told you today. If word were to reach the wrong people's ears, and if they could put the pieces together about your birth, they might use you for their own gain. Take heed that you trust no one but the friends you are sure of."

"I will be careful," she assured him, watching as he closed his eyes; the rise and fall of his chest was labored.

After a while, Tobolt returned to give her father the medicine that would ease his pain.

She sat there long afterward, quietly watching her father sleep. She had much to ponder, and all of it was heart-wrenching. When early afternoon shadows crept across the room, she kissed her father's cheek and quietly left. The knowledge of where her life was taking her was almost more than she could endure — but endure it she must.

It was early afternoon when Danaë found her way to the training grounds. She had grown up watching her father train wild animals. When she was but a young girl, not past her fourth summer, he had taken her into the training pens and begun instructing her how to train the animals.

How long ago that seemed now.

Danaë unhooked the cage that housed the monkeys, and her favorite, Sada, leaped into her arms.

Choking on tears, Danaë placed a kiss on the monkey's head, then put her back inside the cage. Her father had always told Danaë she had natural instincts for training animals and had praised her on how well the animals took to her. She paused before the lions' cage and reached through the bars to stroke the spiky mane of the big male. He licked her fingers, and she smiled sadly, moving down the cages, mentally saying good-bye to each animal, knowing she'd not see them after this night.

Good-byes were so painful — the servants she'd known all her life, the animals she'd loved and trained, and most of all, the man she had always thought of as her father.

Sadly she left the training pens and returned to the house. Tomorrow she would leave her home, never to return, and it was breaking her heart.

Ramtat stood at the bow of Caesar's warship, listening to the even rhythm of the drums setting the tone for the oarsmen. He watched the ship cut through the darkened sea, each stroke of the oars taking him closer to Egypt and home after two years at Julius Caesar's side. But he would find no peace there, for war was raging in his homeland, tearing it apart. He studied his hands, thinking of the sword he'd wielded, the enemies he'd slain. Ramtat was weary of war, but when he returned home, he would be forced to once more take up the sword.

Only Caesar could end the bitter squabble between Cleopatra and her brother, Ptolemy.

CHAPTER TWO

Home to Danaë was a villa several leagues from the ancient village of Akhetaten. To her, it had been the best of all possible worlds. Her father's property stretched from the fertile Nile valley as far as the barren desert land. Unable to bear the sorrow of her father's imminent death and of being forced to leave her home, Danaë did the thing she always did when she was troubled.

She ran.

Running usually cleared her head and lessened her worries. Today she had run farther and faster than was her habit, but it hadn't lessened the pain, so she continued to run. Her legs were long, and her body firm from the exertion of training animals. She could run long after others had tired.

A falcon circled above her in the white-hot sky. She dodged thorn bushes and hurdled over the outer crumbling walls of what had once been a mighty city. Time and sand had eaten away most of the structures, and the encroaching desert had done the rest — the history of the city had been forgotten by the passing of time, and it had gradually crumbled back into the desert from whence it came. It always made Danaë a little sad that no one remembered the name of the ruins or the race of people who had once laughed and loved there.

Her beloved Egypt was old — as ancient as time itself; there were probably many such cities buried by the desert sand and forgotten.

Earth met sky on the distant horizon, and Danaë felt small and insignificant compared to the sheer vastness of the land. Her spirit was tied to the desert, and it was there that she felt most alive. But tomorrow she must leave forever this place that was in her blood, in her very soul.

She tried to clear her mind of grief and concentrate on the many honors her father had earned in his lifetime, the most prestigious being that of Royal Animal Trainer — a title bestowed upon him by the late king. Her eyes were swimming with tears, but they dried on her cheeks quickly in the hot desert wind. In the distance were several huge sand dunes, some as high as the great pyramids themselves; one was so huge it blocked out the sky behind it. Danaë paused and bent, bracing her hands on her knees in an attempt to catch her breath.

She'd gone farther than she'd intended — just over the next rise was an oasis frequented by trade caravans. Gauging the distance, she pondered if it would be better to return home or go on to the oasis where she would find fresh water and shade. The desert was a treacherous place with its shifting, changing sands; even those who thought they knew it well could become lost and wander aimlessly until death overtook them.

When she reached the top of the next sand dune, she saw the oasis in the distance. The wide leaves of date palms were waving in the wind, beckoning to her with their promised shade. She leaped over a rock formation that appeared to be honed out of granite and seemed out of place in this desert setting. When she reached the oasis, she paused long enough to take several deep breaths, knowing it would be madness to take a drink of water before she'd cooled down. Dropping to her knees, she splashed water in her face, then cupped her hands and took small sips until her thirst was satisfied. With a sigh, she leaned against the rough bark of the palm tree and watched a lizard dig its way beneath the scorching sand.

Danaë looked up at the falcon that circled above her and watched the bird of prey catch the wind current and drift gracefully downward. With a smile, she extended her arm, and the falcon landed on her leather glove. She stroked the soft feathers at the bird's neck and planted a kiss on his dark head.

"Tyi, what a useless creature you are. Did you stop to devour some luckless prey before catching up with me?"

The falcon cocked his noble head and blinked his amber eyes as if he understood her words. She glanced up at the lush foliage that acted as a canopy protecting her from the burning sun. Although it was only mid-morning, the temperature would be unbearable when the sun hit its zenith. Her gaze skimmed along the sand dunes that rose and fell like waves in the ocean. The oasis was on the caravan route between Bita and Crimea. She tried to imagine what wonders could be found in those faraway cities at the end of the caravans' journeys.

Danaë could tell by the spicy aroma that still lingered in the air, and by the deep impressions left by camel hooves in the mud, that a caravan had passed this way earlier in the day. Shards of sunlight broke through the swaying palm fronds, and she stood, stretching her muscles. Going up on tiptoe, she plucked a fat date, and although it wasn't quite ripe, popped it into her mouth.

Danaë would miss the desert and she lingered for a while saying good-bye. Tyi flapped his wings and gave a cry as he took to the air. Danaë's hearing was keen, and she detected the sound of a large animal nearby. It wasn't until she saw the black leopard appear over the low rise to the west that she became aware of being stalked by the cat.

She turned her head into the breeze and watched the sleek leopard move gracefully toward her, then braced herself as the cat leaped at her with a force that took them both to the ground.

"Obsidian," she said, scratching behind the cat's ear, "get off me — you're much too heavy." The cat was huge, with corded muscles and sharp claws that could rip prey apart, but she was gentle with Danaë. The creature licked her face, making her turn away to avoid the lapping tongue.

"I told you to get off me!" Danaë said, trying to shove the cumbersome beast off her.

Still the cat pressed against her, so Danaë slid her fingers into the thick black fur, and Obsidian purred with contentment. The black leopard was a rare color; most of her species were tawny with darker spots. Danaë shoved against the muscled neck, and reluctantly the animal moved off, turning her back as if pouting.

"You naughty cat — you broke out of your cage again, didn't you?" Danaë scolded.

Obsidian flexed her muscles and turned her sleek head to regard Danaë with a lazy gaze that made her owner laugh. Only last year a committee from a nearby village had presented her father with a petition that the leopard be forbidden to run wild and, furthermore, that the beast be kept penned at all times. Even though they now kept her caged when she wasn't with Danaë, it was too late to change the cat's habits. Obsidian's ways had already been set, and she was accustomed to roaming free.

Danaë tapped the black head with her fingertip, and green eyes stared into hers. "You know you did wrong."

Obsidian stalked to the watering hole and bent to drink while Danaë glanced around to make certain no one was nearby to report the cat was on the loose. "We must go now!" she said in a tone of voice that was meant to be obeyed. "I said now!"

Obsidian showed her annoyance with a subtle hiss that only made Danaë laugh. When the cat brushed against her leg, and her tongue lapped out to lick her fingers, Danaë knew she had already been forgiven.

As she started running toward home, Danaë glanced upward where Tyi gracefully glided on the wind currents. The falcon had always been jealous of the cat, and today he was showing his displeasure by swooping toward Obsidian, and then soaring up to catch another wind drift, then diving at the cat once more. Oddly enough, Obsidian was intimidated by Tyi and flinched with each dive the bird made.

On reaching the fruit orchard at the outer perimeter of the villa, Danaë finally slowed her pace, her hand on Obsidian's studded collar to signal the cat to stay at her side. When she reached the vineyard, the pickers paused in their work to cast terrified glances at the big cat, so Danaë paused only long enough to pluck a ripe grape and eat it. Fields of grain waved in the distance, and Tyi spread his wings and headed in that direction in search of small game.

This was her world, and she knew she was looking at it for the last time. She was heavy-hearted when she and Obsidian passed beneath the shade of the tall, grace-ful cypress trees, her movements scattering birds from their nesting places. They pro-gressed down a well-worn path toward the sprawling, mud-brick, whitewashed house. Step by step, the leopard matched her pace and stayed even with her when they reached the household gardens where the heady scent of sage filled the air. Danaë watched Tyi dip and glide elegantly through her bedroom window where the bird's perch was kept.

Unlike the field workers, the kitchen slaves paid little attention to Obsidian, who often wandered the house. Most of them had watched her grow from a cub to a full-sized leopard. Danaë moved down the narrow hallway to her bedroom with Obsidian at her heels. "In your cage," she said in a com-manding voice. "No — don't look at me like that. In your cage!"

The animal balked.

"Do it!"

With an irritated swish of her tail, Obsid-ian finally complied.

Bending down, Danaë examined the wooden closure that had been chewed through. "I see how you did this. I shall have to get something stronger to keep you in the cage — especially since we will be traveling," she sighed.

Again the black tail swished with displeasure. Danaë laughed and ruffled the animal's fur. "Don't worry, I'll allow you out later, and you can sleep at the foot of my bed tonight." Lifting a stool, she braced it against the cage door, knowing that if Obsidian wanted to escape, such a flimsy barrier would not deter her.

Removing her leather glove, Danaë hung it on a peg, just as her maidservant, Minuhe, entered the room with a fresh jug of water.

Minuhe had soft brown eyes and was tall and thin. She was an attractive woman with nice features, and like Danaë, she cared little for wigs of any kind. She dressed in plain white linen, her dark hair swept back from her face with ivory combs.

"Mistress, the physician asked me to inform you that your father is resting peacefully; he has given the master an herb drink that will let him pass to the other world without pain."

Guilt slammed into Danaë — she should have remained at her father's bedside today instead of running off into the desert. Hurriedly she went down the hallway to his chamber. Long into the night she sat beside his bed, but he never stirred. Twice Tobolt entered, giving her father medication so he would continue to rest.

It was only two hours before dawn when Minuhe came for her. "The animals have been taken to the boat. It is time for us to leave."

Danaë bent to kiss her father's cheek, knowing she would never see him again in this life. Her hand brushed across his brow, but still he didn't stir. "I love you, Father," she said as she moved toward the door. Danaë didn't stop or look back, fearing she would be unable to leave if she did.

A cart was waiting out front, and Minuhe led her charge toward it. Since her leaving had been kept secret, none of the servants had gathered to bid her farewell. Faraji, the guard who would accompany them to Alexandria, was mounted on his horse, and he acknowledged Lady Danaë, while his gaze swept the surroundings, looking for trouble of any kind.

Danaë settled on the cushioned seat, and Minuhe climbed in beside her. It was but a short distance to the boat landing, but with each turn of the cart wheel, Danaë felt the distance yawning behind her. Sweet memories swirled through her mind as she left the only home she'd ever known.

"How long have you known that your master was not my real father?" Danaë asked Minuhe, keeping her voice low so the man who drove the cart would not hear her.

The servant met her steady gaze. "I was but a young woman when the master brought your mother to the villa. I helped the midwives deliver you, and I later prayed to the gods to save both you and your mother. You were given into my care that day."

Danaë looked at Minuhe accusingly. "You should have told me. I've always told you everything."

"I was sworn to secrecy," she said, as if that excused everything. "Your mother kept her own secrets, and though she was afraid for you, she died peacefully after I promised to guard you with my life."

Danaë's mother was a faceless shadow creature to her, and her real father she would never know; the man who had raised her and loved her as his own was her only family. "It's almost more than I can bear to think of Father dying alone. It seems wrong that I cannot stay to see that he's properly interred before I leave for Alexandria."

"That you cannot do! The master fears that Harique will arrive before you get safely away." Minuhe shook her head regretfully. "Your cousin's rage will be fearsome when he finds you gone. He will search for you."

Danaë nodded, refusing to cry for fear she would be unable to stop. "What you say is true, but it will be difficult to leave everything I love behind." She met Minuhe's gaze. "Harique will be cruel to the slaves at the villa — I've seen how he treats his own slaves. If only I were a man, I'd stand up to him — but being a woman, I must run like a coward."

"No one would ever accuse you of being a coward. You will do what you must and leave the others to the care of the gods. They can no longer be your concern."

"How will I live without Father?" Danaë exclaimed, feeling as if the weight of ages rested on her young shoulders.

"Life is hard for you at the moment. But it will not always be so," Minuhe told her, brushing tangled hair from her face. "You have known the love of a father, and he has arranged your future with a guiding hand. That knowledge is what you must carry with you from this place."

"Yes, but —"

Minuhe patted Danaë's hand. "You must let go of the past. When you reach Alexandria, you will begin a new life."

"I'll try to remember that," Danaë said in a whisper. "But I see only darkness in the future."

"Hush now," Minuhe said with the familiarity of a well-loved servant. "Think only of the happy memories you have of the master."

Danaë bowed her head. The future looked very bleak.

CHAPTER THREE

Captain Narmeri impatiently paced the deck of his boat, his hands clasped behind his back, his gaze on the dock as he waited for his passengers. If they didn't come soon, he wouldn't get under way until the heat of the day. It was already sweltering, and he longed for the cool breeze he'd find in the middle of the Nile. He heard voices and moved anxiously to greet the daughter of Lord Mycerinus as she made her way up the gangplank. Lady Danaë was flanked by a dour-faced woman who stayed at the right hand of her charge, while a fierce-looking bodyguard clamped his hand on the hilt of his sword.

Captain Narmeri's gaze rested on Lady Danaë. It was said that she was a great beauty, and the captain was disappointed that she wore a heavy veil so he couldn't judge for himself. Lady Danaë kept her head lowered as she walked past a group of boatmen who were openly gaping at her, while her guard scowled at them and moved protectively closer to his mistress.

Captain Narmeri had often transported animals for the Royal Trainer and had even supped at Lord Mycerinus's home on two different occasions. He had once caught a glimpse of the daughter from a distance as she'd walked in the garden, but the night shadows had hidden her face from him.

The captain was taken by surprise when Lady Danaë paused in front of him, and his heart started pumping at twice the normal rate. No spoken word could pay homage to the beauty that was barely hidden by the thin veil she wore. Her features were delicate, her nose small and well shaped; her dark brows were black and perfectly arched. She somehow reminded him of a statue he'd once seen of a long-dead queen.

The captain wasn't normally sentimental where women were concerned, but this one's beauty was such that he thought she could strike a man dumb by a mere glance. The hair that fell over her forehead was as black as cinder. Her glorious eyes were outlined with kohl, and as green as the grass that grew along the Nile. But no, on closer inspection, perhaps they were more turquoise, like the waters of the Mediterranean

— or perhaps they were both. It was said that Queen Cleopatra had green eyes — but the queen was Greek, while this young woman was the daughter of an Egyptian.

How, then, did she come by those green eyes? he wondered, wiping his sweaty face on his sleeve. "Welcome aboard, Lady Danaë. I hope we can make your voyage as pleasant as possible."

"Thank you, Captain. Are the cats and my hawk comfortably settled?" she inquired softly.

The lady's voice was deep and melodic, and Captain Narmeri could have listened to her talk all day and all night. He cleared his throat and tried to concentrate on her question. "They are, Lady Danaë. I hope you will find everything on board to your liking."

In that moment, when she smiled and her eyes danced with humor, the captain became her willing slave.

"I'm certain to be comfortable. My father has often spoken of you, and as you know, you are the only boatman he ever trusts to transport our animals."

Captain Narmeri bowed to her. "Your father always honored me with his trust."

She nodded her head and moved away, leaving a lingering aroma of jasmine behind.

He knew that from this day forward, he'd never smell jasmine without thinking of her.

Suddenly Captain Narmeri was jerked out of his pleasant musing. One of his crewmen was staring in admiration at the lady, apparently unaware that her guard had whisked out his sword. Captain Narmeri smiled to himself, thinking the boatman was about to learn a valuable lesson that would serve him well, and also keep any other crew members from making such a foolish mistake.

"Dear lady," the boatman said admiringly, dipping into an awkward bow, "allow me to pay tribute to your beauty."

As if by magic, Faraji's sword slashed through the air, the point coming to rest at the poor fool's throat.

"Pay tribute to my blade!" Faraji said in a menacing tone. "For it will open you up from ear to throat if you don't move away. Now!" Faraji glanced about, catching the gazes of other boatmen. "Heed me well, any of you within the sound of my voice. Let no man approach my lady, or it will be the last earthly act he'll ever perform in this life."

Two of the boatmen quickly backed against the railing, while several other men hurriedly turned away to attend to their appointed tasks with renewed dedication.

"Sir, I meant no harm," the luckless boatman pleaded, unable to move without being cut by the blade. He licked lips that had suddenly gone dry. "I . . . I'll not look upon the lady again if you will but allow me my freedom."

"Then move along," Faraji said, sheathing his sword and giving the young fool a hefty shove. "If anyone else would like to test the point of my blade, let him come now. Otherwise leave my lady in peace."

Captain Narmeri shook his head grimly. "Let that be a lesson to all of you. Lady Danaë is my honored passenger, and you would do well not to trouble her or look in her direction. If you do, I will personally pluck out your eyes and feed them to the crocodiles, or maybe I'll just let good Faraji lop off your head."

Miraculously, the deck cleared, and all hands were occupied with their duties.

"Show me what space my lady is to occupy so I can see her settled," the guard said, his smoldering gaze sweeping the deck to make sure his orders had been heeded.

Danaë was grateful to have Faraji with her as she began her journey to her new life. Although she had felt pity for the young boatman who had been chastised and embarrassed before his crew mates, she was relieved that the men no longer stared at her.

The captain motioned for them to follow him across the deck. "Since the *Blue Scarab* is not a passenger ship, there are limits to the comforts I can provide, Lady Danaë. As you see, I've curtained off this area near the bulkhead so you can have more privacy. Notice also I have put the cheetah and the leopard within your reach as I was instructed to do. Your hawk is also there" — he pointed to a smaller cage — "while your trunks have been stowed below deck."

"You are most kind, Captain Narmeri, and have followed my father's instructions as always."

The captain looked pleased. "Please say the word if there is anything I can do for you. We will be getting under way at once."

As the captain left, Danaë bent down to Obsidian's cage and tested the lock, which was of reinforced metal. "This should discourage you from trying to escape." She tested the lock on the cheetah's cage as well and nodded in satisfaction, certain it would hold. She reached inside Obsidian's cage and stroked her soft fur, but the cat merely swished her tail and laid her head on her paws sulkily.

Taking a deep breath, Danaë moved to

the railing, where she glanced at the dock, which was now fading in the distance as the boat caught the wind and moved to the middle of the Nile. Although it was still mid-morning, the heat was already unbearable. She watched with only passing interest as a flotilla of barges drifted past, laden with their precious cargo of alabaster from the Hatnul quarries. If events had been different, Danaë would have looked upon this voyage as an adventure. As it was, her future was filled with uncertainty.

"Come out of the heat," Minuhe urged her. "See, I have made you a soft bed so you can rest."

"I was just thinking, Minuhe," Danaë said achingly. "I cannot imagine where the future will take me." A sudden cool breeze riffled her veil, and she lowered her head in misery. "I have no hope."

Minuhe could only shake her head. There were no words that would comfort her young charge.

Turning her head skyward, Danaë felt the heat of the sun dry her tears. Her gaze drifted down to the mud-colored Nile, and she tried to close her mind to the sadness that was consuming her. "I have always despised Harique for the weak man he is, but I now despise him even more because he has forced me to leave my father and my home."

"Don't speak of that evil man. You'll be safe under Uriah's watch, and you will never have to worry about Harique again."

Danaë felt the boat shift and glide forward as the sails filled, and the ship was soon running with the wind. "By now Harique has probably arrived at the villa, and if he is true to character, he has taken over the running of the place." She made a helpless gesture with her hands. "As I can do naught to stop him, I must leave my father's home to his cunning."

"That seems to be the way of it," Minuhe agreed sadly.

Danaë glanced across the deck of the *Blue Scarab* to her caged falcon, who gave several piercing calls that indicated he wanted to be released. The cheetah was accustomed to being confined in a larger area, but it seemed he had settled down nicely.

Obsidian was still sulking and had turned her back to Danaë, her tail swishing back and forth imperiously.

The captain yelled to his boatmen to put oar to water, and Danaë watched him set a course down the river. Captain Narmeri was a man of wide girth, and his features were fierce, his nose large and hooked as if it had been broken several times. His eyes were almost as black as his wig. A long scar cut deeply on the left side of his swarthy face, and his skin was as dark as old shoe leather. But she had no fear of the man because her father had trusted him.

At sundown the captain anchored the boat just off shore. Because of its sandbars and shallows, the Nile was much too treacherous to navigate at night. Danaë lay on a soft, spice-filled mat, and Minuhe pulled the mosquito net together and lay down at Danaë's feet. Faraji sat with his back against the bulkhead, ever watchful, his hand on the hilt of his sword. Danaë tossed and turned, thinking of her father — missing him and wishing she could be with him. Toward morning she finally fell asleep, lulled by the gentle swaying of the ship.

CHAPTER FOUR

"Lady Danaë," Captain Narmeri said, ambling up beside her, "I hope this first week of your voyage has been to your liking."

When he smiled, the jagged scar spread across his face, and anyone not knowing him for the good man he was might be frightened of him. "All has been very much to my liking, Captain," she said, trying to sound cheerful. "You have done everything to ensure my comfort." She glanced up at him worriedly. "I've never been this far from home, and I don't know what to expect when we arrive in Alexandria."

He looked at her kindly. "Your father said as much to me when he made the arrangements for your transport." His brow knitted in a frown. "Forgive me, Lady Danaë, but I must say that I was saddened to see your father's health failing. I didn't want to speak to you about Lord Mycerinus lest the subject cause you grief."

She had been tracing the progress of a papyrus skiff as it sailed close to shore, and his words renewed her pain. Not knowing how to reply and not wanting to talk about her father, she merely said, "My father is gravely ill. Thank you for inquiring about him, Captain."

"But," he said, watching the wind snap in the linen sails, "I promised Lord Mycerinus I would deliver you safely to Alexandria, and that's exactly what I intend to do." He nodded toward the cages. "The cats seem to be faring well. Although the black devil looks a bit unhappy."

"Obsidian is my personal pet. She is not accustomed to being caged for such a long period of time — and she has never been on board a ship. How much longer until we reach Alexandria, Captain?"

"All depends on the wind." He scratched his chin. "I would say if conditions continue as they are, three days. I don't know if you noticed it, but although the Nile flows toward the north, the wind blows to the south."

She nodded. "My father told me that Mother Nile is a marvel and sends us many gifts."

"Aye. That she does." The captain glanced

down at her, noticing how fair her skin was. "I'd caution you to stay in the shade today. Even with the cloud covering the sun, Ra's rays can burn you to the bone."

"I'll take your warning," she stated, so deep in thought she was hardly conscious of the captain's retreating footsteps until she heard him issue an order to one of his men from the other side of the ship.

Around the noon hour, the Nile narrowed enough for Danaë to see rocks in the shallows. The boatmen were forced to disembark and attach ropes to pull the ship forward. It was a hazardous task, since the shores were infested with crocodiles. There were other hazards as well: hippopotamuses frolicked in the muddy waters, and on many occasions had been known to capsize a ship. A further irritant was the gnats and mosquitoes that pestered them when the wind wasn't blowing to keep them away. As evening approached, the sun painted the sky dark vermilion. A short time later, the wind kicked up, filling the sails, and the *Blue Scarab* lurched forward, much to everyone's satisfaction.

It was almost dark when the captain steered the vessel to the shallows and secured it for the night at a small river port. When full dark struck, Danaë was glad she had a small lantern. She watched the flickering light fall across Minuhe's face and asked, "Do you mind very much leaving the villa and moving to Alexandria?"

Minuhe looked startled for a moment, because she had not expected such a question. A slave did as she was told, and no one ever asked if she minded. "Long ago I began to think of the villa as my home. Then one day I realized that my home will always be wherever you are. You have become the daughter I could never have."

"It seems you and my father both think of yourselves as a parent, but I'm the daughter of no one," Danaë remarked glumly. When she saw the distress etched on Minuhe's face, she forced a smile. "I'm happy to have you with me. Yours is the face I remember from infancy."

"My only wish has always been to care for you."

Danaë lay back and closed her eyes. Sleep soon took her, and she did not waken until she heard loud voices as the crew took on provisions.

Captain Narmeri was glad they had finally left the Nile valley behind and were sailing on the smooth waters of the sea. The sun was at its zenith, and the weather was hot and balmy without the slightest breeze to stir the limp sails of his small merchant ship. With growing concern, he anxiously glanced upward. The azure sky seemed to be reflected on the surface of the mirror-bright Mediterranean, and it was difficult to distinguish where one left off and the other began. Captain Narmeri felt a shiver touch his spine, and his eyes narrowed apprehensively. Last night he'd witnessed a shower of stars falling from the heavens — surely it had been a bad omen, a foretelling of disaster.

The good captain said a quick prayer that the gods would send a stronger wind to fill his sails and shorten the voyage. His men were getting restless and short-tempered — no doubt because there was a beautiful young woman on board, and they weren't allowed even to glance in her direction.

Captain Narmeri had another reason for feeling nervous: Even though his cargo of Nile fish was packed in kegs of salt, it would go bad if they didn't reach Alexandria within a day. He was startled out of his musing when his passenger stepped over a coil of hemp rope and came to stand beside him at the railing.

Until that moment, Danaë had kept much

to herself, and he'd known she was grieving for her father, who had surely passed to the other world by now. The captain couldn't guess why she was going to Alexandria at such a time, but it was not his business to know.

Danaë nodded toward Pharus Island as it appeared in the distance. "My father told me about the great lighthouse. He explained to me that it not only serves as a beacon but also gathers weather information. It is truly a wondrous sight, is it not?" The wind had kicked up, and she watched waves wash over the causeway that connected the island to Alexandria. "One has to witness it to understand how truly magnificent it is."

The captain tried to look at the familiar sight through her eyes. He had seen the lighthouse so many times, it had become commonplace to him. "It has guided me safely home on many a voyage," he said.

"Then you live in Alexandria?"

"I spend most of my life on the Nile, but when in port, I call that city my home."

"What will we find when we arrive?" she asked. "I know the king and queen are at war, and that must put a strain on the citizens."

"Shh," the captain cautioned. "Have a care. Don't speak of such things — you never know who might be listening. You can get your throat slit for merely mentioning either of them to the wrong person."

Danaë frowned, wondering which of the royals the captain preferred to rule Egypt, the brother or the sister. "I'll remember that," she remarked soberly. "Captain," she said hesitantly, "I would ask a favor of you."

At that moment she dropped her veil, and he stared at the loveliest woman he'd ever seen. Her neck was long and slender; her face shaped for beauty. Her eyes caught and held his gaze, and he could hardly bear to look away. In that moment he would gladly have granted her slightest wish. "Say what you want, and it is yours."

"My leopard, Obsidian — the black cat — is growing restless. She needs to be out of her cage." She saw his features harden and hurriedly went on to explain: "Obsidian is quite tame and would never harm anyone. You have observed that these cats eat only cooked meat. Neither one of them has ever tasted raw meat, nor do they crave it. Therefore, no one on board will be in danger from Obsidian." She smiled at him. "You have my word."

His first instinct was to forbid it, but the pleading in her eyes got the better of him. "You'll need to keep the animal on a chain," he said, knowing that this slight woman could not control the leopard if it should wish to escape its bonds. "Keep it at your side at all times."

"Thank you."

He glanced at his men, who were making ready to enter the port. "Stand over there." He nodded toward the bow. "Be warned — if she escapes her chain, I will have my bowman bring her down."

Danaë gave him a smile that made him forget that he was old enough to be her grandfather. "I have given my word."

"Go on," he said, "take her out."

Danaë hurried to the cage, and when she opened the door, Obsidian looked at her hopefully. The cat purred and rubbed against Danaë's leg as she clamped a chain around her neck.

"You will behave yourself, Obsidian," she said in a firm tone. She was so busy with the leopard, she hadn't noticed that ten huge warships, were coming toward them.

"A Roman fleet," Captain Narmeri yelled. "They bear down on us. Look to the oars and steer out of their path," he ordered his men. "Be quick about it!"

The warships had seemed to come out of nowhere, and Danaë watched in surprise as the lead ship gained on them.

"Look you well," Captain Narmeri stated, coming up to Danaë while making sure the leopard was on the other side of her. "Unless I miss my guess, that will be either Pompey or Caesar. Either one of them will only bode ill for Egypt if they are bringing their war to our shores. We have our own battles to contend with." He stared angrily toward the Roman ships and grumbled, "See how they force me to direct my course toward the lighthouse. We will be late getting into port."

Danaë brought Obsidian close to her body and moved to the edge of the deck. She could hear the drumbeat from the lead warship setting the pace for the oarsmen. She stared in wonder at the sight of the red sails with the symbol of a golden eagle — the emblem of Gaius Julius Caesar, would-be master of the world.

The warship sliced through the water, sending spray across the small merchant craft. Obsidian hissed, and the fur on her neck rose as the Roman ship neared.

Danaë noticed a group of soldiers standing near the railing, trying to get her attention, but she haughtily ignored them. Only one man stood apart and aloof, attracting her notice. He was tall, with broad shoulders, magnificently attired in a uniform of leather and bronze. He wore a helmet with a scarlet plume, and a scarlet cloak billowed out around him. He was so splendidly dressed, Danaë suspected he might be the great Caesar himself! But when he removed his helmet, she saw the man was much too young to be the battle-hardened Proconsul of Rome. Her eyes met his; then he boldly smiled at her and made a deep bow. Without thinking, she gave him a slight nod, then stepped back when the other Roman soldiers let out a raucous cheer.

She had never seen a Roman before and did not want to again. But that one had taken her breath away.

Lord Ramtat was distracted, his thoughts focused on the task that lay ahead; he hardly noticed the small fishing craft and merchant vessels as they gave way to the mighty Roman fleet. He frowned when several soldiers standing at the railing started making lewd comments about a huge black leopard and the dark-haired beauty who held its chain.

Ramtat's eyes widened in surprise when he beheld the young woman. She wore a white garment shot through with golden threads, and a wide green sash that was bound at her waist and fell to the toes of her golden sandals. Her upper arms were adorned with golden amulets, and another amulet encircled her shapely ankle.

"Now, that is someone I would like to know," one of the soldiers said, blowing her a kiss.

"Save your efforts," Ramtat said, smiling. "That, my friends, is an Egyptian maiden of some consequence — she will not even acknowledge you." He noticed that her eyes were outlined with kohl, but those eyes needed no adornment, he thought. He flashed her a smile and bowed as the two ships came so near he could almost have reached out and touched her. She returned his bow with a haughty nod of her head, sending her black hair spilling across her creamy shoulders.

Ramtat leaned his shoulder against the gunwale and crossed his arms, his gaze fastened on her, and he wondered who she could be. Although she looked Egyptian, those green eyes said otherwise. He had seen eyes that color before — Queen Cleopatra had that same emerald gaze. Perhaps this woman was also of Greek heritage.

Tribune Hirtius, Caesar's staff officer, jabbed Ramtat in the ribs. "If that lady is a sample of Egyptian females, I cannot wait to get off this ship. Would that I were that cat at her side."

"I would say she would be unusual in any society," Ramtat replied, knowing he would never forget the sight of the sultry beauty.

"Perhaps that is Cleopatra herself."

"Nay, Tribune. I know Queen Cleopatra, and even she cannot touch this lady in beauty," Lord Ramtat asserted, making a final bow to the mysterious woman, who haughtily turned up her pretty nose at him. "Although she is not the queen, I would venture a guess that one of her ancestors stood close to the throne; the resemblance between them is obvious."

"So you don't know who she is?"

"I know her not," Ramtat said quietly, his gaze turning to the papyrus merchant boat where the woman stood watching him. "But if the gods are kind, we shall soon meet."

CHAPTER FIVE

Captain Narmeri shook his fist and swore under his breath as two more Roman warships relentlessly bore down on his small craft, forcing him to give way and sail closer to Pharus Island. He took the helm himself as the boat rocked and swayed on the waves stirred up by the huge warships.

"Roman dogs!" he muttered. "Think you own the world, and that everyone else should give way to you."

Danaë leaned her elbows on the railing, observing the lead ship, which carried Caesar's banner, as it docked at Pharus Island. She watched with interest as one of the Romans disembarked. "Why would anyone connected with Caesar want to go ashore at the lighthouse?" she asked. "Surely they have come to Egypt on important matters. Why do you suppose they want to examine our lighthouse?"

"Who can tell how a Roman thinks?" the

captain muttered. He nodded toward her leopard. "Put the cat back in —" He suddenly broke off. "Son of Ra! Look you — someone on the island has run up the white flag, and we are being hailed. More delays! They want me to dock and pick up a passenger."

"Is it unusual for someone from the island to hail a passing ship?" Danaë inquired, squinting to see who was waiting on the dock just ahead.

"Aye, most unusual. It's never happened to me before." He stood at the rudder and commanded his men to adjust the sails to bring the *Blue Scarab* alongside the pier that jutted out into the sea.

When they had docked, the captain hurried ashore, and Danaë went to the cage and ordered Obsidian back inside. Her attention was centered on getting the balking leopard in her cage, so she didn't hear the captain return with his passenger. Hooking the cage door securely, Danaë became aware of a stranger's voice, and she quickly stepped behind the netting, where Minuhe joined her.

"Thank you for halting your voyage for me, Captain. The lighthouse guard informed me that you were a cargo ship, so I assumed you would not mind taking me on board since you had no passengers to be inconvenienced."

The captain was standing between Danaë and the newcomer, so she could see no more than a pair of sandal-boots laced high on a pair of muscular legs. When the captain shifted his weight a bit, Danaë noticed the scarlet plume on the Roman's bronzed helmet. He was without doubt a high-ranking officer. The tone of his voice was deep, and it puzzled her: Why would a Roman speak pure Egyptian without an accent?

Captain Narmeri said in an irritated voice, "I saw you when you left the warship, and it made me wonder what a Roman would be doing on Pharus Island. There is not much to see there unless you climb to the top of the lighthouse for a better view of Alexandria."

The newcomer's voice came out like the crack of a whip. "You saw naught, Captain." His tone went lower and became quieter, more menacing. "There was naught to see — do you understand me?"

Recognizing the danger that confronted him, Captain Narmeri took a hasty step backward. "You're right. My eyesight is not as good as it once was, and the glare from the sun was reflecting off the sea. Under those conditions I could see nothing clearly."

Danaë heard the fear in the captain's voice, and now that he'd stepped away from the soldier, she had a clearer view of the man. He wore a bronzed breastplate and a scarlet cloak fastened on each shoulder with golden disks. She realized he was no ordinary soldier, but a lord of men. He was the same man she had noticed on the Roman warship. His expression became grave, and his dark eyes penetrating as he stared at the captain.

"I see by your uniform you are ranked a general. What can a Roman general want of me?" Captain Narmeri asked. "Where am I to take you? I have produce on board that will spoil if I do not make it to Alexandria this day. I'm but a poor captain; I owe my living to the cargo I transport. Surely you can appreciate my dilemma."

"My good captain, If you don't stop your tongue from wagging," Ramtat warned, "it may very likely cause you to lose your head."

A gasp from Danaë drew the Roman's attention, and he stepped toward her with a quickness that took her by surprise. She froze when he brandished a dagger and sliced through the thin netting she stood behind, the point of the blade poised close to her breasts.

Time stood still as Danaë met Ramtat's gaze — she watched as his anger turned to confusion, and then he smiled, shoving his knife back into a bronze sheath.

"My lady, I did not realize this was the same vessel that passed us in the harbor." He bowed low, but his gaze remained watchful. "I ask your pardon if I frightened you in any way."

Several things happened at once. Sensing that Danaë was in danger, Obsidian hissed and clawed at the cage, trying to get out and protect her, and Faraji stepped forward with drawn sword, ready to defend her.

"It will be the worse for you if you do not step away from my lady," Faraji warned menacingly. "General or no, leave my lady in peace."

Ramtat, the seasoned soldier, drew his sword so quickly, the movement took Faraji by surprise. With a wide thrust, Lord Ramtat's blade tore Faraji's sword from his fingers and sent it swirling in the air to slide across the deck out of the guard's reach. The tip of Lord Ramtat's blade landed at Faraji's throat, pricking the skin and drawing blood. "One more move from you and you are a dead man," he warned.

Danaë quickly stepped forward and angrily shoved the blade away, wedging her body between Faraji and the Roman. "You will not touch him. We have done naught to you!"

Ramtat stared into her turquoise-green eyes for a long moment, and then smiled, shoving his sword back into his scabbard. "Bravery should always be rewarded, not punished."

Before Danaë could react or guess the man's intentions, he lifted her chin and lowered his head, his lips brushing lightly against hers at first, and then pressing hungrily. At first Danaë struggled, but when he deepened the kiss, her mouth softened against his.

Something fluttered inside her, and she forgot that everyone was watching and that she didn't even know this man's name.

Ramtat pulled back quickly, wondering what had just happened between them. He hadn't intended to kiss her, but now he wanted to kiss her again. He swallowed deeply and stared at her. "Perhaps I'm the one who's been grandly rewarded."

A blush stole up Danaë's face, and she regained her composure. Out of the corner of her eye, she saw Faraji hurry forward, and she knew she had to do something quickly or her brave guard would fall victim to the Roman officer's sword. "Step away from me, Roman," she commanded. And to her surprise, the Roman did just that.

Ramtat was bemused. He wanted to see this woman again. "Who are you? Where can I find you?"

She frowned at him, but she couldn't help staring at the mouth that had just given her so much pleasure. "Who I am and where I live are no concern of yours," she said, turning her back to him.

Faraji gripped Danaë by the shoulders and shoved her behind him, and Minuhe pulled her farther away from the officer. "Never come near my lady again," the guard told Lord Ramtat. "I will kill you if you do."

There was a long, tense silence while Ramtat and Faraji stared at each other. Ramtat knew the bodyguard was feeling shame because his lady had been forced to protect *him.* The maidservant was gripping her mistress's arm to keep her behind the guard.

Suddenly Ramtat laughed. "Perhaps, beautiful lady, we'll one day meet under different circumstances." He then turned and strode to the bow of the boat where he stood staring out at Alexandria in the distance, trying to pull his mind back to duty.

Danaë's heart was still pounding as she watched the Roman stand so still and impressive, his armor gleaming brightly in the sun, his head held at a proud tilt. Minuhe pulled Danaë farther into the netted area, and, after retrieving his sword, Faraji took up his stance as guard, his face red with shame.

"I thank you for protecting me," Danaë told him kindly, knowing he was suffering because the Roman had bested him. "You were very brave to put yourself between me and that man." When Faraji made no reply and wouldn't meet her eyes, she continued, "That man is a seasoned soldier and is trained to kill — you are not."

Faraji still kept his rigid stance, his sword unsheathed, and she watched him drop his head in shame.

With a sigh, Danaë settled beside Obsidian's cage and spoke soothingly to the cat, who had been disturbed by the confrontation. But her gaze kept going to the Roman, who seemed lost in his thoughts and gave little notice to anyone aboard the *Blue Scarab*.

Danaë was startled when she saw the Roman unhook his scarlet cape and toss it over the side of the boat. She was even more startled when he unbuckled his armor and tossed it over the side as well. His helmet was the last to go into the sea. The man now wore only his white tunic and leather sandals, and she realized he wanted to blend in with the populace when they reached Alexandria.

Why should he want to do such a strange thing? she wondered. None of it made sense to her — but then, she could not guess how a Roman thought. She touched her mouth and remembered his kiss. He was just a man who had accidentally crossed her path and would disappear from her life forever.

Even without his splendid armor, it was easy to see he was not a common man. But he looked younger, and less fierce, in the garb of a civilian. His black hair was clipped short in the Roman style. He was tall and lean; his body was quite beautiful. In that instant, he turned to look in Danaë's direction, and she wondered if he could see her behind the netting. Probably he could, since he gave her a bow, his expression mocking.

As soon as the boat bumped against the pier, Danaë watched the Roman toss a leather bag of coins to the captain, and she drew in a relieved breath when he leaped over the side of the boat and was soon swallowed up in the crowd. It puzzled her that he'd gone to such lengths to make sure no one knew he had sailed to Alexandria with the Roman fleet. She decided to dismiss him from her thoughts, and to hope she would never see him again. The last-minute activity of the boatmen drew her attention — the sails were tied off, and the crew was making ready to unload cargo.

Captain Narmeri came up beside her. "I am sorry about what happened. If I'd known it was a Roman who wanted passage on my boat, I would have sailed past the island without stopping."

"There is no reason for you to apologize, Captain. I have only praise for your actions. You made a long and difficult voyage a pleasant and safe experience for me and my servants."

With a serious expression on his face, the captain bowed. "Lady Danaë, I hope our paths will one day cross again. If you are ever in need of my assistance, you have only to send me word and I'll come to you. This is not an idle offer. I stand ever your friend."

She was touched by his sincerity. "I shall always remember that." Danaë looked up at him with uncertainty. "You will have the men take great care unloading the animals?"

He bowed. "As always, lady."

"May the gods smile upon you, good captain," she said, turning and moving across the deck. It didn't escape her notice that the crewman still kept their gazes averted, especially when Faraji moved beside her.

She watched the dockworkers busily loading and unloading cargo onto camels as well as ox-drawn carts. Throngs of people competed for space on the narrow road leading away from the harbor. Merchant ships from all over the world rode at anchor, and there were also the newly arrived Roman ships with well-armed soldiers crowding their decks.

Danaë doubted that anyone would challenge Caesar's right to go ashore. In the distance she saw the immense marble palace gleaming beneath the midday sun. Guards stood before the tall arched gateway, denying anyone without permission entrance to the sanctuary. Danaë could only imagine the magnificence that lay behind those walls.

Everything else went out of Danaë's mind when she spied Uriah, her beloved teacher, standing among the crowd. With a happy smile, she waved to him and rushed down the gangplank. Her first step on land was jarring, and it took her a moment to adjust to the strange sensation. She watched Uriah approach, his gaze sad.

"Lady, my heart is gladdened at the sight

of you, but I am saddened by the reason that brought you here."

She went into his arms and laid her cheek against the roughness of his woolen robe. "Have you had word of my father?"

"Nay, lady." He raised her head so he could look into her face. "Your arrival precedes any word from the villa."

She nodded. "I am not surprised."

"I have a cart for the trunks and the animals. You and Minuhe will go by litter."

"It is good to see you, my dear friend," she said, reluctant to move out of the comfort of his arms. He had been her teacher and her friend. He had taught her mathematics, history, Greek, and so many other things about the world around her — his knowledge had always seemed endless to her.

Uriah looked her over carefully. "How are you faring, my child?"

"There is nothing wrong with me except for the pain of leaving Father when he needed me most."

"I know. All will be well in time." He gently guided her toward a litter and saw her comfortably seated inside. Minuhe climbed in beside her, and they both reclined on silken cushions. Once they were away from the docks, Danaë allowed her

72

gaze to move over her surroundings. They were in a poor part of the city, where people lived in huts thatched with palm leafs and wore reed sandals instead of leather. As they moved away from the wharf, there were shops for stonecutters, weavers, carpenters, and potters. She now had a clear glimpse of Alexandria, and she thought it was a magnificent city with its shining golden domes and buildings with carved obelisks.

Eventually they passed down a long, tree-lined avenue with marble temples on both sides. At one point the litter bearers halted abruptly, and Danaë was irritated that they had to stop to allow a troop of Roman soldiers to pass. On land, as on sea, it seemed everyone had to give way to Rome. She caught a quick glimpse of a purple cape sweeping by and realized she had just caught a glimpse of the great Caesar himself. She wondered if he would meet the man who had entered Alexandria aboard the *Blue Scarab.*

When the sound of tramping feet faded in the distance, the litter bearers continued down the wide avenue, where there were shops selling everything imaginable — silversmiths labored alongside leather craftsmen and goldsmiths. Turning down a side street, they passed through a teeming marketplace. The scent of flowers, spices, and fish mingled in a not-unpleasant aroma. The noise was almost deafening as hawkers called out to passersby and motioned for them to draw near. Danaë missed the quiet serenity of the villa, she met Minuhe's gaze and suspected the other women was having similar thoughts.

By the time they reached their destination, the sun was sinking low in the western sky. The bearers plodded through an arched gateway and down a stone walk, setting the litter down before the massive front door.

Danaë wasn't sure what she'd expected, but it certainly wasn't this lovely home, hidden away from the city noise amid pathways that led to gardens she would love to explore. The house was white sandstone with a red-tiled roof, and much larger than she'd imagined.

After they had settled in, Danaë insisted on walking in the gardens. The evening air was cool, and the gardens were peaceful after the long voyage.

"I was not aware that Uriah had such wealth," Danaë remarked as Minuhe dusted off a marble bench so they could be seated.

Minuhe looked startled. "Uriah has no wealth of his own. He is your father's slave, just as I am."

Danaë could feel her face redden with embarrassment because she had not known this. "I . . . nay. I never thought about it." She was stunned. "I have always thought of you and Uriah as family."

Minuhe knew that her charge had been protected from the harsh realities of slavery by a father who had shown great tolerance to his slaves. "Nonetheless, we are slaves."

"Then this house —"

"Belongs to our master, your father." The statement was made without regret or bitterness. To Minuhe, it was just a fact of life.

Danaë lowered her head. "In truth, Minuhe, I'm also one of my father's slaves."

Minuhe could not deny it.

CHAPTER SIX

Danaë went directly to bed, refusing even the delectable tidbits of nourishment with which Minuhe tried to tempt her. Danaë's quarters had every comfort: The floors were of white marble, and so bright she could see her reflection in then, the bed had such soft linen sheeting, it almost felt like lying on a cloud. It was obvious that Uriah had instructed everyone to be attentive and to attempt to distract Danaë from her sorrow.

She tossed and turned restlessly, though sleep eluded her. She touched her lips, remembering the feel of the Roman officer's mouth on hers. Even now her stomach clenched, and she felt weak all over just thinking about him. She was haunted by his face and wished she could put him out of her mind. Not until the first morning breeze stirred the bed hangings did Danaë finally slip into a dreamless sleep.

It was mid-morning when she was awakened by the sound of Minuhe instructing one of the servants to set up the mistress's bath and lay out her clothing. A short time later, Danaë had bathed and dressed, wondering how she would fill the long hours that stretched ahead of her.

She was accustomed to being active, and now she seemed to have no purpose.

After Danaë had eaten her fill of honey cakes, a chilled mango, and a slice of goat cheese, Minuhe spoke. "Uriah has asked if he might speak with you this morning. He awaits you in the courtyard."

The first thing Danaë noticed when she stepped into the beautiful courtyard was the splendid splash of color from flowers of every hue known to man. Uriah had been pacing the flagstone walk and hurried in her direction when he saw she had arrived.

"Lady Danaë, thank you for seeing me so promptly."

Danaë frowned at Uriah's formal attitude and wondered at the reason for it. After her education had been completed and Uriah had been sent to Alexandria, she had missed him dreadfully and had always looked forward to his quarterly visits.

As Uriah walked toward her, she noticed that his back was not as straight as it had once been. He was not a tall man, and his gray beard was the same color as his balding hair. Kindness softened his dark eyes as he smiled at her and swept her a bow.

"Please make yourself comfortable." With a sweep of his hand, he indicated she should be seated on the marble bench.

"Have my cats been any trouble for you, good Uriah?"

"Not in the least, lady. As your father's instructions, I had had an enclosure built for them. And Tyi has his own large cage. The cats have been fed only cooked meat as Lord Mycerinus instructed, and they have a large space to roam about in." He smiled. "I will admit the others of the household have been avoiding the back part of the garden where the cats have been penned."

Danaë knew that Obsidian would attack the cheetah if she had the chance. "You kept them separate?"

He bowed. "As I was instructed."

She noted for the first time how tired he looked.

"Will you not sit beside me, Uriah?"

"If it pleases my lady, I prefer to stand. I have much to tell you."

"Then tell me while you are resting beside me," she insisted.

With a weary sigh, he dropped down onto

the bench next to her. "I have sad tidings."

Her head dropped. "It's my father, is it not?"

"The messenger came but an hour before sunup. Your father did not live past the day you left the villa."

Hot tears scalded her eyes, and her body shook with emotion. "My dear father — what will the world be like without him in it?"

Uriah did not attempt to stem her grieving, because he knew she loved his master well. He was shocked, however, when her head dropped onto his shoulder, and with a rough hand he wiped his tears away before his arms went around her, and he patted her back. Time passed, and the sun rose high in the sky before her trembling stopped and her crying ceased.

At last she raised her head and looked at Uriah with tears still swimming in her eyes. "I wanted so much to stay at my father's side, but he sent me away. It's bitter to think of him passing from this world without me there to comfort him. It shouldn't have happened in such a way."

The old man unashamedly wiped his tears away. "Bitter indeed for both of you."

Danaë regained her composure, knowing she would later grieve in seclusion. "Have arrangements been made for Father's mummification?"

"I am told that Harique arrived the evening of your departure and has taken the matter into his own hands. The messenger assured me the plans were going forward for a proper burial. Harique will do the right thing only because he will want to foster goodwill among his neighbors."

Pain stabbed at her. "Would that my father's final journey could have been arranged by loving hands. My father's nephew loved him not.

"Is there any more news?" she inquired.

"Only this." He handed her a scroll.

She looked curious. "Do you know what it is?"

"As you can see, your father's seal has not been broken. It was meant for your eyes alone. I do, however, have official documents that he charged to my care. I shall tell you about them as soon as you have read your father's words."

It was difficult for Danaë to read the uneven ciphers caused by her father's unsteady hand. Fresh tears flooded her eyes as she began to read:

Dearest daughter, it was difficult to send you away, but you know in your heart I had no other recourse. I have given into Uriah's hands the official document that makes you legally my daughter. Be warned, this does not mean you should return here to the villa. My land and property in Alexandria I leave to you, and a good living that will make you a most respected lady. Look to Uriah for counsel. Know that no father ever loved a daughter more than I have loved you. Grieve not my passing, but celebrate the time we had together. Your proud and loving father.

Before she could speak, Danaë had to clear her throat. Nothing, not even a legal document, could make her feel more her father's daughter than she already did.

With a sad gaze, Uriah waited for her to compose herself. She handed him the scroll and waited for him to read it.

After a moment he raised his head and nodded. "This house and property are deeded to you. There is also a textile work-shop here in the city that brings a hand-some profit."

She shook her head and fought fresh tears. "Surely you know none of that matters to me."

"It will when you no longer grieve. One day you will understand that your father took great care for your future."

"We both know Harique will dispute any property rights my father has given me. He will want everything for himself."

"To do that, he must first petition the young king." Uriah's smile made crags along his jaw. "I believe you have a handsome gift for King Ptolemy meant to soften his heart to your plight." His smile deepened. "Your father was a wise man — Harique is not so wise."

Danaë began to fully understand the reason her father had insisted that she present the cheetah to the king, and why he'd bequeathed the albino tiger skin to the High Priest of Isis. "Let us hope the gifts will bring about the results my father intended." She frowned. "But what would happen if Queen Cleopatra took back her throne?"

Uriah shrugged his shoulders. "A man could forfeit his life for voicing such thoughts, but Cleopatra has not the manpower to win against the armies of King Ptolemy. However, we now have a new player in the mix — who knows which way the mighty Caesar will jump?"

"If Caesar throws his might into the fray and should decide to set the queen back on the throne of Egypt, the balance of power would shift," she said.

"Who can say what is in the Roman's mind? As it is, let us hope King Ptolemy reacts to your gift the way your father predicted. But with this king you can never be sure what he will do — or so I'm told. Let us hope the High Priest of Isis will help us establish your identity. I've already asked for an audience on your behalf with King Ptolemy. I've let it be known that Lady Danaë, of the House of Sahure, has a priceless gift for him."

She placed her hand on his gnarled, blue-veined one. "How can I thank you, Uriah?"

He stood, but not before she saw how pleased he was. "It's been my honor to serve the noble House of Sahure." He bowed his head. "I'm now pleased to serve you."

"Have you never craved your freedom? I ask this because I've lately had cause to think of myself as a slave."

The old man smiled. "Your father never made me feel like a slave. He always treated me as a treasured friend and allowed me to be the overseer of his house and lands. With Lord Mycerinus as my master, I had a better life than I would otherwise have had."

"You are free now that my father . . . dwells among the dead."

"Nay, lady. I now serve you." He smiled

with great affection. "I trust you will not deal too harshly with me." Her gaze met his, and he could see the confusion reflected in her eyes. "It is as it should be," he reminded her.

"If I offered you freedom, would you take it?"

"Yea, lady — I would."

"Would you leave me?"

His brows met across his nose when he laughed. "Nay, lady. Where else could I go that I would have such an easy life and be made to feel that I am part of a family?"

Danaë had been in Alexandria a mere six days when word came from the palace that King Ptolemy demanded she appear before him. Particular attention was paid to her appearance on that day. Danaë had soaked in perfumed water, and then oil of myrrh was rubbed into her skin. Golden beads had been threaded through her dark hair, and each time she turned her head there was a slight tinkling sound.

Danaë stood before her beaten-brass mirror draped in a white silken gown that was gathered beneath her breasts, the hem resting just above her golden sandals. Making certain her mother's pendant was tucked beneath the neck of her gown so it wouldn't show, Danaë nodded for Minuhe to fasten a gold and turquoise collar about her neck.

"I'm nervous," Danaë admitted. "These new shoes are stiff and uncomfortable. If only I could wear my soft leather sandals."

"You must be grandly dressed for an audience at the palace," Minuhe said in a shocked tone. "You would not wish to bring disgrace to the House of Sahure."

Danaë shook her head as she studied her reflection critically. "I look pale; do you think the king will notice?"

Minuhe smiled to herself, thinking how lovely her mistress was. "I do not think anyone will notice."

CHAPTER SEVEN

Uriah assisted Lady Danaë into the litter while he climbed into the ox-driven cart that held the caged cat. As a precaution, and to keep the curious public from disturbing the cat, the cage had been covered with a large piece of linen. When they finally reached the outer palace wall, a guard halted them. Uriah presented to the man the proper documents embossed with the royal seal. After the cage was inspected, he waved them through the gate.

Nothing could have prepared Danaë for the majestic fountains and gardens behind the walls. When they passed through a second gate, the beauty of the landscape took her breath away. There were a myriad of fountains tinkling like music while brightly colored flowers spilled over the walls and lined the marble walkways.

Danaë felt her heart lurch and skip a beat when she stepped out of the litter and faced the wide, sweeping steps that led to the main part of the palace. She pressed her hand against her stomach, feeling so nervous she feared she was going to be ill.

Uriah must have known what she was feeling because he patted her shoulder. "Have courage, child. Although I can go no farther with you, I'll be waiting right here for your return. The king already knows who you are, and you will be welcome."

Uriah had explained to her that the palace was built in the Greek style, and she saw huge columned structures that reached skyward. There were many sections and buildings that she assumed held apartments, banqueting halls, and reception areas. If there was a more beautiful place in the land, she had yet to see it. In the distance she could hear the sound of harps and flutes blending sweetly.

Danaë was still trembling as she climbed the black marble steps, hoping no one would notice how badly her hands shook. It seemed the sound of her footsteps echoed loudly against the marble walls of the corridors. When she reached her destination, a long line of people were ahead of her, each waiting his turn to see the king.

She forgot her fear for the moment and became absorbed in studying the tall columns that supported the ceiling of the room; they were covered in hieroglyphs carved in gold. The ceilings swept upward to such a height, she was unable to decipher all the figures in the mosaic patterns. She stared at the tall bronze doors that led to the throne room, reading the hieroglyphs that proclaimed the Ptolemies the chosen of the gods and —

"Lady Danaë, of the House of Sahure, oh, Mighty One," a man in a blue and gold uniform called out, motioning her forward.

Feeling as if a hundred butterflies were beating their wings inside her stomach, Danaë moved forward, and then stepped down the six steps that took her into the throne room. Silently she prayed she wouldn't trip and disgrace herself before she reached the bottom. She halted at the base of the steps until a man waiting there motioned for her to follow him until he handed her over to the court scribe. The older man had bushy eyebrows, and for some reason, she kept staring at his ink-stained fingers.

There were other people in the audience chamber, some courtiers, and others who had come to seek the king's wisdom. Danaë was aware she had become the center of their attention. She heard murmured voices speculating on her identity.

The vivid colors of the courtiers' clothing swirled about her like a kaleidoscope of patterns. Some were dressed in the traditional Egyptian linen, while others had chosen the Greek costume preferred by the Ptolemies. What drew her eye from the crowd was the huge golden cobra head that loomed upward and cast its shadow across the golden throne.

Although Danaë had known the king was but fourteen years old, she was still unprepared for the small boy who was seated on a throne intended for a much larger and more imposing person. For some reason, he struck her as a tragic figure, and she felt a flash of pity for him. Dressed in white, he was bedecked in gold and jewels enough for ten people. His kohl-lined eyes made him look like a young boy playing at being an adult. She watched him move his head to converse with one of the men who stood to his right.

"Declare your reason for seeking audience with King Ptolemy, Lady Danaë," demanded a lavishly dressed man with a wide girth. By the description Uriah had given her, she knew the man to be the prime minister and eunuch, Parthanis. He had long, oily ringlets, and he wore an elaborate jeweled robe that was even finer than the one the king wore. It was rumored that the prime minister was the true ruler of Egypt. It was easy to see that he enjoyed gorging on food. Because he was a eunuch, his voice was high-pitched, and he apparently tried to compensate by speaking loudly. He looked somewhat grotesque because he was sweating profusely and the sweat had smeared streaks of kohl beneath his eyes.

Again drawing on the descriptions Uriah had given her, she judged the other man who hovered near the king to be Theodotus, the royal tutor. The teacher's eyes were watchful and cunning as he leaned possessively toward the king. "The king does not speak Egyptian, young woman," Theodotus announced. "Will you require an interpreter?"

"Nay, sir. I speak Greek," Danaë said, bowing low.

"Then state your business."

Danaë dropped to her knees and bowed her head. "Most Gracious Majesty, I was asked by my father to present you with a most wondrous gift."

"You may rise, young woman, and approach me," Ptolemy said with curious interest. "You are the daughter of my Royal Animal Trainer, are you not?"

She avoided looking into his eyes, thinking it was forbidden to do so. "I am, Majesty. Sadly, my father has left the land of the living and dwells in the land of the dead." Saying it aloud brought a dull ache to her heart.

"What is this!" the king demanded angrily, casting an accusing glare at Parthanis. "My animal trainer is dead, and I was not informed. Why is that?"

Taking a deep breath, and with much trepidation, Danaë moved toward the young king as he motioned her forward. When she raised her gaze to his, she saw the pout on his lips.

"Explain why I was not told of this," he said, turning to his teacher.

Theodotus merely shrugged as if the matter were of no importance. "His death was unknown to me, Majesty."

"It is your function to know these things," the eunuch Parthanis stated, and in that moment, Danaë noticed the animosity between the two men who stood closest to the throne. She had the feeling they fought over the young king like two dogs with a bone.

The boy king brought his fist down hard on the arm of the throne. "I will have my animal trainer! Today you will start a search to find someone adequate to replace Lord

Mycerinus."

The king seemed focused not on the death of Danaë's father but with replacing him so he wouldn't be inconvenienced. The young boy was ranting so loudly, Danaë was shocked.

She suddenly felt as if the walls were closing in on her, and she longed for a sip of water.

As she glanced to the left of the king, her gaze collided with a pair of probing dark eyes, and she suddenly discovered what terror felt like — for the man was none other than the Roman officer who had boarded the *Blue Scarab* at Pharus Island! The man who had kissed her. She saw something that frightened her even more. The man seemed to be sending her a silent message that was an unmistakable threat. She lowered her glance, wondering what reason he would have to be standing beside the king.

Confusion took over her reasoning because the Roman wore a fine robe of state with gold bands around his upper arms and a wide golden collar about his neck. What shocked her most was the fact that his eyes were outlined with kohl, in the Egyptian manner, and he wore the ceremonial wig of a great lord. Anger snapped inside when she realized he must be a spy for Caesar.

"You say you are brought me a gift." Ptolemy said in irritation. "What is it? I don't see a gift."

"Before my father died, he asked me to present to you a rare and wonderful animal. Jabatus is a hand-tamed cheetah."

The king leaned forward, his eyes suddenly bright with excitement, and he looked very much like the young boy he was. "I want to see him now. Did you bring him with you?"

"Yes, Majesty. He is in a cage in the outer courtyard."

The king turned to his guards. "Bring the cage to me at once." He motioned to Danaë. "Approach me and tell me more about this marvelous creature."

She took several steps, but halted at the dais. "The cheetah was raised from a cub and is very gentle. As Your Majesty knows, there is no animal faster than the cheetah, so he can accompany you even when you ride on horseback."

The young king's eyes glistened. "Is he dangerous?"

"No, Majesty. If you knew my father, then you would be aware he would never present you with an animal that might do you harm."

The prime minister had come down the

steps and had stopped in front of Danaë. "Do not speak so familiarly to the king, Lady Danaë. Remember where you are and whom you address."

The king held up his hand to silence the man. "I like you, Lady Danaë. I have too many people who pander to me. Promise you will always speak truth to me."

"It is a promise easily given and easily kept, Majesty." Her gaze went to the man she believed to be a Roman, and she focused on his hand, which rested up on the hilt of a golden dagger. Did the king know that the man was a Roman?

"Clear everyone out of the room. I want to see my cheetah," the boy commanded. "Parthanis, Theodotus, you may both leave, and all the others with you."

"But —" Theodotus protested. "I never leave you alone."

"Do so now!" the king ordered harshly. "Lord Ramtat, you may stay," the king said, interrupting Theodotus. "I will rely on your knowledge of animals. Everyone else, except you and Lady Danaë, get out!"

"I am eager to please, Majesty," Ramtat said, stepping closer to the king and resting his arm across the back of the ornate throne. His gaze was focused on Danaë as if daring her to speak of what she knew.

Anger battled with confusion inside her. Why did he stand so near the throne when he was one of Caesar's men? Danaë was so deep in her troubled thoughts, she had not noticed that the room had emptied. She turned around when the bronze doors swung open and four guards entered, carrying the caged cheetah. She vaguely heard the king order the guards to place the cage on the floor and depart.

"Show him to me," the king commanded Danaë, excitement threading his tone.

Danaë unlatched the cage, took the golden leash off a hook inside, and clipped it to the jewel-studded collar. The cheetah yawned and scratched, rubbing his body against Danaë like an affectionate house cat.

Ptolemy had raised himself on his knees and was grinning. "Will he come to me?"

"He has been trained to respond to certain commands, Majesty. You must clap your hands once and say *'come,'* and he will do so."

Ptolemy did as she instructed, and the cheetah lumbered toward him while Danaë kept a firm grip on the chain.

"If you want him to lay his head on your knee, you must say in a firm voice, *'lay.'*"

The boy scrambled to a sitting position and did as she instructed. At that moment, the two-hundred-pound cat dropped its head on the king's knee and licked his hand.

A fresh bout of pity hit Danaë as she watched the lonely young boy's face light up with happiness. "If I take him when I go out riding, will he attack other people or animals?"

"Nay, Majesty. Jabatus has never tasted raw meat, so he has no desire for it."

Ptolemy's face brightened as he buried his fingers in the animal's thick coat. "This is a wondrous animal indeed. Can I trust him enough that he can sleep in my room?"

"He would never harm you, Majesty. I have only to give him the command that will make him know he belongs to you, and then he will guard and protect *only* you and act on your commands. But have a care," she cautioned. "For if you give the command for him to attack someone, he will strike to kill."

"Say the words that will let him know he belongs to me," the boy commanded impatiently.

Danaë went down on her knees and took the cheetah's face in her hands. "Jabatus, this is your new master." She motioned to the king. "Do just as I did, Majesty. Hold his face in your hands and let him get your smell."

Scrambling to the steps, Ptolemy fearlessly went to his knees, just as Danaë had instructed.

"Jabatus, this is your master — you will heed only his words. He is your master!" She nodded to the king. "Tell him you are his master."

Ptolemy took the cat's huge head in his hands and smiled. "I am your master."

The cat merely blinked.

"It did not work," Ptolemy stated, his green gaze seeking Danaë's. "He shows no sign that he understood me."

"He understood you, Majesty," she assured the king. "If you give him a command, he will obey you."

"Not you?"

Danaë hesitated before she said, "He will always remember me, but he knows who his master is."

The cat turned his big head and stared at the king. Then he lapped the boy's cheek and settled down at his feet.

"He will belong only to you from this day forward."

Ptolemy's face lit up, and he laughed like a small boy. "I have something that only I can command."

Lord Ramtat, who had been silently watching the whole event, now spoke, "But surely you can command whomever you will, Your Majesty."

"Yes, yes, but that does not matter. It is no fun to have people fumbling around to please me." His gaze met Danaë's. "I am sorry about your father. He did well when he trained this animal."

"Thank you for honoring my father, Majesty. But it was I who trained the cheetah."

"I may consider bestowing your father's title on you," he stated absently. Then his gaze shifted to the man beside him. "I am glad you have returned to court, Lord Ramtat. I need all my loyal friends beside me with the Romans lurking about." Then he glanced back at Danaë. "You may leave, young woman. I will send word if I decide I want to see you again."

Danaë bowed her head, but not before she saw the threatening look in Lord Ramtat's dark eyes. Something was very wrong, but until she knew what it was, she would remain silent. Egypt was in turmoil, and to speak against a man as powerful as Lord Ramtat would surely bring about her death.

First she would discuss the matter with Uriah — he would know how to advise her. Before she bowed and backed away, she gazed once more into Lord Ramtat's eyes, hoping she was wrong about him. But his dark gaze burned into hers, and she knew he was dangerous.

Danaë backed quickly away, hurrying from the throne room. As she rushed down a long marble corridor, her heart was beating so fast, she could feel the blood throbbing in her temples. Two guards were posted at the double doors just ahead, and she could see the reflection of the sun on the black marble floors. If she could only make it outside, perhaps she could take a clear breath.

"Lady Danaë, wait. I would speak with you."

With dread, she recognized Lord Ramtat's voice and realized he had followed her. Some inner voice warned her of danger. She had only two chances to escape him: she could approach the two guards and ask one of them to take her to the king at once, or she could run.

She did neither — she turned to face Lord Ramtat. "Yes?" she asked.

Ramtat nodded at the guards, who saluted him. Then he casually took Danaë's arm, but his grip was strong. "I would have a private word with you, Lady Danaë."

She wanted to jerk her arm free and rush outside to find Uriah, but instead she raised her head and met his gaze defiantly. Looking into his brown eyes, she noticed they were flecked with gold. "I must . . . hurry or my servant will be concerned about me."

A smile curved his lips. "A mistress concerned about her servant's feelings — a dangerous notion if it took root and swept across Egypt," he said with humor; then his expression became serious. His grip tightened painfully on her arm. "I insist on speaking to you."

Danaë had no choice but to allow him to lead her back down the hallway into an empty room. Ramtat did not relinquish his hold on her until he was sure no one could overhear their conversation.

"Lady Danaë, I noticed your . . . confusion when you saw me with the king today."

She stared at him, feeling more angry than frightened at the moment. "But I was not confused when I saw you on board a Roman ship, wearing the uniform of a Roman officer," she said.

He pulled her closer, and Danaë knew she was in real danger. "You shall forget you saw me before today," Ramtat insisted in a quiet voice that held warning. "Is that understood?"

"I understand you want the king to believe you are his friend."

"You tread on dangerous ground," he warned.

"And you tread the path of a traitor."

He gave her a small shake. "I'm no traitor."

"Yet you would have me forget I saw you that day on the deck of the *Blue Scarab.*"

"The gods know I have not been able to forget you."

He brought her against him, and she could feel the hard muscles beneath his robe. Her eyes half closed when he raised her chin and gazed down at her. Then he dipped his head to whisper, "Have you thought of me?"

Danaë felt his breath on her lips, and her body went weak, but not from fear. She wanted to be in his arms and feel his lips pressed to hers once more. But this man was not to be trusted — he was a danger to the king, and most certainly to her. Pulling away, she shook her head. "How could I *forget* you when you insist I have never seen you before today?"

His eyes narrowed as he tired to decide whether she would expose him to the king and ruin Caesar's plans. "Do not meddle in matters that don't concern you," he cautioned. Then he gave her a courtly bow for the benefit of any onlookers who might happen by.

Before she could reply, he turned and walked away.

Theodotus stepped out of the shadows, his teeth bared. He had overheard the end of the conversation between Lady Danaë and Lord Ramtat, and he wished he could have heard the whole exchange. One thing was certain: For some reason, Lord Ramtat had threatened Lady Danaë. But why?

But the royal teacher had other matters on his mind. He was sick of paying homage to the sniveling boy who held the throne of Egypt. For years, he'd pretended to be Ptolemy's friend, and where had it got him? Today, the child had sent Theodotus out of the throne room, humiliating him. In all the years he had been the king's tutor, Theodotus not been able to instill much knowledge into the boy's head.

Theodotus had no idea he was glowering as he moved steadily down the corridor, but the guards on duty saw the frown, and they stiffened, avoiding his gaze. If anyone was to be feared in the palace, it was the royal tutor.

Theodotus's thoughts were centered on the man he despised most. He had devised many plans to be rid of Parthanis, who had been hailed as prime minister by all Egypt.

Theodotus knew he was more intelligent than Parthanis and deserved the office more than the fat eunuch.

But Theodotus was patient and willing to wait until the right moment before he struck at Parthanis. Otherwise the fingers of blame would point at him since it was well known that he despised the man. Because the boy was weak and easily led, the person who controlled the king wielded the power in Egypt.

After he had been sent from the throne room, Theodotus had listened in the hidden passage while Lady Danaë had presented the cheetah to the king, and in that moment, he knew how he would finally be rid of the eunuch.

Poison was what most people used to dispose of an enemy, but Theodotus would devise something ingenious, and something that could never be traced back to him. It would be very simple to make friends with the cheetah — Ptolemy would like that. Theodotus smiled — he would secretly begin feeding the animal raw meat. The cheetah would grow to trust him, and he would slowly train it to strike against his enemy.

He could hardly contain his joy, just thinking what a glorious day it would be when the cheetah tore the prime minister's throat out!

Ramtat found it difficult to keep his mind on the affairs of Egypt when all he could think about was the sultry beauty who kept crossing his path. She was brave, and the gods knew she was stubborn, but she was also as exciting and unpredictable as the exotic cats she trained. He had seen a flash of anger in her green eyes, and it made him wonder what color those eyes would be if they were darkened with passion. Her body was lean and muscled, and he wondered what beauty lay beneath her robe. Still, she was a problem for him; as of yet, he had not decided what to do about her. She could expose him if she decided to. That she had not told the king what she knew about him was merely because she had been taken by surprise when she'd seen him today.

When she had time to think about it, she might very well go straight to Ptolemy with the truth.

Danaë could not stop trembling. She had made a powerful enemy in Lord Ramtat — one who would not hesitate to take her life if he thought her a threat. She remembered his warning. He already saw her as a danger.

What should she do?

She rushed out of the palace, and in her haste, she took a wrong turn and ended up near a private garden where a guard barred her way. Carefully she retraced her steps and finally discovered a door that led to the outer courtyard, where she found Uriah waiting for her.

"Was the king pleased?" he asked, helping her into the litter, and then settling in beside her. He had already sent the empty cart home.

It took Danaë a moment to compose herself. "He seemed excited. He was very well pleased."

"Yet you are worried about something," Uriah stated with his usual perception. "Do you want to discuss it?"

She hesitated, knowing the litter bearers could hear every word they said. "Later. When I've had time to think and get everything straight in my mind, I'll want to ask your advice."

He nodded. "Did you meet someone other than the king?"

"Yes." She lowered her voice. "A Roman."

Uriah was puzzled. He could see that Danaë was more than worried, she was frightened of something, or someone, and

he wondered what had happened to upset
her.

CHAPTER EIGHT

A cloud bank covered the moon, and only torchlights along the walkway illuminated the high pylons and thick marble walls of the palace. Ramtat, having the advantage of being a frequent visitor to the place in his younger years, was familiar with its layout, and he knew many of the secret passages and hidden gardens. He cleverly avoided the two sentries posted near the palace steps, and pushed aside a climbing vine so he could enter the hidden gate that led to an inner courtyard.

Hearing someone approaching, Ramtat flattened his body against a wall, blending with the shadows. Moments later, he reached the inner garden where Caesar was quartered, and the Roman sentries waved him through. They had been told to expect him.

As he entered the well-lit chamber, Ramtat's gaze went directly to the man whose head was sagging into his hands.

Wearily the Proconsul of Rome raised his head and nodded at the young Egyptian who had fought at his side through the last campaign and had covered himself with glory, bringing honor to an already honored name.

"You're late."

"There are spies everywhere, Caesar. I had to double back twice to avoid being seen. And I had to make my way to your armory so I could pay the men in my legion and disburse them."

"Yes, yes," Caesar said in irritation. "That had to be done. And as for spies, young King Ptolemy has his spies watching me, and my spies watch him while he watches me."

"Are you ill?" Ramtat asked with concern upon seeing the older man's pallor.

"Sick at heart. Your Egyptians murdered a noble man when they beheaded Pompey. He would have come to a better end at my hands. You must have heard that Pompey was married to my daughter until she died giving birth to their child."

"I did know that." Ramtat had also been horrified by the murder of Pompey. "And you must know the men responsible for Pompey's death are not my Egyptians, but rather that festering lot attached to King Ptolemy."

Caesar pounded his fist on the desk in front of him. "They thought to please me, but by beheading Pompey, they have merely sealed their own doom, as they will discover in the days to come."

Maps were spread out in front of Caesar, and he began rolling them up and shoving them into goatskin tubes.

Unconsciously Ramtat rolled one of the maps and shoved it into a tube while he observed Caesar. Although the Roman leader was in his fifties, he had the appearance and physique of a much younger man. He was battle-hard and muscled from years of war. Though not handsome in the conventional sense — his nose was large, his brows too heavy — there was something magnetic about his personality, and when he spoke, he drew people to him.

"If King Ptolemy had his way, you would meet the same fate as Pompey," Ramtat warned.

"Which is precisely why I have you at my side, son of Egypt. You bring me luck, and now I expect you to win your people to my side. It falls to me to heal this split between Cleopatra and Ptolemy. It is in Rome's best interest that they rule jointly."

With a satirical glance at the man he admired above all others, Ramtat shoved the last map into a cylinder and placed it with the others. "King Ptolemy is a mere puppet, his strings pulled by that eunuch, Parthanis, as well as Theodotus, who masquerades as the royal teacher, although I have never observed him implanting any knowledge into the boy's head. The civil war between brother and sister will most probably end in Cleopatra's death, and Egypt will be the worse for it."

Caesar rubbed his forehead. "Little would I care who wins or loses if the war did not involve Rome. The way it is, I find myself being pulled into their war against my will. I will need you to glean information for me in the next few weeks." His eyes narrowed on the young Egyptian. "Tell me everything you know of these two rivals for the throne of Egypt. I must know their weaknesses, for surely they have them."

"Cleopatra is nothing if not cunning. When her brother had her deposed and set himself up as sole ruler, she did not accept defeat. She used her knowledge of languages to draw people to her, and has gathered quite a force to march against her brother."

"She cannot win."

"Nay. Her troops are outnumbered by

Ptolemy's army."

"What of her character — what is she like?"

"I knew Cleopatra well when she was younger, and nothing about her at that time drew special attention. Of course, no one expected her to be queen. But I noticed she was always studying and reading, gleaning all the knowledge she could. It was easy to see that she was her father's favorite child — all the court knew how he indulged her and had her educated by the best scholars from all over the world. She speaks several languages fluently, and is the first of her house to bother learning our Egyptian language, a point that has always pleased her people."

"And Ptolemy?"

"His ambitious mother kept him in his father's eye at all times and never allowed the king to forget who should succeed him on the throne." Ramtat looked thoughtful for a moment. "Ptolemy is no great scholar. His temperament is childish, bitter, and he always insists on having his way in everything. He is growing into exactly the kind of person one would expect when a child has been spoiled and pampered from birth."

"And what about the two men who stand closest to the throne? What are their

111

weaknesses?"

"Parthanis and Theodotus are both dangerous; it must have been at their orders that Pompey was beheaded. Their real interest is in lining their pockets with gold and directing the power of Egypt. They even bicker among themselves to obtain that glory."

"As I recall, the king's father was no great scholar either," Caesar said disgustedly. "When your own people drove him out of Egypt, he raided the treasury and gave most of it to Rome to buy back the throne for him. What do you say of such a king?"

"The dead cause no trouble, my lord. It is the living that concern me."

The Proconsul of Rome gave an uproarious laugh. "Well said. Let us keep a sharp eye on the living and guard our own backs. Be my eyes and ears — keep me informed of all that goes on behind these walls."

Ramtat bowed. "I will do what I can."

"It is good that the king trusts you. Continue to flatter him, remain at his side, be a friend to him. I want to know which way his armies are going to jump before he does."

Ramtat lowered himself onto a leather stool. "My position may have been compromised today."

Caesar jerked his head up, and his eyes became hooded. "In what way?"

"There was a young woman aboard the boat that brought me to Alexandria. I saw her today, and she recognized me."

Caesar looked thoughtful for a moment and then shrugged. "You have merely to find out who she is and silence her."

"I know who she is, so I should have no difficulty locating her. But what do you mean when you ask me to silence her?"

"If your position is compromised, you will be of no use to me — and you will be in grave danger from those who serve their own interests." Caesar rubbed his forehead in weariness. "Most probably we have nothing to worry about. The woman surely cannot reach the king with her tale."

Ramtat flexed his shoulders to ease the tension. "She had an audience with the king today while I was with him."

Caesar stood and began pacing. "She didn't tell Ptolemy about you at that time?"

"Not today. But I think after she has had time to reflect, she will seek another audience with Ptolemy. She has no liking for me."

"Who is she?"

"Lady Danaë of the House of Sahure. Her father was the Royal Animal Trainer."

"Eliminate her!"

Ramtat was stunned by such an order and shook his head. "That I will not do."

Caesar glared at him. "Do you dare defy me?"

"In this instance I do. Lady Danaë is a noblewoman of some import and has done naught to warrant such action. As an Egyptian, I cannot allow harm to come to her unless I see harm in her."

Caesar clasped his hands behind him and glared at the younger man. "Why must you always challenge my authority?"

"If you will remember, when you sent for me in Gaul, I told you I would never do anything that was not in Egypt's best interest."

Caesar waved him away. "You are one of the few I ever allow to dispute my orders and live to tell about it." He stared at Ramtat in annoyance. "Surely we can meet on common ground, and you can do something to silence the woman. Too much depends on my knowing what the king is up to, and only you can find that out for me."

"I can take measures to prevent her from talking," Ramtat suggested. "That shouldn't be too difficult."

"Then do it," Caesar snapped, dropping down onto a cushioned stool and waving his hand around the opulent room. "Look at this — how does one sleep in such a place? Golden beds, golden footstools, strange writings on the walls. With half of what it took to furnish this room, I could have taken Gaul."

"Egypt is a very wealthy country."

Caesar nodded in agreement. "I am about to relieve your Egypt of some of her wealth. But no matter about that — tell me what transpired between you and the king."

"I let it be known that you were my father's good friend and that I knew you well. That pleased those two vultures who circle around Ptolemy."

Caesar nodded and gave a deep laugh. "The fools play right into my hands. When we meet tomorrow in the throne room, I shall put on a great show of affection and make them believe I haven't seen you in years."

Ramtat nodded in understanding. Caesar was not called the "great strategist" without reason. "So I am to play both sides of the coin."

"Precisely!" Caesar looked even more weary and eased back onto his stool. "I need to know the reason the king chased his sister into the desert. Use friendship, flattery, or whatever it takes to win the boy to your side. But keep your eyes open in my service."

Ramtat was thoughtful. "Again I must remind you that I love Egypt well, and will never do anything to the detriment of my people. In this campaign, you may ask something of me which I will be unwilling to do."

Caesar gave Ramtat a look of grudging respect. "Your honesty is one of the first things I admired about you. I know that, no matter what, you will be truthful with me."

Ramtat started to say something, but Caesar silenced him with a wave of his hand. "What makes you think you have to keep reminding me where your first loyalty lies? You have convinced me of that on several other occasions."

"My country must see an end to this war. It is my heartfelt wish for Queen Cleopatra to be exclusive ruler of Egypt when it is over."

"Have a care, young Ramtat, for you walk over an abyss. One wrong step will cause your downfall, and if you fall, you may very well drag Egypt down with you."

"I know that."

"Are you sure you are not allowing the affection you felt for the queen when she was younger to color your judgment?"

"Nay, Caesar. I had no real affection for her at that time. I was more interested in strengthening my sword arm than being a royal sycophant like many of my friends."

"Then heed this," Caesar stated forcefully. "The ruler of Egypt will be whom I choose. Only I can make that decision."

Ramtat bowed. "As is your appointed right. With your permission, I should leave right away. Dawn will be breaking within a few hours, and the courtyards will be swarming with people."

"Have a care. Look for that young woman and make sure she doesn't talk. See to it immediately."

Ramtat nodded. "I'll find out what I can, and then I'll report to you. But I must caution you to guard yourself at all times. You have few friends here in the palace."

"Your concern is appreciated. Just make certain to keep that woman away from the king."

Ramtat bowed. "Your word is my command."

Caesar gave him a skeptical glance. "Get out of here, you young rogue. You serve me only because you think it is in Egypt's best interest."

"I would never dispute your words, mighty Caesar."

"You would, and you have." Caesar turned away. "Leave me so I can find my bed before the duties of the day demand my attention."

When he turned back, Ramtat was already gone, melting into the shadows.

After Danaë had settled Obsidian down for the night and fed the hawk, it was too late to seek Uriah's council. And she needed to think everything through. Why would a man of Egypt want to help Rome? She could not understand what Lord Ramtat's motive could be. The king knew Ramtat from the past and trusted him enough to send his guards out of the room and leave himself undefended with the man.

She went to the window and watched the moonlight appear and disappear through the scattered clouds. If she had been just an ordinary woman, and Lord Ramtat an ordinary man, she could so easily have opened her heart to him.

A cloud passed over the moon, devouring the light and leaving the night in darkness, and Danaë was afraid. But Ramtat was not an ordinary man — the gods had cast the two of them in opposite camps, and that made him her enemy.

CHAPTER NINE

It was early morning as Danaë made her way down the curved garden path, inhaling the sweet scent of the flowers that were in full bloom. She moved hurriedly across the courtyard in search of Uriah. She had been awake for most of the night wondering what she should do about Lord Ramtat, and she was still uncertain. When she found her former tutor, he was seated beneath a tree, his head bent over a scroll. He was so engrossed in what he was reading, he had not heard her soft tread.

"How are you faring, Uriah?"

He quickly rose to his feet and bowed respectfully. "Well enough." He looked her over carefully and noticed the shadows beneath her eyes. "I hope you are settling into your new life."

She sat down on the bench and tried to gather her thoughts, not yet ready to discuss Lord Ramtat. "I am. However, Obsidian paces her cage and is restless since she is accustomed to a certain amount of freedom, which she cannot have here in Alexandria."

"That would not be wise," Uriah agreed, smiling as if he were contemplating something humorous. "If Obsidian were allowed freedom on these grounds, your servants would flee in fear."

"It's hard to know what to do about her."

Uriah looked at her speculatively. "The problem of the leopard is not what really eats at your mind, is it?"

Danaë raised her gaze to him. "There is something that troubles me greatly, and I don't know what I should do about it."

"Are you ready to tell me?"

She plucked at the blue trim on her gown. "On the sea voyage to Alexandria, just before we reached the Great Harbor, several Roman warships overtook us. I told you about the man we encountered, and how we had to dock at the lighthouse to take him on board."

"Yes. As I recall, you said he was a Roman general."

"And so I thought he was at the time. Now I don't believe he's a Roman at all. The king called him Lord Ramtat. He stood as a friend to the king in the chamber yesterday, but I do not think he is Ptolemy's friend at all."

Uriah looked worried. "Lord Ramtat is of the Tausret family, they are very powerful and stand close to the throne." He paced forward and then back to stand before Danaë. "I can see why he might not want the king to know of his connections with Rome." He watched her face as he asked, "Did he speak to you?"

Her bottom lip trembled. "After I left the throne room, Lord Ramtat caught up with me and . . . and threatened me."

"Does he know who you are?"

She watched Uriah's brows meet across the bridge of his nose as he frowned. "Yes, he does. My name was announced to the king."

Uriah looked worried. "He is a man of great power and standing. If he wants to find you, he will."

"You don't think I am making too much of this, do you?"

"He may be searching for you even now." Uriah's frown deepened. "There is some plot afoot, and he knows you can place him in league with the Romans. Therefore, we can assume he'll soon find his way here."

"Do you think I should leave Alexandria?"

"Aye, I do — at once." He glanced toward the house as if deciding what to do first.

"There is no time to squander. There is treachery afoot, and you have unwittingly become a part of it. We must hurry!"

"Where can I go? Where can I hide that he cannot find me?"

Uriah closed his eyes a moment; when he opened them again, he gave Danaë a troubled glance. "I know of a place you will be safe. But it is far away, and you must prepare for a long, hard journey across the desert. It will not be easy."

Even as Uriah was speaking, there was a pounding on the front gate, and a loud voice demanding entrance. "Wait here," Uriah warned. "Stay in the shadows and do not show yourself until I determine whether you are in danger."

Danaë knew in her heart that Lord Ramtat had found her.

Who else would come pounding on her gate, unless it was Harique?

She flinched when she heard the clash of swords. Faithful Faraji would be resisting the intruders. She ran in the direction of the front gate, fearing for her guard's life.

Uriah stepped into her path and grabbed her arm. "You must come away with me at once!" His linen robe flapped against his legs as he hurried Danaë toward the stable. "The men fighting their way past your guards wear the blue and bronze Egyptian uniforms and carry the banner of Lord Ramtat. Hasten, hasten! We have not a moment to lose."

Lord Ramtat was accompanied by five of his personal guards, and they had easily subdued Faraji and two other men who had fought bravely in defense of their lady.

"Restrain them if you must, but do not hurt them if you can help it," Ramtat ordered, making his way toward the house. When he brought the household servants together and tried to question them, he found them sullen and uncooperative. One, a woman who identified herself as Minuhe, was hostile and ordered them to leave the premises. Ramtat's men went through every room, shoving aside furniture and breaking pottery in their search. An angry order from Ramtat halted the destruction, and the men meekly righted the furniture they had over-turned.

When it became clear to Ramtat that Lady Danaë was not there, he called the servants in again and lined them against the wall. "Who among you is willing to tell me the whereabouts of Lady Danaë for payment?"

"No one will tell you anything," Minuhe declared.

"Anyone who can give me the information I seek will be rewarded with twelve silver pieces." Lord Ramtat nodded at the woman called Minuhe. "How about you — would you like to have silver of your own?"

"I scorn your offer. I'll tell you naught, and neither will any of the others. You'll leave with no more than you had when you came."

Ramtat fixed his gaze on a young kitchen maid who was trembling with fear. "How about you — do you know anything?"

"No . . . lord. The last I knew of the mistress, she'd gone into the courtyard."

"And how long ago was that?"

"Just before you came."

One of the guards entered, dragging a boy of no more than twelve summers. The soldier shoved the grimy-faced lad forward. "He says the lady left on horseback accompanied by a man named Uriah."

"Is that true?" Ramtat demanded of the boy, who trembled with fear.

"Yes, lord."

"Do you know where they went?"

"Did I hear you offer silver for information?" The boy asked, avoiding the great man's gaze.

Ramtat smiled. "Now I have the rat that will spring my trap. Yes, if you tell me what

I need to know, I will pay you well."

The boy looked down at his feet. "If I tell, I'll be punished. Faraji will pluck my eyes out to feed to the crows."

"I will take you away from here if you cooperate with me." Ramtat watched relief appear on the boy's face. "Tell me what you know."

The boy wiped his grimy face with an equally grimy hand. "I heard Uriah mention something about joining a caravan — that's all I know."

Ramtat bent down so he was at eye level with the boy. "Did he say when?"

"Not that I heard."

"There are many caravans leaving the city. For which one should I look?"

"I know not, lord." The boy looked at Minuhe, whose gaze was poisonous, and he shifted uncomfortably. "Truly I don't."

"Bind him and bring him with us," Ramtat ordered. "If he speaks true, he shall have his freedom and the promised silver. If he speaks false, he'll not see another sunrise."

Minuhe spoke, reaching for the boy, who cringed away from her. "You cannot free a slave who belongs to Lady Danaë."

Ramtat watched his guards lead the boy away. "Then let your lady come for him."

■ ■ ■ ■

Danaë hurried down the clay-packed streets in the direction of the Golden Horn Tavern, where she was to meet Uriah. He had gone ahead to find a caravan to take them out of the city. The streets were clogged with humanity; shepherds herded their flocks into the city to sell at the slaughterhouses, and many two-wheeled donkey carts rumbled past, hauling fruits and vegetables for the next day's market. Throngs of people were trying to make it out of the gates before they closed for the night, and several camel caravans waited by the high arched gateway for their turn to pass through.

Since Danaë had fled from her home, she'd been unable to bring anything with her. Uriah had managed to sell the horses and borrow money from a silversmith friend. Danaë had purchased plain garments and a black headdress, hoping to blend in as a Bedouin.

Just as she reached the front of the tavern, people began scattering to the side of the roadway, and Danaë heard the sound of riders approaching. Soldiers in bronze armor over light blue togas passed by — Lord Ramtat's men were on her trail! With fear driving her, she slammed her body against a mud-brick wall. When the guards began shoving men aside to question their women, she knew without a doubt they were searching for her. Slowly she eased her way toward the door of the tavern, taking great care to stay in the shadows. With trembling hands, she pulled the coarse linen headcovering over her face, hoping to go unnoticed.

A hand landed on her shoulder, and she spun around, relieved when she saw it was Uriah. "We must get you out of the city now."

She shook her head sadly. "It wouldn't be wise for you to come with me. I'm sorry that I pulled you into this intrigue. Perhaps you can return to the house, and if questioned say you know not where I went."

"I'll not leave you, Danaë," he said earnestly. "But it must not seem that we are traveling together. I have made arrangements for you to ride with the harem of an aged friend of mine. You'll be safe under Sheik Mardian's banner." Uriah took her hand. "Quickly, lower your head so no one can see your face."

She nodded toward the guards. "It doesn't seem possible to get past all of them."

Uriah pressed her forward, ducking behind the stall and heading away from the tavern. "Our caravan has already been searched and is not likely to be searched again."

They heard other riders arriving, and Uriah pushed Danaë into the doorway of a leather shop just in time to avoid the hooves of Lord Ramtat's horse. Uriah urged her out the back door and led her to the caravan on which they would be traveling. She was soon mounted high on a camel, which she shared with two other women. A canopy of fine linen was their shade, and thin gauze allowed them to see out while no one could see them. It took Danaë only a moment to discover she did not understand the language the two women spoke. They giggled and offered her sweetmeats, which she accepted, not because she was hungry but because she did not want to offend them.

She cringed and pulled back when she saw Lord Ramtat ride by again. She felt sick inside — it seemed he would stop at naught to find her.

Ramtat had delayed the departure of three caravans until his men could search among them for Lady Danaë. He'd been told that two caravans had already departed. Certain that Lady Danaë must be traveling with one of them, he sent men to search for her. One of his guards had reported that a woman at the linen market had described a beautiful lady who had purchased the weaver's humble clothing and left her fine robes behind.

Ramtat clutched the white gossamer gown that the shopkeeper had turned over to his guard. There was no doubt in his mind that the garment belonged to Lady Danaë. He pressed it to his cheek and smelled the sweet scent of jasmine that still clung to the fabric.

Disgusted with himself, Ramtat shoved the garment into a leather bag. Lady Danaë was mistaken if she thought she could escape him by fleeing into the desert. He would seek her even there.

By late morning the next day he still had no word on Lady Danaë. He stared into the distance while something he could not explain ate away at him. He had to find her — had to have her under his power. She was becoming an obsession with him. No woman had ever lingered in his mind more than a few days. But this one had haunted him since the moment he'd first seen her standing on the deck of the *Blue Scarab,* her fierce leopard at her side.

He had to rest his horse, so he reluctantly dismounted and motioned for his men to do the same. If Lady Danaë was not ahead of him, she must be behind him. Either way, he'd find her.

He had to.

Theodotus cautiously entered King Ptolemy's bedchamber, knowing the boy had ridden away from the palace earlier and wouldn't return until late afternoon. As he had hoped, the cheetah was in the cage near the bed. But when he approached the animal, it growled; the fur on the back of its neck stood up and it gazed pointedly at Theodotus with menacing yellow eyes. Apparently the cat had been trained to protect its owner; it might be difficult to win its trust.

But Theodotus was nothing if not determined.

"Good Jabatus, you will soon realize I'm your true friend," he said in a soft voice meant to gain the animal's trust.

The big cat rose on its hind legs and snarled, swatting at the cage.

"Here, pretty one, smell what I have for you."

The cat shrank away as Theodotus unwrapped a chunk of raw meat and held it against the cage. "Soon you will become accustomed to raw meat and will balk whenever you are offered cooked meat." Theodotus poked the meat through the bars and jumped back as the cheetah lunged at it. At first Jabatus merely sniffed at the meat and turned away from it. Theodotus knew his attempt to gain control of the cat would fail unless it took to the raw meat.

He held his breath expectantly as he watched Jabatus slowly turn back and nose the meat. Then its tongue lapped out and the animal took a small bite. With a snarl, Jabatus tore into the bloody tidbit, devouring every morsel.

Theodotus watched in satisfaction as the cat licked its paws, and then lapped everywhere blood had splattered, leaving no trace of the evidence. He bent to rub the cat behind the ear so the animal would become accustomed to him. It wouldn't be long before the bloodlust would take the animal completely, and it would no longer accept cooked meat.

"I will teach you whom to trust —" he said, wrapping a small piece of raw meat in one of the prime minister's sashes "— and who is the enemy. Smell the scent — grow accoustomed to it — this is the scent of the man you will one day kill!"

CHAPTER TEN

Once the sun had dropped behind the distant sand dunes, night shadows crept across the land. A slight evening breeze was stirring, but it brought little relief from the heat. For most of the day, the caravan had traveled across rugged wasteland where the earth was hard-packed and there was neither shade nor water.

At first Danaë had been annoyed by the constant tinkling of the tiny bells attached to the camels' harnesses, and the motion of the swaying beasts had made her feel ill. Now she was accustomed to the sound of the bells and even found it soothing, and she had discovered that if she swayed in rhythm with the camel, the motion was not so bad. She found the strong perfumes of the two older women overwhelming, but the women were kind to her, and she was grateful that they had allowed her to travel with them.

She was bone-weary and wondered when they would reach their destination.

The farther they traveled from Alexandria, the safer she felt. Surely Lord Ramtat would be satisfied that she had left the city and would not pursue her into the desert.

Danaë wished she could talk to Uriah and find out what he had planned. But since she was hiding among harem women, no man was allowed to approach them. He had warned her that if they met, she was to treat him as a stranger — Uriah was concerned that Lord Ramtat might have him followed. Danaë had listened to the mumbling and giggling of the women until her head ached. How was it, she wondered, that not one of them could speak Egyptian?

It was nearing dusk by the time the caravan leader called a halt for the night. Danaë lurched forward when one of the men tapped her camel's knees and the beast knelt on the ground. The other two women were helped by their husband's eunuchs as Danaë had been for the first two days. She thought nothing of the man who offered her his hand, assuming he was one of the sheik's minions.

Danaë was startled when his hand lingered too long on hers, and she pulled free as she gazed into suspicious brown eyes.

"Lady, I have been watching you since I joined the caravan yesterday. Why is it that you are much younger than the other women in Sheik Mardian's harem and you do not act like you belong in his household?" he asked, trying to peer past her veil.

In that moment Danaë suspected that she was staring into the eyes of Lord Ramtat's man, and she trembled in fear. Summoning all her courage, she glared at him. "Be warned that I am being watched over, and my protector is quick to anger. If you treasure your life, you will move away as quickly as possible, and you won't approach me again."

The man stepped away, smiling as if he knew something she did not. "A thousand pardons, lady. I was merely making an observation." He bowed. "I'm sure we shall meet again."

Trembling, she watched him disappear into the shadows. The harem women grouped together, but she backed away in fear.

Uriah — she had to find Uriah.

As if she had no conscious thought of what she was doing, Danaë walked quickly away from camp, and then she ran and ran until she dropped to her knees, gasping for breath.

Suddenly Uriah appeared, dropping down beside her, a little winded himself. "I saw you run. Is something the matter?"

"He's found me, Uriah. One of Lord Ramtat's men is here, and he knows who I am."

Uriah handed her a waterskin and watched her take a sip. "Are you certain of this?"

"Aye. We must get away as soon as possible. The man said he'd been watching me since his arrival yesterday. He's probably already sent word to his master."

Uriah whipped his head around and stared back toward the encampment. "We must not act in haste," he cautioned. "It's possible that you are being overly suspicious."

"Nay!" Then Danaë hesitated, wondering if he could be right. "Perhaps I did overreact."

At that moment a loud shriek pierced the night air. Danaë jumped to her feet and stared toward the encampment, watching as riders in flowing robes entered it.

"Stay here," Uriah warned, shoving Danaë to the ground. "I'll find out who they are."

"Could it be that Lord Ramtat has found me?" she asked in a quivering voice, brushing sand from her face.

"I'd say not. From here it looks like

ordinary Bedouins. They sometimes demand tribute from the caravans that trespass on what they think of as their private territory. All the same, stay here out of sight. If I do not return right away, hide yourself among the sand dunes, and I shall find you when I am able."

Fearing for his life, Danaë watched Uriah hurry toward the camp. By the light of the campfires she watched several of the Bedouins dismount and speak to the head man of the caravan. One of the men drew her notice because he was taller than the others, and he was dressed all in black while the others wore white robes.

Danaë heard voices raised in anger, and she watched, horrified, as several of the men entered the tents as if searching for someone. Some primal survival instinct warned Danaë that this was no ordinary Bedouin tribe. She knew they were searching for her.

Although it was no more than a shadowy outline, she glanced toward a tall sand dune some distance away, wondering if she could make it to the other side before the men came looking for her. The sound of swords clashing urged her into action. With sand filling her sandals and slowing her progress, she fled. It was so dark she could hardly see her hand in front of her face, but she managed to reach the dune and started climbing. The sand seemed to collapse beneath her sandals, causing her to slide back down the mound. But she rallied enough to climb upward once more.

Danaë had almost made it to the top of the dune when she heard the rattle of a bridle and glanced back to see that the Bedouin dressed in black was riding directly toward her.

Had he the eyes of a cat? she wondered. How could he see her in the dark? She slipped and fell, rolling back down.

Danaë felt crushing fear when the rider overtook her and dismounted before she could gain her feet. Knowing it was useless to run, she slowly stood and waited for him.

The night was so dark, the Bedouin was no more than a shadowy outline. He said not a word as he reached for her and swung her into his arms. With aching clarity, Danaë knew it would do her no good to struggle. There would be no escaping this man.

She was his prisoner.

Fear loosened her tongue. "If it is money you seek, I can give it to you. If you will allow me to go free, I can give you gold."

He said nothing. Strong fingers tilted her face upward, and she shrank from him. When he carried her quickly toward his horse, she slid her hand about his shoulders to steady herself and felt the corded muscles beneath her fingers. She would not be able to fight her way free of such a man, so Danaë decided to use cunning instead.

She tried to think of what she'd been told about the Bedouin — they were desert dwellers, a nomadic people, and some tribes possessed great wealth. Maybe her offer of gold meant naught to this man. Perhaps he thought he could get more if he sold her at the slave market. Or worse still, maybe he wanted to add her to his own harem!

"Sir," she said desperately, not knowing if he understood Egyptian, "you should beware. I have a man of great power searching for me. If he should find me, you will suffer the same fate as I, which will probably be death."

He remained silent as he carried her to his waiting horse. Smoothly he swung onto the saddle with Danaë in his arms. Before she could protest, she was enfolded in his black cape, and he nudged his horse down the sand dune, then into a gallop as they raced across the desert.

Danaë was terrified, and tried to crane her neck in an attempt to locate Uriah. Her captor gave a sharp command, and although she did not understand the words, she felt a chill climb up her spine and ceased her resistance. At the moment she was not sure which would be worse — to be the prisoner of Lord Ramtat or this wild Bedouin tribesman.

After an hour of continuous riding, Danaë grew weary and her head dropped back against the man's shoulder. There was no moon or stars to guide them, but the Bedouin seemed to know exactly where he was going. They had been joined by other Bedouins, and their fine desert horses galloped through the sand as if it were no obstacle.

Danaë felt the man's breath stir her hair and she forced herself to sit stiffly away from him again. Soon however, she became too weary to care and once more fell back against his hard body.

She felt his grip tighten about her, and he whispered, his breath touching her ear, "Sleep, green-eyed one. You will be the better for it."

How could she sleep when she was riding off into the night with a man who probably meant her harm? Her life had been naught but upheaval since she had left her father's home. She was weary of running, first from Harique, then Lord Ramtat; now she was the captive of this man of the desert. It was unlikely Uriah would ever find her. Her fate rested with the gods, and up until now, they had not served her well.

Sleep?

Not likely!

Danaë was too weary to think, too frightened to dwell on what would happen to her once they reached their destination. Her eyes were heavy, and her head seemed to nestle against the man's shoulder. She didn't care that she could feel his breath against her cheek, or that his arms held her like tight bonds. Her eyes drifted shut, and she fell asleep.

Drowsily Danaë wondered what had awakened her; then she realized they had halted at a small camp where men seemed to be waiting for them and helped them quickly change horses. Her captor handed her down to one of his men until he was mounted on a fresh horse; then she was handed back up to him. She tried to struggle and kick, but he forced her against his body until she was unable to move.

They continued on through the night, to what destination Danaë could not guess. After a while she drifted to sleep once more. When she awoke a short time later, she jerked forward, and the Bedouin loosened his grip on her. Struck by renewed fear, she fought and twisted, trying to slide off the striding horse, but the man roughly clamped her arms and held her fast until she finally ceased her struggle.

"Do not try that again — you will only injure yourself," he told her. "I'm stronger than you; to struggle is futile."

He was right, of course. She had felt his strength and tested his resolve. Even if she could manage to escape, he would overtake her.

"What do you want with me?" she demanded.

"Not what you may think." He laughed in amusement. "In truth, I would wish you anywhere else but on this horse with me."

"Then let me go."

"Nay."

Soft moonlight now fell across the countryside, and Danaë turned to glance at him. The lower part of his face was covered, and all she could see was the gleam of his dark, piercing eyes. Fear crept into her voice. "What are you going to do to me?"

"Woman, I have no intention of harming you." His voice was muffled, but she could tell he was irritated. "Take comfort in the fact that you are under my protection."

He settled her into the crook of his arm, and she felt the intake of his breath. Something wild and wonderful stirred within her, and that frightened her more than any threat he could have made. "Please let me go," she pleaded.

"Impossible! Speak no more of it."

Danaë fell silent, her thoughts in a quandary. What could this man want with her? Then she thought she knew. "Did Lord Ramtat hire you to capture me, or was it Harique?"

She felt him stiffen. "I know of no one by the name of Harique. I act on my own."

None of this made sense to her. "Then what can you want with me?"

He was silent for a moment, and when he did speak, it was with feeling. "What I want of you, and what I can have of you, are two different matters."

His words were not reassuring. The man spoke in riddles she could not understand.

Her mind filled with turmoil, Danaë tried to relax in the Bedouin's arms as the horse traveled on through the night. When the sun tinted the eastern sky with streaks of gold, they reached an encampment where some twenty tents were clustered among large date palms. Her captor rode straight to the center of the camp and halted before a magnificent tooled-leather tent.

When he placed Danaë on her feet, she

was immediately surrounded by curious women and children. Several women poked at her, and one pulled her hair. But a crisp order from the Bedouin made the women move away and scatter.

She watched as the others quickly dispersed. If there had been any doubt in her mind that this man was the leader of the Bedouin, it no longer existed. He turned to her and held out his hand, but she shook her head and moved away. He issued orders to those who stood nearby, and one of the men led his horse away.

Turning his attention back to Danaë, he took her arm and guided her resisting body toward the tent.

"No!" Danaë cried, struggling to free herself from his grip. But he merely swung her into his arms and carried her.

"I beg you, let me go."

He glanced down at her, and for a moment she stared back at him, her heart racing. The lower part of his face was still covered, and all she could see were dark eyes that showed no mercy. She knew it would do no good to plead with him. "Whoever you are, and whatever your reasons for making me your captive, I can mean naught to you. Give me a horse, and I will find my own way home."

"Consider this your home," he said crisply. "I cannot allow you to go free."

This time when Danaë struggled, he placed her on her feet abruptly. She was still stunned by his words. She was trembling with fear as she watched him move across the soft rug and walk toward an inner room, shoving the tapestry aside and disappearing behind it. She was left alone — pondering her fate and fighting her fear of the man's intentions.

In the seclusion of the inner room, Ramtat removed his dark robe and tightened the belt of his tunic, all the while aware that his hands were shaking. How could she not recognize him? He had purposely disguised his voice, but she should have known him anyway.

He closed his eyes, wondering why he always had such a passionate reaction to Lady Danaë. When he was near her, when he touched her, he realized his feelings for her were inexplicably deep. When he was not with her, all he did was think about her.

Now she was under his power, but he dared not give in to the urge to take her in his arms and confess his need for her. It was easy to see she feared him as the Bedouin, and she certainly despised him as

Lord Ramtat. If she only understood the depth of his desire for her, Danaë would be even more frightened of him.

The night ride through the desert had been torture for him. The feel of her soft body against his had stirred something deep within him — he had wanted to be her protector, not her tormentor.

He had to remember his duty to Egypt, and the reason he had been forced to take her prisoner. Caesar had wanted her dead; to hold Lady Danaë captive was the only way he could save her life. If she found her way back to Alexandria, she would go straight to the king and expose his ties to Rome. If that happened, there would be no way he could save her from Caesar's fury.

Ramtat straightened his shoulders and stared at the tapestry that separated him from Danaë. He had always thought that love was the one trap he would never fall into. Now he had fallen hard.

How could he expect to save Lady Danaë when he could not even save himself?

CHAPTER ELEVEN

For a long time Danaë stood in silence wondering what she should do. It was useless to think of escaping — she heard men talking just outside the tent, and they would never allow her to slip past them. Even if she could, where would she go?

With a resigned breath, she dropped down onto a cushioned stool, all the while keeping a wary eye on the tapestry area where the Bedouin had disappeared. She feared he'd return at any moment.

Trying to remain calm, she glanced around the interior of the tent. Several lanterns cast their warm glow against the beautiful hand-tooled leather walls. The silken rug beneath her feet was mostly red with slashes of blue and white; it fit so snugly against the sides, it must have been designed just for the tent. There were silk hangings and colorful tassels across the entrance, as well as the tapestry that shielded the inner room into which the Bedouin had disappeared.

Danaë was so surprised by the richness of the interior, she forgot for the moment to be afraid. She had been inside many tents, but certainly none was of this size and grandeur. There were several white goatskin couches scattered about. She walked to a small curtained area and pulled back the filmy netting to find a bed. Hastily she let the netting drop and stepped back. Her heart pounded with fear as she sank down onto a stool. Drawing a deep breath, she turned her attention to an ebony desk piled high with what appeared to be maps and charts. What kind of man was this Bedouin?

Danaë leaned forward and braced her chin in her hands. Life had handed her almost more than she could bear. By now, Uriah would be sick with worry, and so would Minuhe when she found out what had happened. Would she ever see them again? She thought about Obsidian and Tyi and how they must be grieving in her absence, especially the leopard, which had never been separated from her.

Once more, she heard the murmur of voices just outside the tent, but she did not understand anything said. She was frightened, and alone, and she had not yet seen the face of the man who controlled her fate.

Her father had taught her to be strong and to think for herself, but she felt powerless in her present circumstance and was angry at herself for giving in to fear.

Danaë tensed when she heard a commotion at the outside opening of the tent and steeled herself to face whomever entered. She was surprised and relieved to see four young women; one carried a large copper tub while the others carried earthen jars of water.

"Do any of you understand me — will you talk to me?" she asked in Egyptian, searching each face. The young woman who was giving instructions to the others shook her head, looking confused.

In frustration, Danaë smacked her fist into her open palm. "Can you find me anyone in this camp who is willing to talk to me?"

The young woman's dark eyes widened with sadness, and again she shook her head.

Danaë felt alone in a hostile world. Another woman entered carrying several fine robes and draped them over one of the couches, then left. Danaë felt hot and gritty, and she glanced longingly at the steaming copper tub. Two of the women helped her disrobe, and she readily eased her body into warm water smelling of exotic spices. As she bathed, her gaze kept going furtively to the tapestry at the entrance to the inner room, for she was fearful that her captor would enter while she was bathing.

That thought made her quickly dunk her head, rinsing a sweet-smelling balm from her hair. When she climbed out of the tub, her gaze still on the other room, she quickly dressed. Although her own garment was soiled and made of rough linen that chafed her skin, she refused the soft robe one of the women held out to her.

The women looked at her in distress so she tried to explain, not knowing if they understood her. "I prefer to wear my own clothing. I want naught that isn't mine."

The women finally left, but shortly one of them returned with food. Danaë relished the sight of fresh dates, and she would have loved to sink her teeth into the creamy slices of goat cheese, but she did not want to eat the food of her enemy. The fruit nectar was especially difficult to resist — she turned her face from it so she would not be tempted.

As morning changed into afternoon, no one disturbed Danaë, and she began to relax, hoping her captor had forgotten about her. Since she heard no movement coming from the inner room, she assumed it must have its own entrance, and that the Bedouin had left.

Later in the afternoon, a woman appeared. She was older than the others had been, and she looked Danaë over carefully as she placed a tray of food on the low table.

Danaë ignored the food as a plot formed in her mind. If she refused to take any kind of nourishment, perhaps the Bedouin would fear for her health and allow her to go home. "You may take that away," she said, pointing to the food.

The woman's dark gaze swept placidly over Danaë's face as if she cared little whether the captive ate or not.

"If you understand me, tell your master that I will not eat his food."

"Sheik El-Badari is not my master," the woman stated haughtily before sweeping out of the tent.

Danaë was not surprised to discover that the man who had captured her was a sheik. From the beginning, he had exuded power and confidence that his every command would be obeyed.

What continued to puzzle her was why he had brought her to his camp and refused to free her.

The evening meal was brought by the same older woman, and Danaë's stomach rumbled as she looked longingly at the spiced meat and block cheese. She tried not to think about the cakes dripping with honey. But she stiffened her spine, determined not to eat. "I will not partake of this food. Take it away."

The woman shrugged and withdrew before Danaë could question her. Danaë lowered her head, completely despondent. She was at the sheik's mercy — helpless, alone. But she could still control what food she put in her mouth, and to her that was a small kind of victory.

Lord Harique knocked against the high gate with the handle of his whip. When no one came to admit him, he called out loudly, "Open to your master or I'll have the gate ripped off its hinges!"

After a short wait, the gate creaked open and a thin young man bowed, his frightened eyes darting from Harique to the twelve armed guards who accompanied him. "You are not master here," the young man announced in a shaky voice. "This is the home of Lady Danaë, and she is away at the moment."

Harique dismounted and pushed past the lad, his eyes snapping with anger. "You will learn soon enough who your master is.

Think on this, and you will live a lot longer: *Lady* Danaë, as you call her, is not your mistress; rather, she is my slave."

The servant backed away, not knowing what to believe. He barely avoided being trampled by the guards' horses as they rode through the gate. "My mistress . . . er, Lady Danaë is not expected back for some time."

Harique glanced about him, liking what he saw. This was a rich property to add to his holdings. It was by mere chance he had learned about this place. He soon discovered that no one at her father's villa would tell him where Danaë had disappeared to. Either they didn't know, or they were keeping quiet because of misplaced loyalty.

At the time, Harique had become enraged when none of the household slaves would tell him what he wanted to know. Threats had not loosened their tongues. Nor had the beatings he had administered to the most stubborn of the slaves. When nothing else worked, he craftily inquired about Uriah's whereabouts, realizing that Danaë was probably with the old man. A foolish kitchen slave had blurted out the location of the house in Alexandria. In that moment, Harique knew he had Danaë!

His gaze swept the courtyard, and he smiled smugly — everything here, including

Danaë, belonged to him. "Search every-where," he commanded his men. "Surround the house and allow no one to enter or leave." Harique then turned his attention to the young man who had opened the gate for him. "If she is hiding on the grounds, you would be wise to take me to Danaë at once."

There was confusion in the young man's eyes, and fear. "I spoke the truth when I told you she is not here. But you could ask Uriah. He has just returned this very morn-ing."

Slapping the handle of his whip against his palm, Harique ordered, "Take me to him at once."

Uriah was still dusty, bruised and sore, and most of all worried about what had happened to Danaë. After her disappear-ance he'd had no other recourse but to return to the city and gather more men to help him search for Danaë.

When Harique entered the room, Uriah knew that matters had just become a lot worse, and he wondered whether Lord Harique was responsible for Danaë's abduc-tion. The man, young though he was, was capable of any atrocity. Uriah had observed Harique from his childhood and watched him grow more vicious and greedy with the passing years.

Planting his body in front of Uriah in a threatening manner, Harique motioned for two companions to aim their spears at the Jew's chest. "Tell me where she is if you want to live, old man," Harique said coldly.

Harique had a physique that any man would envy — he was muscular, with broad shoulders and a narrow waist. His face was handsome, though most of the time his mouth was twisted into a cruel line. The black-hearted young man's handsomeness was only a facade. Uriah looked into eyes so dark they were almost black, the irises mere pinpoints, and he knew he was looking into the eyes of pure evil. It was no secret to Uriah that Harique had always been obsessed with Danaë. But Uriah had sworn an oath to the dying Lord Mycerinus that he would keep Danaë safe from the nephew, though it cost him his life.

"Perhaps *you* can tell *me* where she is," Uriah said accusingly, refusing to bow or show deference in any way. "If you do not know where Lady Danaë is, I cannot tell you."

"Do not speak to me as if you were my equal, slave!" Harique shrieked, striking Uriah across the face with the handle of his whip, bringing blood. "Produce her immediately, old man. If you value your life, you will bring her to me at once." He ran his fingers across the whip, eyeing Uriah. "And tell her there is nowhere she can hide that I cannot find her."

Uriah touched his bleeding cheek but still showed no fear. It was clear to him that Harique had had nothing to do with Danaë's disappearance. He felt almost relieved — but if Harique was not responsible for her abduction, who was? "I cannot deliver your message because I am searching for her myself."

"You lie to protect her," Harique snarled.

"I would. But in this instance I am telling the truth."

"Do you expect me to believe you? I knew that if I could find you, she would be with you. Produce her now!" The whip lashed out and sliced into the old man's shoulder, and Harique smiled with sadistic pleasure as Uriah staggered backward. "I can hold out longer than you can in this game of wills between us."

Uriah struggled to keep his footing and stood defiantly before his tormentor. He would reveal what he knew about Danaë's abduction, for it would do Harique no good. The man had no chance of finding her; Uriah knew he had little chance of that himself. "Lady Danaë was forced to flee into the desert to escape a certain high-ranking nobleman who was causing her trouble. We had traveled but two days out of the city when our encampment was attacked, and she was spirited away." His shoulders hunched. "I returned here to gather men and horses so I could search for her."

"You expect me to believe this outrageous tale?"

Uriah shrugged his frail shoulders. "Whether you believe it or not, 'tis the truth."

"Who would have done such a thing?" Harique asked suspiciously. "Who would dare?"

"All I can tell you is there were more than a dozen Bedouins from a tribe I have never before encountered. I do not know where they took Lady Danaë, or why, because they took no one else. They were not interested in capturing any of the other women, and they did not rob the caravan. More than that, I cannot say."

Harique was beginning to believe the old man's story. "Who is the high-ranking lord she was running from?"

"I cannot say."

"Cannot — or will not?"

"I do not know the man," Uriah stated, which was true as far as it went — he'd never met Lord Ramtat in person, though he knew of him.

"You know more than you are saying. If you took her out of the city, you knew who she was running from. Is the man she feared responsible for her abduction?"

"That I cannot say, but I do not believe so. What dealings would an Egyptian lord have with desert dwellers?"

Harique looked into defiant eyes. "Just know this, old man: She is my slave, and so are you."

"Neither of us belongs to you," Uriah stated, trying not to smile. "Harique, you have been outsmarted by your uncle. Before he died, he made Lady Danaë his adopted daughter. You cannot touch her."

"I do not believe you. Show me proof."

"That I will never do. The document is in a safe place. If I were you, I would have a care about persecuting someone with the standing of Lady Danaë. She has made a friend of the king."

"The king's friendship did little to help her in her present situation, did it?" Harique stated sarcastically.

The muscle in Harique's jaw twitched with anger. For so long he had imagined

Danaë as his slave, subject to his every whim, and just when that desire was about to be realized, he had been thwarted. "Enough! Restrain the old man," he ordered. "I want the house thoroughly searched for documents, even if you have to bring it down stone by stone. This room is as good a place to start as any."

Uriah watched warily. Harique would have no trouble finding the adoption scroll, because he had not hidden it. Everything had gone wrong so quickly. His lips tightened, and his gaze went to the satisfied grin on Harique's face when one of the guards produced the document from a stack of scrolls on a shelf.

Harique saw Uriah's face whiten, and his satisfaction deepened. He quickly scanned the document and nodded. "My uncle did not love me, nor did I have any love for him. But I have outsmarted him, and he must be gnashing his teeth even in the afterlife." He handed the document back to the guard who had found it. "Burn it," he ordered. His voice hardened as he watched the document disintegrate into ashes. "There goes your proof, old man. Danaë is now my slave, and when I find her, she will be forced to do whatever I say."

"There are two other copies in safe

hands," Uriah stated. "You cannot find and destroy them both."

Harique smirked. "Do you think me a simpleton? I have already destroyed those two copies of which you speak." He pointed to the pile of ashes. "That was the last written proof that my uncle took Danaë as his legal daughter."

When Uriah struggled to free himself, Harique brought the handle of his whip down on his head, and Uriah crumpled to the floor.

"For that matter," Harique stated, kicking Uriah's ribs to see if he was unconscious, "you have lost, fool."

CHAPTER TWELVE

Danaë had spent two days waiting for the Bedouin sheik to reappear, but when he finally did, he came without warning, taking her completely by surprise. The tapestry parted, and she held her breath as he walked slowly toward her. He was tall and still draped all in black — the lower part of his face covered so all she could see was his eyes. His penetrating stare made her drop her gaze to concentrate on his dusty black boots. Apparently, he'd just returned from riding in the desert. After a long, uncomfortable silence, she finally raised her head to find him staring at her intently.

His silence, more than anything else, unsettled her. Warily she watched as he removed the *agal* that held his headcovering in place. Shock must have registered on her face as she stared in disbelief at the last man she ever wanted to see again.

He made a deep bow. "Lady Danaë."

She was astonished that Lord Ramtat was the one who had abducted her. In truth, she feared her captor more now that she knew who he was than she had when he was only an unknown Bedouin sheik.

"I trust you have been made comfortable," he said, his hot gaze sweeping across her face.

"You are a traitor and a deceiver," she said.

"A deceiver, perhaps, but a traitor, never — not to Egypt."

"You are a traitor to the king, and you deceive everyone who trusts you. The Romans think you are one of them; the king thinks you are his friend; and you deceived me into thinking you were a sheik." Her courage rose as her anger heightened. "How dare you make me your prisoner!" She backed toward the curtained area, her fingers gripping the filmy material. "You had no right to abduct me!"

He looked at her gravely. "Unfortunately, it was necessary. I could not take the chance that you would tell Ptolemy you had seen me sail into Alexandria on a Roman warship."

"I should have told the king that day at the palace, even though you threatened me," Danaë said decisively. "How could you have stood at the king's side pretending to be his friend? I denounce you as an impostor and a traitor to Egypt!"

Lord Ramtat frowned. "My allegiance is to Egypt, not to a spoiled boy-king who is naught but the puppet of those two evil men who control him." He found himself wishing he could make her understand his motives. "If not checked, Ptolemy will eventually bring Egypt to its knees."

"You will not find me a sympathetic ear if you wish to talk against King Ptolemy." Anger exploded inside Danaë. "And who are you to decide what is best for Egypt? You would hand everything over to your Roman masters as a gift." Danaë watched Ramtat's eyes darken and narrow, but that did not deter her. "In truth, it's you who is the real puppet — and it's your mighty Caesar who pulls your strings."

"You are free to think what you will. Your views will cause no one harm here in the desert, where only the scorpions can hear them."

"I'm not without powerful friends who will come looking for me. Do you think my servant Uriah did not go immediately to Alexandria when he discovered I was missing? I'm sure he sought an audience with King Ptolemy immediately. Even now the king's troops could be scouring the desert for me."

"The king has other pressing matters that consume his time," Ramtat informed her, his hard gaze sweeping across her face. "Not only is he fighting his sister, Queen Cleopatra, but he has now also foolishly waged war against Caesar and his legions."

"If the gods are with him, none can stand against him."

Ramtat looked at her impatiently, and when he spoke, it was as if he were explaining the situation to a child. "The gods would have done well to warn him not to divide his troops, or to fight on two fronts."

Danaë was actually shocked to learn that Ptolemy was in open warfare with Julius Caesar, the most powerful man in the world. "I admit," she said grudgingly, "it might not have been wise for the king to take up arms against Caesar." She frowned as she met Ramtat's gaze. "And what of Queen Cleopatra? Is she safe?"

"Caesar has sent men out to search for her. When last I heard, she had not been found. When she is, Caesar will place her under his protection. Egypt stands in great need of her."

"I scorn your notion of what's good for Egypt. If Queen Cleopatra is found by the Romans, she will probably be placed under

Caesar's *control,* not under his protection. What is the difference between King Ptolemy being controlled by the two imbeciles who counsel him, and Queen Cleopatra being owned by Rome? Can you answer me that?"

"What would you like to happen?" he snapped. "Would you want to see the queen slain on the field of battle?" He watched Lady Danaë's eyes sadden, and her sorrow struck him to the heart, though he could not have said why. Still, he tried to make her understand. "You saw Ptolemy — talked to him. You know Egypt will never fare well under his rule."

"I believe that with the right advisers, Ptolemy could become a good king."

"You do not really know the boy."

She was becoming annoyed. "And you do?"

"I know him well, and trust him not at all."

She raised her gaze to his. "When I met Ptolemy, I found him pitiable. He has no one to stand as his friend."

"Open your eyes and look around you — the country has been torn apart by a spoiled child playing at being king. Ptolemy must be stopped, along with his two evil advisers. If he does not accept his sister as co-ruler, he must die."

Danaë raised her chin even as she felt it tremble. She no longer knew what to think — there was sound reasoning behind Lord Ramtat's arguments. But she did not want to think about the young king losing his life. "Would his death not bother you?"

"Sometimes I feel as if I am bleeding inside because of the choices I have been forced to make. But every Egyptian will soon have to decide between the king and the queen." He gazed into her eyes. "Be very sure you choose the right one."

Danaë doubted she and Lord Ramtat would ever agree on who should rule Egypt. What she really wanted to know was what he was going to do with her. "How long are you going to keep me prisoner?" she demanded.

"I will only detain you for a time."

"Be warned, I will escape if I get the chance. And if I reach the king's ear, I will warn him you are no friend of his."

He stared at her through half-closed lashes. "It would not be wise to set one foot outside this tent. Should you attempt to do so, you will be restrained by my guards." He took a deep breath. "Should you somehow succeed in slipping past my men, there is nowhere you can go."

She had already come to that conclusion on her own. In her anger, Danaë struck out at him. "Should you not go back to your lord Caesar and ask what else you can do to serve him?"

She was not watching him, so she did not see him flinch. "I will speak to you no more on this matter," he said harshly. "I am only here because I was informed that you have refused to eat."

Danaë's chin rose to a defiant angle. "I choose not to eat your food, Lord Ramtat."

He walked toward her, and her hand tightened on the curtain netting as if it were her lifeline.

Ramtat regretted that she was frightened of him, but there was naught he could do to change her mind while she was his captive. "You have only to say what you would like to eat, and it will be provided for you."

"I just want to go home."

He lifted one dark brow and smiled slightly. "For now, consider this your home."

Danaë met his gaze. He was standing so near, she could feel the heat of his body. His eyes were dark brown, sensuously deep and hypnotic. He was more than handsome, and he probably knew it. Somehow the Bedouin robes made him look younger than he had appeared as a high-ranking Roman officer or as an important Egyptian lord standing beside the king. Whatever disguise he wore, he exuded power. She had to say something, anything to break the tension between them.

"How did you fool these people into believing you're a Bedouin sheik, and the king into believing you're an Egyptian nobleman?"

He drew in his breath. "At least in this I can defend myself. My mother is a Bedouin, and I inherited the title from her father, my grandfather; therefore, I *am* a Bedouin sheik, Sheik El-Badari. My own father was Lord of Tausret — I inherited his title on his death." He removed his outer robe and tossed it onto one of the couches, which left him wearing only a blue-trimmed toga that came to his knees. "In those two things I have practiced no subterfuge."

"Why should I believe you?"

She had a way of nettling him. He didn't know whether he wanted to throttle her or kiss her into submission. Running a hand through his short-clipped hair, he said in exasperation, "I am not here to talk about me — I came to make sure you take nourishment. I would not want to have the charge of starving you added to my other crimes."

It was difficult for Danaë to concentrate on anything but Ramtat when he was standing so near. He held himself in a regal manner that set him apart from other men. She had felt the touch of his mouth on hers, and just thinking about it caused a dull ache inside her. But he was her enemy, her captor, and she must not feel any softening toward him. "Go away — I shall eat what I want, when I want. You're wasting your time with me."

Angrily he shoved aside the tapestry that led outside. Danaë could not see the person he was talking to, but whoever it was handed him a tray of food, which he placed on a low table before turning back to her.

"You think to defy me by not eating?"

"At the moment, you have taken away my freedom in almost everything. But I can still refuse your hospitality." She watched him carefully, expecting those glorious brown eyes to flame in anger. She was unsettled when he smiled indulgently.

"If you will eat but a little, I will tell you how the war is progressing." His voice was cajoling. "You have an interest in the battle that is now taking place, do you not?"

He thought to induce her to eat by offering her information, but she was not so easily fooled. "Why should I care?" She shrugged. "I'm just a prisoner."

Undeterred, he sat down on the couch and looked at her. "How would you like me to tell you about the fire that burned many of the buildings along Alexandria's waterfront?"

She gasped and took a step toward him. "Was there much destruction?"

He patted the seat beside him, indicating she should sit. "Have a bite of honey cake, and I will give you details."

With a guarded look, Danaë dropped down next to him. "I know what you are doing."

Ramtat smiled. "Do you?" His gaze moved over her dark hair, which looked like a river of shimmering black silk. Her green eyes — how they had haunted him. He could gaze into them all day and never wish to look away. He had felt her firm, lithe body when they'd raced across the desert. She stirred emotions within him that he'd rather not feel. But at the moment, all Ramtat could think of was pressing his mouth against those trembling lips until Danaë surrendered completely to his will. She thought she was his captive, but in truth, she was close to enslaving him.

Ramtat would not allow himself to be conquered by a woman — he must bend her to his will. "Will you not take a bite?" he coaxed, breaking off a piece of honey cake and offering it to her.

With a resigned sigh, Danaë leaned forward and took a bite; a shock wave went through her as her lips touched his fingers. She detested this man who had driven her into the desert and then made her his prisoner. She was also drawn to him as she had never been to any other man. "There," she said, wiping crumbs from her mouth. "I hope that made you happy."

He smiled, thinking that what would really make him happy was licking those crumbs from her lips. Instead he took a bite of the cake himself. "This is very good."

"You said you would tell me about the fire," Danaë reminded him.

He held a slice of cheese out to her and resisted smiling when she took it from him and nibbled slowly, all the while glaring at him.

"Actually," he mused, "I am not sure who was responsible for the fire. Caesar issued orders that all ships in the harbor be burned so Ptolemy could not put up a barricade from the sea. I was told that a high wind carried the flames ashore."

Danaë thought of Captain Narmeri and hoped the *Blue Scarab* had not been burned.

"Where — what part of the city?"

"Mostly along the docks. Unfortunately, one of the buildings damaged was the Great Library."

She was shocked when she thought of the irreplaceable scrolls housed in the library. "Your Caesar is a barbarian."

Ramtat watched her unconsciously take another bite of cheese. "Even Caesar cannot command which way the wind blows. I'm sure he's feeling remorse about all the destruction. But such is war."

"Tell that to the people who've lost their homes and businesses." She glared at him. "You claim to love Egypt, yet you serve a man who destroys our treasures and burns our city."

Ramtat studied her for a moment. He had been sickened by the loss of the library, but Egypt stood to lose everything unless Ptolemy was checked. Why could she not see that?

"It's hardly fair, Lady Danaë," he said, "that you *think* you know everything about me while I know so little about you. Will you not tell me something of yourself?"

Danaë stared at him. "Why would I do that?"

Ramtat thought she looked adorable with her eyes flashing and her fists curled in her lap. "So I can know you better. I didn't realize Lord Mycerinus had a daughter. It seems your father kept you in the country, making you a mystery — no one seems to know anything about you." His voice deepened. "I've always had an inclination to solve mysteries."

"Then do your best. But you will get no help from me."

There was a long silence while Danaë chose to look away from him and examine the luxury of the surroundings. "This is your tent, is it not?"

He bowed his head. "It is when I have occasion to be with the tribe. You see, Lady Danaë, as half Egyptian and half Bedouin, I must divide my time between my two peoples. For the last few years I have been out of the country and could not fulfill my duty to either of them."

She turned her head back toward him. "You must find it hard to know which way to jump first — Caesar, Egypt, the royal court, or your Bedouins. You are a very busy man."

He was angered by her assessment of his character. "Perhaps you should feel sympathy for one in my position and try to understand how difficult it is to be tied to so many duties and not know which way to 'jump,' as you put it."

"I have little doubt you jump fast enough if the great Caesar calls."

"I don't play these political games for my amusement. We live in dangerous times. You may think of me as your enemy, but I am more friend to you than you know."

She looked at him in disbelief and started to say something, but he held his hand up to silence her.

"I've tried to explain to you why I appear to wear many faces, but you willfully refuse to understand. When the wars are over, Egypt will need Rome as an ally, and I can best plead Egypt's cause by being Caesar's friend."

Danaë felt in her heart he might be right, but she would never admit it to him. Instead she tried a different approach. "If I promised on my father's honor not to reveal anything I know about you to the king, or anyone else — then would you release me?"

Though she was making his life difficult, Lord Ramtat admired her courage. No other woman he knew, and not many men, would make such a worthy adversary. And it seemed that adversaries were what they were destined to be, though in a different time and under different circumstances, he would have liked it to be otherwise.

He leaned forward and took one of her hands in his, causing her eyes to widen hopefully. Knowing he was about to dash her hopes, he said, "When you will be free to return home, Lady Danaë, I cannot tell you, for I do not know myself."

Angrily she jerked her hand free and jumped to her feet. "Whether you free me or not, I do not accept your authority over me. Beware — I shall devise a way to escape your prison. And neither you, nor your guards, nor the desert will stop me."

"Enough!" he ordered, rising to his feet and towering over her. "You test my patience. You will remain here as my *guest.* Obey me and eat the food that is brought to you, and I will not trouble you with my presence."

She was relieved that he did not intend to share the tent with her.

He smiled at her mockingly, as if he knew what she was thinking. "Though my people might expect me to stay with you here in the main tent, I have settled quite comfortably in the inner room and will not disturb you." Already his mind jumped ahead to his duties. "In any case, I shall be leaving tomorrow. Does that put your mind at rest?"

"I don't trust you."

Other than kidnapping her, which he'd

done to save her life, he had done nothing to warrant her distrust, and he was tortured by her words. Had he not purposely stayed away from her the last two days so she would feel secure?

"If you believe nothing else about me, Lady Danaë, believe this: I would never force my attentions on any woman." He touched one of the golden beads that had been woven into her hair. "I prefer my women willing." His hand drifted down to her cheek, then to her throat, and he felt her pulse throbbing against his fingers. He leaned forward slowly, his mouth inches from hers. "I have tasted the nectar of these lips and am sorely tempted to find out if they are as sweet as I remember."

Danaë's lips parted, and she moved in his direction as if some unseen hand guided her movements. She ached for his lips to touch hers.

"But," Lord Ramtat said, pulling away and dropping his hand to his side, "that will have to wait until another time."

Feeling embarrassed because she had so easily surrendered to his touch, Danaë raised her chin. "I doubt you ever have to worry about finding a willing woman. I'd be more inclined to believe you have to keep a guard to discourage women from storming your bed."

Ramtat suppressed a smile at the implied compliment she had unwittingly bestowed on him. The more time he spent with her, the more she delighted and bedeviled him. Danaë could not know how provocative she was, or how, with just the tilt of her head, she could send hot blood pounding through his body. Suddenly his eyes narrowed. "And what about you? I crossed swords with your guard on the deck of the *Blue Scarab,* and then again at the gates of the house where you were staying in Alexandria. Does he keep all suitors away from you?"

She cried out, overwhelmed with apprehension, remembering the sound of clashing swords when she had fled from her home. "You didn't hurt Faraji, did you? Tell me he still lives!"

"He lives. No matter what your opinion is of me, I would not allow such a loyal servant to be harmed." He gazed into her troubled eyes. "Unfortunately, I did have to wound him, but be assured it is no more than a scratch. Your man fought for you most valiantly."

She dropped back onto the sofa and looked up at him. "What will happen to my people in Alexandria?"

"They will stay as they are and await your return."

She lowered her head. "You speak to me of duty. I also have a duty to my people. There are many who will be worried about me. Can I not send them word that I am well and ease their fears?"

Ramtat frowned and glanced away from her. "That would not be wise. But have no worry for your own well-being. When I feel it is safe to do so, I shall see you back to your home in Alexandria."

"And when will that be?" She looked up at him challengingly.

"Eventually."

As he gazed into her eyes, Danaë felt the pull of his magnetism. He was a man of great power, and it radiated from him. She suddenly had the urge to touch his face, to ease away the care lines that fanned out from those glorious eyes. He was weary; she could feel it in him. Mentally shaking herself, she turned away, lest she act on her impulse and embarrass herself further.

"You have eyes like emeralds, and your skin is like the white lotus blossom."

She felt warmed all over by his compliment, but when she turned to glance behind her, she found that Lord Ramtat had left the main tent and disappeared behind the tapestry that hid the inner room, leaving her once more alone.

Anguish came crashing down on her. With a feeling of helplessness, Danaë stalked to the tent opening, but quickly stepped back when she saw two men standing guard, blocking her exit.

She felt frustrated.

And frightened.

She had been loved and protected by her father. But he was gone now, and she was alone. It seemed that every direction she took, danger lurked.

Pacing across the rug, she shoved the netting aside and sank down onto the soft bed. Who was this man who had taken her prisoner? Was he Lord Ramtat, Sheik El-Badari, or Caesar's spy?

What frightened her the most was that she had been drawn to him in all three guises. With a wary glance at the tapestry that separated her from Lord Ramtat, she wondered if he slept alone, or if a woman shared his bed. Maybe one of the women who had waited on her — they were all certainly pretty enough to be his wife, or wives. The thought of him holding a woman in his arms just steps away from her devastated her — tore at her heart.

Therein lay the real danger to her.

■ ■ ■ ■

Theodotus stepped down from the cart and yanked the tarpaulin off Jabatus's cage. The horses sensed danger and reared, pulling on the reins when he unhooked the latch to free the cat. It had been easy to sneak the cat out of the palace, since these days Ptolemy's mind was focused on war. There was no doubt the king would be in the company of his generals for most of the day and long into the night.

Theodotus had finally won the cat's trust, and it had become accustomed to raw meat. He smiled to himself when he recalled the king moaning that his cheetah refused to eat, and he feared it might sicken and die. Theodotus kept the cat well fed on raw meat, so it was natural the animal would refuse the cooked meat the king offered.

He reached for the sack at the side of the cart, which held a squawking goose he'd pilfered from the royal kitchen. "Drive the horses to the top of the hill and wait there until I call for you," he told his slave Nute, who was eyeing the big cat with trepidation.

Jabatus swished his tail, his gaze expectantly on Theodotus.

"No, no, my beauty, I have no raw meat for you. Today, you must make a kill of your own."

Theodotus removed the goose from the bag, his hand circling the long neck to keep it from escaping. "This is your kill," he said, holding the fowl out to the cat.

Jabatus merely blinked and gazed at the flopping goose.

The day was sweltering; Theodotus was uncomfortable and longed for the cool gardens of the palace. "You must kill the bird if you want to eat," he said, losing patience.

Still, Jabatus showed little interest in the live fowl.

Suddenly Theodotus understood what the trouble was: The cat could not smell blood. The animal knew nothing about hunting and making a kill. With a grumble, the tutor gripped his dagger and slit the bird's throat. While it flopped around scattering blood, Jabatus became alert. With a swiftness that took Theodotus by surprise, the cheetah launched itself at the goose and grabbed it in his strong teeth.

With glee, Theodotus watched the cat devour the goose. Though Jabatus had not exactly made the kill, he had tasted hot blood. Theodotus shivered, thinking how easy it had been to turn a gentle animal into a killer.

His next step would have to be a human victim — it was one thing to attack small game, and quite another to kill a man. His gaze went to the top of the hill where his slave waited for his signal. Nute had been a good slave, but he was expendable and could be easily replaced.

But the hour was late, and that would have to wait for another day.

Chapter Thirteen

Danaë stirred and opened her eyes, stiffening with fear.

She listened intently to a windstorm that pelted the tent with sand and rattled the rings stabilizing the support posts. But the wind was not what had awakened her — it was the sound of murmuring voices outside the tent that had dragged her from sleep. She heard horses neighing and stomping their feet. Ramtat had told her he would be leaving today, but she had not expected him to depart so early. It was not yet sunup.

Danaë shoved aside the bed netting and hurried across the soft rug to the tent opening. When she shoved the tapestry toward the side, the wind tore at her hair and sand pelted her face. Blinking several times, she finally became accustomed to the darkness. When she saw the ominous shadow of the guard set to watch her, she stepped back inside so quickly she almost stumbled.

With trembling hands, she yanked the tapestry in place. Unthinking, she sank onto the couch. For some reason she did not comprehend, her heart felt heavy. As she heard the horses ride away, loneliness fell on her like a weight, and she hunched her shoulders, suddenly realizing what was bothering her. With Ramtat leaving, it was as if a part of her had been torn away.

It shocked her to discover she missed him. How was that possible? She hardly knew him, and the times they had met, they'd disagreed on everything.

She remembered the hasty kiss he had given her on board the *Blue Scarab.* It had probably meant nothing to him, but it had been her first kiss, and hard for her to forget. If she was honest with herself, she had to admit she wanted once more to feel the touch of his lips on hers.

Danaë listened to the wind intensify, slamming sand against the tent. Lord Ramtat would be riding through that sandstorm. Although he had not said so, she knew he was joining the war. She felt tears spill down her cheeks at the thought he might be wounded, or even killed.

Then another thought occurred to her.

Perhaps Ramtat had a woman waiting for him in Alexandria. He could be married —

he could have several wives, as she had thought the night before. She was disgusted with herself — what did it matter who shared that man's bed as long as it was not her? But thinking of lying beside him spread warmth through her body like hot honey.

She imagined him touching her, and it was almost more than she could bear. It made her ache with need.

"Stop it!" she told herself, gazing at the brightly patterned rug as the sound of the wind died away. Moodily she dropped her head in her hands. How could she have such feelings for so dangerous a man?

She thought of what he'd said about Ptolemy's weaknesses. It was true the boy was spoiled and too easily influenced by his advisers. If she had not met Ptolemy and felt such pity for him, she might be able to be more objective about who should rule Egypt. She had never met Cleopatra, so how could she judge which sibling would be the right one to sit on the throne?

For eight days Danaë tried to find something to fill her time. Hours passed, and she began pacing.

What was going on in Alexandria?

When would Lord Ramtat return? And

when he did, would he allow her to go home?

Out of boredom, she took her courage in hand and decided to enter Lord Ramtat's private domain. Moving to the inner tapestry, she jerked it aside and paused at the entrance. This area was much smaller than the outer room. There was a large bed, a desk and some of Ramtat's personal items of clothing, but this space had none of the splendor of the main room. It seemed that Lord Ramtat lived a simple life in the confines of his own quarters. She took just one step inside at first, and then several more as her courage rose.

Her attention was caught by a scroll Ramtat had left unrolled on a small ebony table. Tentatively she glanced at it and soon realized the writings were Latin. It was a language Uriah had urged her to learn, but one that had never interested her, since she hadn't expected to be conversing with Romans. If only she had listened to Uriah, she would be able to read the scroll.

Danaë had just turned to leave when she heard a commotion outside the tent. She stood frozen as the tapestry leading to what she assumed was an outside entrance parted, and Lord Ramtat entered, wearing his *kufiyya* and robe and looking every inch a Bedouin sheik.

There was a long silence as they stared at each other. Then Lord Ramtat gave her a mocking smile.

"Were you waiting to welcome me home?"

"Nay!" she said, backing away from him. "I . . . was merely curious about —"

His hard gaze went to the scrolls on the table. "If not to welcome me home, then why else are you here in my private chamber?"

"If you are implying I was spying on you, the thought never entered my mind."

He shrugged. "It would not matter if you were — you would find naught of importance here."

Danaë was reluctant to leave. "You were not gone as long as I expected," she said softly, slowly moving toward the tapestry that led to the quarters she occupied.

"I accomplished what I set out to do." He smiled slightly, intrigued by the heightening color in her cheeks. "Tell me, have the women made you comfortable in my absence?"

She paused in mid-stride, realizing she was happy to see him, that the days had seemed endless when he was away. "They have tried, but I'm not as comfortable as I would be in my own home." When Danaë saw his eyes darken, she realized he was annoyed. His chest rose and fell as he took an irritated breath. She moved as far away from him as she could get without actually stepping into the outer room.

"Stop acting as if I'm going to hurt you. You have nothing to be frightened of. Have I not said you will come to no harm under my care?"

"Your idea of harm and mine are very different."

Ramtat unwound his head wrapping and tossed it aside. He had ridden hard to get back to her, and at first he had thought she was pleased to see him, but she was still as unapproachable as ever. "I haven't slept in two days. I'm too weary to spar with you."

She pushed aside the tapestry and hurried into the outer room. She was startled when she felt Ramtat's hand on her shoulder, and he spun her around to face him.

"Why must every conversation between us end as a confrontation?"

Danaë straightened to her full height, but that brought her only to the level of his chin. "Could it be because I am not here by invitation but am forced to endure your company?" she remarked sardonically, shoving his hand away. "What would you do if I made a run for freedom right now?"

"You would regret it."

"Because you would have your guard run his sword through me?"

Ramtat rubbed the back of his neck as weariness swamped him. "Nay. I merely meant I have had a long few days, and I would prefer not to chase after you through this heat."

"Please leave me alone," Danaë said, raising her chin stubbornly.

Ramtat reached for her and brought her close to his body. Something warm and unsettling stirred her blood, and she ached inside with emotions she did not want to feel.

"I wonder if I could change your mind." Ramtat's thumb moved across her lips, and he watched her eyes close. His fingers moved into her hair, and he caressed the dark strands. He watched a blush steal up her cheeks, and he smiled. "I am sorely tempted to try," he said regretfully. "But now is not the time." And he released her.

Danaë's eyes snapped open. She took a stumbling step backward and would have fallen if not for his steadying hand. What was this game he played with her, bringing her alive to his touch and then pushing her away? Why did she care? Had she not told him to leave her alone? She tried to blink back tears and turned away from him so he would not see.

Ramtat saw her tears and was almost undone. "I have no right to touch you since you are under my protection."

She took several quick steps away from him. "How can I trust you now? If you can't keep away from me, then let me go home!"

Ramtat stalked across the rug to stand before her, capturing her face between his hands and turning it toward the lantern. "The gods have given you the face of a goddess, the green eyes of our queen, and a temper that would sour goat's milk."

She stared at him coldly. "I'm glad you dislike me. I would consider it an insult if you thought well of me."

Overcome with weariness, he sat on a couch. "I never implied I disliked you." He looked at her, totally confused. He had commanded legions, conquered nations and been covered with glory, but nothing had prepared him for his encounters with Lady Danaë.

"I am no longer surprised that your father kept you hidden in the country," he said. "In the few weeks I've known you, you have made an enemy of the most powerful man in the world, and if you hadn't left Alexandria when you did, you might have toppled the whole Ptolemaic Dynasty."

Danaë was shocked. "Why is Julius Caesar my enemy? I don't even know him!"

Ramtat had not intended to tell her about Caesar, but it was done now. "He knows you have discovered my connection with Rome, and until he is ready to disclose it, you are a threat to him."

She paled. "I begin to understand. You really are his man, and you captured me on his command. You are worse than I thought."

He had lost again, and there was no way he could defend himself without telling her that Caesar wanted her death. "Think what you will, Lady Danaë."

"And what you said about my father — no matter what you think, he didn't keep me hidden away in the country."

"Then tell me about him."

"I don't know you well enough to share my life story with you," she replied. "You are more of a deceiver than I thought. I don't know who you are."

He was pensive for a moment, and his tone deepened when he spoke. "Is anyone truly what they seem? Are you?"

She thought of her own situation. Lord Ramtat believed her to be the blood daughter of Lord Mycerinus; in that, she was deceiving him. "Probably not," she admitted.

His dark gaze swept her face. "The man who partakes of your final surrender will be fortunate indeed," he said, staring at her mouth.

"That man will not be you."

"Nay," he admitted regretfully, rubbing his aching head. "It will not be me. I assume your father had already chosen a husband for you before he died."

She hung her head, and the words slipped out before she could stop them. "There is no husband chosen for me. My father would have let me decide on my own. You are the only nobleman I have met since leaving my father's home, and if you are a sample of what I would have to choose from at court, I would rather remain as I am."

Her opinion of him did not bother him; in fact, he smiled, feeling suddenly lighthearted. Briefly he wondered why he should care that she was not tied to another man. "Perhaps one day I shall endeavor to change your mind about me." He laughed at her startled expression. "But do not distress yourself — this is not that day."

Before she could answer, he stood, make her a bow, and said, "I will leave you for now. There is much that requires my attention."

She watched him depart, wondering if the matter that required his attention was a woman. A man who looked as he did, and was as important a lord as he was, must have many women. Again she wondered if he had a wife, and that thought left her feeling strangely empty.

Danaë dropped down onto the couch Lord Ramtat had vacated and stared at the intricate patterns on the rug without really seeing them. She leaned back and closed her eyes, wondering what was the matter with her. She was drawn to a man who had proven to be her enemy. She had to remember that he had abducted her and refused to allow her to return home.

Her head jerked up when someone pushed the outer tapestry aside and a woman entered, balancing a tray of food, which she set on the table. She was tall and slender, perhaps Minuhe's age or a few years older. She wore a very fine linen robe of a green hue Danaë had never seen before.

The woman moved forward gracefully before she spoke.

"My name is Zarmah, and I have come to inquire if there is anything you need. I was told by my lord to do what I can to please you."

Danaë was relieved to have someone she could converse with at last. "I do need something," she said, staring into the woman's watchful eyes. "A horse and a guide to get me out of here."

The woman looked shocked. "You must know that isn't possible. And my lord would only chase after you if you attempted to leave."

"I would pay you well if you helped me escape. If you are a slave, I can buy your freedom."

Anger appeared on the woman's face, and Danae realized she was insulted. "There are no slaves in this tribe. And certainly not I. I am Sheik El-Badari's aunt, the sister of his beloved mother."

Embarrassed, Danaë nodded. "I ask your pardon if I have offended you — but think how I feel being held here against my will."

Zarmah looked indignant, and her dark gaze bore into Danae. "You are my nephew's honored guest. Has he not given you respect by quartering you in his own tent?"

"Honored guests are allowed to come and go as they like, while I am not even permitted to step outside."

The woman looked grimly at Danaë but

made no reply until she moved to the tent opening. "I will have a bath prepared for you."

Danaë was weary of people telling her when to eat and when to bathe. In frustration, she shoved the table away and a bowl of honey overturned, dripping onto the beautiful rug while slices of cheese scattered in every direction. The fruit drink soaked into the rug, making a wide stain. The woman looked at Danaë in horror, but bent to clean the remains of the meal in silence.

Feeling contrition and shame for her outburst, Danaë bent to help the woman. "I'm sorry."

"It was a childish thing to do," Zarmah stated.

"Aye," Danaë agreed, "it was."

The woman stood and hesitated. "In truth, I might have reacted in the same way under like circumstances. I'm surprised it took you this long to strike back."

"I want to go home."

Ramtat's aunt shook her head. "It is not within my power to grant you your request, Lady Danaë. All I can do is make certain you have every comfort while you are among us."

"You could speak to your nephew on my behalf," Danaë suggested hopefully. "Surely he would listen to you."

"I would not dare. Nor would he welcome such interference from me. If you want to leave, this you must ask El-Badari yourself."

Danaë merely stood, looking dejected.

"I'll bring you more food," Zarmah said kindly, sweeping out of the tent.

CHAPTER FOURTEEN

Three days passed, and in that time Danaë did not see Lord Ramtat. There were times when she heard voices coming from the inner room, and she supposed he was tending to tribal affairs there, but he and his visitors always spoke in the Bedouin language, so she did not understand anything said.

She was seated on the sofa, restlessly drumming her fingers against the cushion. She would lose her mind if she had to endure this solitude much longer. The only people she ever saw were the young women who brought her food and prepared her bath, and they never spoke to her.

Danaë stared grudgingly toward the tapestry at the entrance. She felt confined, smothered, her movements restricted. What she wouldn't give to go outside and feel the sun on her face! She would love to run through the desert as she had before she'd left her home. She missed the antics of

Obsidian and Tyi, and she wondered who was caring for them, especially the temperamental cat. Of course it would be her faithful Minuhe.

Hearing a slight sound, she glanced up to see the tapestry flung aside and Lord Ramtat walking toward her. She no longer feared him, but the anger she felt toward him was increasing with each passing day.

He smiled. "Can you ride a horse, Lady Danaë?"

Her anger was forgotten as hope took root. "Of course." She held her breath, almost afraid to breathe. Perhaps today was the day he was going to take her back to Alexandria.

Ramtat watched uncertainty play across her face. "How would you like to go for a ride with me?"

Danaë was disappointed that he would not be taking her home — but only for a moment. At least she would be able to leave the confines of the tent. "Aye, I would." She slid to her feet. "When can we leave?"

He laughed at her exuberance. "Not until you're properly attired. I will have one of the women bring what you need. I'll be waiting for you outside the tent."

The clothing turned out to be very strange to Danaë. There was a green tunic that fell just below her knees, and a pair of yellow goatskin boots that fit above her knees. The veil she looked at with distaste and decided against wearing. When she was dressed, she was delighted with how unrestricted she felt in the Bedouin clothing; although she was completely covered, she had great freedom of movement.

When she stepped out of the tent, Lord Ramtat was astride a prancing black stallion and holding the reins of a beautiful white horse for her. He looked Danaë over and nodded with approval.

"You make a very fine-looking Bedouin. Perhaps you might want to consider joining my tribe."

"I would join anything you say and do almost anything if it would get me out in the open."

Ramtat dismounted and gripped Danaë's slender waist, lifting her onto the soft leather saddle. He could see by the way she sat the horse that she had riding experience. "You will find it quite different riding here," he cautioned as he swung onto his own mount. "My horses are trained for the desert, and the sand doesn't impede their stride in any way."

"My father also had very fine horses, and I learned to ride in the desert," she said, laughing. Joy burst through her as she nudged the spirited white stallion forward, noticing that Ramtat stayed even with her.

"Come," he said, urging his horse to a faster pace, "Let's see what kind of horsewoman you really are."

As they rode away from the encampment, Ramtat could not keep from staring at Danaë. Never had he seen her more lovely than with the wind tearing through her long, dark hair, and her cheeks flushed with excitement. His heart felt like it was being squeezed by a tight fist when he heard her laugh. His gaze dropped to her breasts, which were clearly outlined by the flowing robe that had become entangled on the saddle and pulled tightly across her shoulders. She wore her ebony hair without ornament, hanging loosely about her shoulders as he had often imagined it. For the first few moments of their ride, he could not speak because his breathing was constricted.

Danaë was smiling as she bent low over the horse and raced alongside Lord Ramtat. The desert air kissed her cheeks as her knees gripped the horse's flanks, urging the stallion on to a faster pace. Side by side, Danaë and Ramtat galloped into the desert.

"You're as fine a horsewoman as any Bedouin," Ramtat admitted at last, as they slowed their pace to let the horses rest. "My sister is the only woman I know who could keep pace with you. Being half Bedouin, she sometimes likes to ride bareback."

Danaë was pleased by his compliment. "My father put me on a horse when I was but three years old. We have . . . we had every kind of animal you could imagine at the villa. He insisted I interact with them all. Horses and big cats are my favorites."

"The day I first saw you, a huge black cat stood at your side. I will never forget the sight of the two of you."

"Obsidian is my own personal cat."

"Is the animal dangerous?"

"Not unless I give her the command to attack." She glanced at Ramtat with a mischievous smile. "If I ordered her to rip you apart, she would obey me without hesitation."

"Would you order her to attack me?"

"Nay," she admitted. "My father taught me it was wrong to use any of our animals to do harm to a person." She laughed, feeling lighthearted. "So you see, Sheik El-Badari, you're safe from Obsidian."

"I know you miss your father," he said.

Danaë looked directly at him, and it was as if the light left her eyes. "I mourn him still."

In that moment, Ramtat despised himself because his actions had added to her pain. He also realized that his motives for capturing her and bringing her to his camp were not all that pure, and not entirely to keep her from talking to the king. He'd wanted her — it was as simple as that. She stirred his senses, and he was awed by her courage, and something more. He resisted the need to scoop her off her horse and hold her against his body to give her comfort.

"Lady Danaë, please accept my deepest sympathy. Losing your father could not have been easy for you."

"The hardest part," she admitted, meeting his steady gaze, "is knowing I can never again hear my father's voice or benefit from his wise counsel." Her throat tightened, and it took her a moment to speak. "It's difficult to know that I belong to no one, and no one belongs to me."

Ramtat could no longer bear to look into Danaë's expressive green eyes because he saw pain there, and her pain had somehow become his.

How could that be? he wondered. He was changing because of Danaë, and he was dazed and unsure of what to do about her. She had every reason to hate him, but oddly enough, she did not. Could she ever forgive him for his treatment of her? He found he wanted her respect, but he didn't think she gave respect easily. And love — what would it feel like to be the man she loved? He was shocked, but it was true. He wanted nothing more than to love her and have her love him in return — but was it too late for him?

They rode in silence for quite a while. Shadows had lengthened across the sand by the time Ramtat called a halt and handed Danaë a waterskin.

After she took a deep drink, she wiped her mouth on the back of her hand and gave the skin back to him. "I have told you about my life, yet you have said little about yourself."

He motioned for her to dismount so they could walk the horses. "Growing up as I did, I was introduced to the best of two worlds. I had a good life, and a fine education under my father's guidance. When he died, I was sent to my mother's father to learn the ways of the Bedouins."

Danaë frowned. "How long ago did death claim your father?"

"When I was in my twelfth summer. To me, he was the best of men. I was devastated when he died."

She glanced down at her boots and

vaguely noted they were dusted with sand. Then she inhaled the distinct, heady smell of the desert. "What about your mother?"

Ramtat smiled as if he were amused. "She's very much alive. And I mentioned my younger sister, Adhaniá. She's perfect in my eyes."

Dazzled by the bright sunlight, Danaë shaded her eyes with her hand. "And you have your Bedouin family," she reminded him. "That makes you fortunate. Tell me more about your time with them."

There was a long pause before he spoke. "Under my grandfather's guidance, I was instructed by the finest horsemen in Egypt, and trained to throw a dagger from a great distance and hit the mark. I learned much from the Bedouin people, and I am proud to be of their blood. If you only knew them as I do, I believe you would like them as well."

"Under different circumstances, perhaps. As it is, I see them only as your watchdogs."

Ramtat glanced into the distance at the setting sun. "We should go back to camp now."

Danaë nodded. She was not ready to return to her solitary existence, but what choice had she?

When they arrived at the encampment,

Ramtat asked, "Would you like to ride again tomorrow?"

She nodded. "I would wish it above all things."

Ramtat couldn't help noticing the glow in her cheeks, and the happy light in her eyes. "Then you shall have your wish. Tomorrow we must get an earlier start — there is something I would show you that is a long ride from here."

Danaë had thought she would be unable to sleep because of the excitement of the day, but she fell into a deep slumber almost the moment she lay down, and didn't wake until the early morning sun poured into the tent.

Ramtat was waiting for Danaë as she emerged from the tent. As he walked toward her, the sun was behind him. In its bright glow, she could not help thinking he had taken the form of the sun god, Amun-Re, so brilliantly did he shine.

"I have a surprise for you," he said. "I'm going to show you something very few know about. How would you like to camp overnight?"

His offer was altogether unexpected, and she eagerly nodded. "Some of my fondest memories are times when my father and I camped in the desert." She looked reflective. "The servants prepared the same food they would have served us at home, but somehow it tasted better in the desert."

He lifted her onto her horse, his hands lingering at her waist. "I will be your servant tonight, for we go on our adventure alone." He arched his brow. "Unless you would prefer to have servants wait upon you."

Danaë was filled with delight at the prospect of being alone with him but was afraid to let it show on her face. "I'm no pampered maiden who needs someone to wait upon me."

"Then let us go — it is almost a full day's ride to this place I would show you."

In no time at all they had left the encampment far behind and were racing across the desert. They stopped at the noon hour and broke their fast, rested the horses, and then were on their way once more.

Danaë loved the feel of the wind blowing in her hair. Her white stallion raced up the side of a sand dune without pausing. She glanced over at Ramtat and laughed. "Would you dare race me to the next dune?" she asked, issuing him a challenge.

With a nod of his head, Ramtat allowed Danaë's horse to break out in front before he spurred his own stallion forward. She was laughing as she bent low over the saddle. She saw Ramtat come up beside her and urged her mount faster. But try as she might, she could not catch him when he overtook her, and his black stallion maintained his lead. Ramtat had dismounted and was waiting for her when she reached the top of the dune.

She slid off her horse and crossed her arms over her chest, glowering at him. "You purposely gave me the slower horse — you knew I couldn't win."

Ramtat lowered his gaze to her compressed lips. "Would you expect me to set you on a horse that could outrun mine?" He pushed a wayward strand of hair behind her ear. "Nay, Danaë — I am not a fool. If you found you could outrun me, you would have left me behind." His dark gaze challenged her. "Is that not the right of it?"

She lowered her arms. "You are wise not to underestimate me. I was testing you, and if I had won, I would have kept going."

His eyes narrowed. "But you didn't win, did you?"

They stared at each other challengingly.

At last Danaë spoke: "You think you know me, but you don't."

His lips twisted mockingly. "If I lived two lifetimes, I would never fully understand you — you're too complicated."

Danaë plopped down on the sand and looked up at him. "And you think you are uncomplicated? You, who has so many identities. Probably you forget who you are to be on any given day unless you consult a list."

Ramtat was tightening his horse's girth and could not keep from laughing aloud. "It isn't as complicated as it might seem to you."

She gazed into the distance, the desert reminding her of home. "Tell me where you are taking me."

"That would spoil the surprise." He held out his hand and assisted her to her feet. "We should leave now."

"I could outrun you on foot," she told him as he lifted her onto her horse.

He stroked her horse's mane, and her gaze followed his long, lean fingers.

"Is this another challenge?"

"If you like." She tossed her hair proudly. "Of course, you mustn't let it sting your pride if I outrun you. I am accustomed to running with big cats."

He swung onto his horse and spun the animal around. "Why don't we test that tonight?"

"If you like," she said smugly, almost

certain she had him now. He was probably not in the same physical condition she was — most likely he was spoiled by riding everywhere he went. A smile touched her mouth, and she could hardly wait to best Ramtat at something.

Anything.

CHAPTER FIFTEEN

They had ridden some time in silence when Lord Ramtat halted. "We'll soon be leaving the desert behind. If you want a footrace, this would be the place."

Danaë could hardly contain her excitement as she slid off her horse. "You may choose the starting and ending points."

Laying down his pack and bow and arrows, he put his hands on his hips and glanced around. "Suppose we walk to the top of the low dune and race to the next one."

"That's not far enough. Suppose the stopping point is the second dune — the tall one?"

"Done."

She watched him strip down to his short tunic, and she noticed how muscled his legs were. For a moment she wondered if she had underestimated Ramtat. Of course he was not out of condition — he was a soldier, strong enough to wear massive armor and wield a heavy sword.

What had she been thinking?

Nay, she would not allow him to beat her! This race became the most important thing in her life at the moment. It was more than just a race; in some way it was a bid for freedom.

They walked to the top of the low dune, and Ramtat shaded his eyes against the sun. "Would you like a head start on me?"

Danaë shook her head. "I don't need it, but I'll give you the same offer."

"We start out even, then."

"There is one thing I want you to promise me before we start: Don't hold back because I'm a woman." She tapped his arm. "Give me your word."

"You have my word." He bent down and scooped a handful of sand. "When the last of this sifts through my fingers, it will be the signal to run."

She nodded, carefully watching the sand drift away.

With the last grains, they both burst down the hill, and for a time they stayed even. But Danaë felt a sudden surge of energy from somewhere inside her, as she always did, and she hurtled over the top of the first dune. Running full out, hardly winded, she began to pull ahead of Ramtat. In that moment, she knew she would win.

Lunging forward, she lengthened the distance between them, and she smiled.

Ramtat had not really expected Danaë to be much of a challenge — after all, she was a woman and accustomed to a more sedentary life than he. But as he ran beside her, he realized she was beginning to outdistance him. Determined to match her steps, he ran full out, but she was pulling still farther ahead of him. To watch her run was a delight — she was graceful, leaping over the obstacles in her path with ease. As the distance between them widened, he realized he could not catch her, try though he might. She raced up the last hill and stood smiling down at him, waiting for him to catch up with her.

He was breathing hard and fell down on the sand at her feet, laughing. "If I hadn't seen you with my own eyes, I would never believe your amazing speed. You won, and I'm proud to salute you."

"I like a man who is gracious in defeat." She dropped down beside him. "You did give it your all, did you not?"

He turned his head and looked at her. "I gave it more than my all. Maybe you can teach me how you do it."

She lay back, staring at the blue sky. "It's quite easy — you have to run every day. I may not be as fast as I usually am because I haven't run in a while."

Ramtat stood up and helped her to her feet. "I have never seen anyone who could beat you in a race."

"Neither have I." This was said without conceit — she was merely stating a fact.

"Was this another test to see if you could escape?"

Danaë laughed. "Nay, though I was sorely tempted. I'm not a fool — even if I could outrun you, I couldn't outdistance your horse."

It was early afternoon when they reached level ground and left the desert behind. At first there were only sprigs of green bursting from the cracked earth where nothing but the hardiest plants could survive. As they descended a steep hill, thick grass cushioned their horses' hooves.

Danaë stared at the valley that stretched before them and was taken by surprise at its beauty.

She slid off her horse and stared at tilled green fields that gave way to vineyards, and beyond that, orchards for as far as the eye could see.

She turned to look at Ramtat. " 'Tis as beautiful a land as I've ever seen. Surely it must belong to some noble family."

"It belongs to my family," he told her, his gaze skimming with pride over the countryside. "But this is not what I brought you to see."

He surprised her when he took the bridles off both their horses and removed the saddles, dropping them on the ground. He then slung his bow and quiver of arrows over his shoulder and untied the linen bag that was packed with supplies. When he saw Danaë's questioning look, he explained: "The terrain where we are going is too rugged for the horses to climb."

"Can you just leave them here? Will they not wander away?"

He hoisted a pack on his back and swatted the rump of his horse. The slap started the animal galloping away, and the white stallion followed closely behind. "They are well trained, and they know where to find food, water, and a good rubdown. When I want them, I have merely to whistle, and they will find me."

He started moving in the direction of the sunset, and Danaë followed. He helped her up the steepest formations. They crossed a narrow stream until he paused and nodded at the small rise. "My surprise is just beyond that grove of tamarisk trees. I think you'll like it."

The sun had sunk low in the west, and the land was washed in a golden glow. Danaë held her breath, unable to believe her eyes. Cutting its way through the gorge of a steep rock-face cliff, a waterfall splashed its way down to a shimmering pool. She was afraid to move lest it be only an illusion and disappear before her eyes.

"How is this possible?" She met Ramtat's eyes. "What can be the source of such a phenomenon?"

He helped her over a rock and watched her sit upon the edge, happy that he had pleased her. "When I was but a boy," he said, placing his pack on the ground, "I wondered the same thing — so I climbed the waterfall to discover it was fed by a stream that comes out of a mountain. Since there was no exit other than the one I found, I imagine it is fed by an underground stream." He braced his leg on the rock and rested his arm on his knee. "Of course, the waterfall is seasonal — in dry years it does not flow at all."

Danaë stretched her arms toward the heavens, feeling joy wash over her. If she could choose a moment in time, it would be this, this moment — here in this beautiful valley with this man beside her.

She turned to him and found him watching her with a soft expression.

For a long moment, they listened to the sound of the rushing water plummeting to the pool below. "I should like to bathe in the pool," she said wistfully. "But the sun is going down and taking the warmth with it."

"Then you shall have your wish on the morrow."

"But," she said, frowning in confusion, "where do we pass the night?"

"There is a grassy valley just beyond the waterfall. I spent many boyhood nights in just that spot. And sometimes, when I am troubled about something, I have come here even as a man."

As if by natural instinct, she held her hand out to him. "Show me."

His fingers closed around hers and he aided her down the embankment. She paused for a moment when they reached the waterfall, bent, and cupped her hands, taking sips of water. "This is cold."

"It always is."

Ramtat felt his heart swell — the more time he spent with Danaë, the more his need for her grew. How had he lived before she came into his life? he wondered. His existence had been filled with uneventful moments, colorless and without meaning, aside from his duty to Egypt. Now that he knew her, life without her would be a torment.

One day, when Egypt's political problems were settled, perhaps he could make her understand that he had brought her to the desert to save her life.

But not now.

After they had climbed farther down the embankment, Danaë ran toward the meadow. "This is the place I would build a house if this land belonged to me." She looked at him and smiled. "I'm surprised you haven't already done so."

"Perhaps until now I had no reason to settle here. You are the only one I have ever brought to this place."

She settled on the grass. "If it were my land, I would keep it to myself as well. Surely the gods must dwell in this valley."

Ramtat sighed. She had missed his whole point that she was the only one he had ever shared this refuge with. Was she that innocent, or did she choose to misunderstand him? "Are you hungry?" he asked, opening his pack and laying food on a linen cloth.

She moved closer to him, sitting back on

her folded legs, and nodded. "What have you to tempt me to eat this day?"

He caught the sweet scent of her hair and could hardly concentrate on what he was doing. "Dried meat, cheese," he said, taking stock — "honey cakes and bread."

"I'm hungry," she said breaking off a chunk of cheese and popping it in her mouth. Smiling, she took another chunk and held it up to him.

Ramtat bent his dark head and took the offering, his gaze on hers. Even in the near darkness, he could see the brilliant green color of her eyes.

Danaë stared up into the sky. Surely there had never been such a night. The stars were lustrous, the moon bright, and Ramtat was beside her. She never wanted to leave this place.

"Danaë, you are far away from me," he said, watching her stare into the distance.

She pulled her attention back to the food. "Did you say you had honey cakes?"

He nodded. "Aye."

She stood, and his gaze followed her slender form, the swell of her breasts, the silkiness of her hair.

"I find I am not so hungry after all. Will you allow me to dunk my feet in the pool?"

Again he nodded, only this time because

his throat had closed off and he could not have said a word if his life had hung in the balance. He watched her until she reached the water, where she sat down to remove her boots. He still watched her as she waded into the pool. Closing his eyes, he lay back on the grass, wondering why he had brought her here. He should have known it would be torture for him, and perhaps for her as well, though he really could not decipher what she was feeling.

He lay there for a long time until he heard her soft tread. His eyes remained closed when she sat down beside him.

"Why did you bring me here?" she asked softly.

"I was just asking myself the same thing. Perhaps because I thought you would like the freedom you could have here."

"I'm cold."

He rolled to his feet and reached for his pack. Withdrawing a soft wool blanket, he draped it about her shoulders. "This should keep you warm until I can make your pallet."

"You have thought of everything," she said, shivering. "I should never have put my feet in the water."

Taking one of her dainty feet in his hand, he rubbed it vigorously, then gave the same attention to the other. Then, without a word, he went about spreading their sleeping mats.

Danaë curled up on one of them, tucking her feet into the woolen coverlet. "Are there wild beasts in these parts?" she asked sleepily.

"Lions have been spotted from time to time — there are jackals, and, of course, snakes. But don't be afraid; I won't let anything harm you."

"I'm not afraid." She turned her head in his direction and saw he had dropped down onto his pallet. "You forget I tame wild animals."

"Nay, I have not forgotten."

Danaë yawned and closed her eyes, falling asleep almost immediately. But Ramtat remained awake long afterwards. He watched night shadows play across the most beautiful face he had ever beheld. But it was not just her beauty that drew him, it was her untamed spirit as well. She had become so much a part of him, he did not want to spend one day away from her.

He pulled his bow and quiver closer to him and watched the rise and fall of her breasts until he, too, fell asleep.

Ramtat opened his eyes, squinting as sunlight fell across his face. He looked quickly at Danaë's pallet, thinking she would still be asleep, but it was neatly folded, and she was nowhere in sight. He jumped to his feet, looking in every direction, fearing Danaë had taken it into her head to run away.

But he relaxed when he heard musical laughter and the splashing of water, realizing she was in the pool. He hurried in that direction and was surprised to find her floating on her back. Most women could not swim, but obviously she did. She waved at him and turned over to swim to the edge of the pool.

"You were sleeping so soundly, I didn't want to wake you."

"My hearing is keen; I should have heard you."

She smiled as she crossed her arms over the rock edge of the pool and rested her chin atop them. "But I can move as silently as the big cats. No man can hear me if I don't want him to."

Her hair hung about her like shimmering onyx, and he could see the swell of her breasts through the wet linen of her tunic. "So it would seem. I could use you as a spy to slip in and out of the enemy camp."

She gave him a dubious glance. "First we'd have to agree on who exactly is the enemy."

He ignored her barb and waded into the water. "It's still cold."

She laughed and splashed water on him. "Big, bad warrior — what's a little cold water to Caesar's fiercest fighter?"

He dove under the water and pulled her down with him. She kicked her feet and slid out of his grasp, laughing as she made it to the edge of the pool. "I also learned how to swim alongside a fish that is bigger than you are."

Ramtat tossed his hair to keep it from dripping in his face. "Is there anything you don't know how to do?" He swam toward her but stopped before their bodies touched. "Is there any challenge I can offer where you can't best me?"

"You might be able to shoot an arrow truer than I. Although my father did engage his finest archer to teach me. You've met Faraji on two occasions."

He seemed to be watching her intently, and Danaë was glad she had taken the precaution of removing her mother's pendant because it would have shown through the damp material. And Ramtat would surely have wanted to know about it.

He slowly moved closer, and she froze as their flesh touched. Her eyes widened, and his eyelids lowered.

"I want to hold you," he said in a deep voice.

Without hesitation, she pressed closer to him, her arms sliding around his shoulders. Sunlight reflected off the water, the birds trilled in the nearby trees, and their bodies strained to get even closer. Then his mouth was on hers, and she whimpered with need.

Ramtat tore his mouth from hers. "I didn't mean for this to happen." He pressed his cheek to hers. "Or did I? I don't know anymore."

She brushed a wet strand of hair out of his face. "Why does this happen when we are together?" She pulled back. "Or does this happen when you are with any woman? Can any female resist you?"

He tried not to laugh. "They have, and they do." He suddenly became serious, his gaze heavy upon her. "But I have never wanted any woman the way I want you." He swept her hair off her neck and rested his lips there. "I believe you know of what I speak."

She laid her head against his shoulder while his hands spanned her small waist. "We are enemies," she said, reminding herself of the rift between them. "That you cannot deny."

His hand moved gently to her breasts, and she gasped as if hot honey ran through her body. "Nay, not enemies, sweet green eyes. It's my belief that the gods created you for me."

Danaë tilted her chin, parting her lips. "If only it were so."

Barriers broke! He pulled her body against his, pressing her to the side of the pool and grinding his lower body against her. His hardness slid between her thighs, and she went limp in his arms. His mouth touched her ear, and she quivered.

"Please don't torture me so," she pleaded.

She had thrown her head back, and he kissed along the length of her throat. "You have only to say the word, Danaë, and I will take the ache away."

She jerked her head up, and they stared into each other's eyes for a long moment. He wondered what she was thinking as he watched the passion drain from her gaze. When she pushed against his chest, Ramtat immediately released her and watched her smoothly lift herself out of the pool.

"I don't like the way you make me feel," she said with her back to him. "Why it must be you that brings out this yearning in me — I cannot guess. Sometimes the gods can be cruel."

"Danaë, you can neither deny this attraction between us, nor can you explain it away. If we gave ourselves to each other, it would be more wondrous than you can imagine."

She turned her face back to him, her dark hair swirling about her shoulders. "You have felt this with other women?"

"Nay. Not like this, Danaë. I would speak only the truth to you. I want to be much closer to you — my need is so great, I tremble from it."

She moved away reluctantly. "There are already too many chains that bind me to you. I will not give you another."

He came out of the pool, and she turned to look at him. He was the most beautiful man she had ever seen, his body perfect, his eyes mesmerizing and bright with passion. He said he wanted to be closer to her, and she, too, trembled from the thought of surrendering to him completely.

Ramtat moved some distance from her. "Perhaps now is not the time for us, Danaë. But my hope is that one day all the barriers between us will be removed."

She dropped her head. "My life was uncomplicated before I met you. Everything was calm; I knew peace."

"And I was dead before I met you," he

said, bending to fold his bedroll and stuff it in the bag. "I believe we should leave now."

Danaë ignored her wet tunic and sat on a fallen log to pull her boots on. She refused to let the tears that burned behind her eyes fall down her cheeks.

They were both silent while they packed the rest of the supplies. Ramtat offered her a slice of cheese and some figs, which she ate because she knew she would have to keep up her strength.

The barrier between them was well in place by the time Danaë followed Ramtat up the hill. She paused to glance back at the waterfall, almost wishing she had given herself to Ramtat. But it was too late to recapture what could have been — the moment had passed.

When they reached the place they had left the saddles, just as Ramtat had predicted, his sharp whistle brought both horses racing up the hill toward them.

It was a long and silent ride back to the encampment. Ramtat was locked in his own misery, and he was sure Danaë was as well.

CHAPTER SIXTEEN

Ramtat seemed to push the horses hard on the ride back to the Bedouin camp. The silence between him and Danaë was painful, but neither knew what to say.

When they reached the encampment, Ramtat lifted Danaë from her horse and was struck by the thought that if he let her go like this, they could be lost to each other forever. His hand was on her shoulder, and she was staring up at him as if she expected him to say something.

"I wonder," he said at last, "if you might consent to dine with me tonight?" He had asked casually but searched her eyes for her reaction. "I'd be pleased if you would."

She considered for only a moment before answering. "Aye, I would like that."

Ramtat watched Danaë move gracefully toward the tent, wishing he could change the past. How differently he would have treated her if he had another chance. He could have pressed her further when they were at the waterfall, but he wanted her willing and aware.

When she disappeared inside the tent, he led the horses away. Danaë's innocence stood between them like a sharp-edged sword. She would probably be shocked if she knew how difficult it had been to let her leave him when they were in the pool. She was ripping him apart inside.

Tonight he would be his most charming. He would woo her and change her opinion of him — if he could. Never before had a woman been so elusive, but Danaë was unlike other women and kept him bewildered most of the time. In the past, he had not given much thought to spiritual love between a man and a woman, but lately that was all he seemed to think about.

Her body responded to his, but he knew that if he did not win her mind, he could not possess her heart.

Ramtat did not want Danaë for just a night or two; he wanted her beside him for the rest of his life.

Tension filled Danaë as she nervously sat beside Lord Ramtat on the white couch. After all the intimacy that had passed between them, it was hard to know how to react to him.

Danaë's eyes widened when she saw the low table laden with food; never in her life had she seen such a feast. At the center of the table were a roast duck, a fish wrapped in palm leaves, and wedges of honey cakes. This bounty was surrounded by a mound of figs dipped in honey, and platters with every kind of fruit she could imagine.

"This seems like a waste of food for only two people."

He smiled. "Perhaps I wanted to impress you."

"You could have done so with half the fare you have here."

Ramtat showed her deference by serving her from his own plate, something an Egyptian rarely did. She kept her lashes lowered as she took a bite of fig dripping with honey. She was aware of him with every beat of her heart, and she dared not look into his eyes lest he see what she was feeling.

Her gaze settled on his long, tapered fingers as he took a date from his dish and her eyes followed his hand to his lips — which was a mistake. He had the most beautifully shaped mouth she had ever seen, and she remembered what it felt like to have that mouth pressed against hers.

It gladdened Ramtat that she had worn the gown his aunt had chosen for her. When he had seen Danaë on board the ship and in the royal palace, she'd been dressed as an Egyptian rather than in the Greek style that the royal family had made popular in Alexandria. The gown she now wore was jade green and draped about her in the manner worn by Bedouin women — it outlined her curves in a way that heated his blood.

"You are very lovely tonight."

She blushed. "It isn't me," she stated demurely. Her hand brushed against the soft material. " 'Tis this lovely gown."

"We won't go into that, or it might tempt me to speak unwisely, as I seem to do so often with you."

"In what way?"

He had just put a fig in his mouth, and he looked down at her. "I would reply that even if you wore a miller's sack, you'd still be lovely. 'Tis not the gown — 'tis you, Danaë."

Amused laughter spilled from her lips. "You are right, you are speaking unwisely."

"Do you not know you are beautiful?"

"I don't know," she said honestly. "My father always told me my mother was beautiful, and that I look very like her."

"I don't doubt that."

She looked up at him, frowning. "Because

my father saw me as beautiful does not make it so. He loved my mother so much, he saw her as beautiful, and, in turn, he saw me in the same way."

Ramtat lowered his gaze, resisting the urge to look at the swell of her breast. "Your mind is too quick for me. I have difficulty keeping up my side of the conversation with you."

She nodded. "See, that is what I have always known about myself. You wanted to give me a compliment, and I ruined it by analyzing it. I don't know why I do that."

"Because you have the mind of a person wise beyond your years, and you're always seeking answers."

"Another compliment?"

"Another truth. Do something for me," he said, leaning against the couch, his arm stretched across the back, almost touching her shoulder. "Finish telling me what it was like growing up with so many animals. It must have been very adventuresome."

She relaxed a bit, because her girlhood was a safe subject as long as he did not inquire about her mother. "I cannot recall one day of my life at home when I was not happy." She gazed past Ramtat's shoulder, concentrating on the tapestry at the entrance, which was stirring from a sudden wind. "Except, of course, when my father became ill. It was very difficult to watch him grow weaker and to see his pain worsen with each passing day."

Ramtat watched the glint of tears in her eyes, and it stabbed at his heart. He needed to move their conversation to safer ground. "Tell me about training the animals. Surely you have many tales to relate."

She smiled at him, and he felt his heart lurch. This one slight girl had shaken the foundations of his world.

"As I told you, Obsidian is my personal pet. Like the albino tiger, she is one of the rarest animals we have ever trained." She giggled and covered her mouth. "The silly cat was always in trouble because she was allowed the run of the house. She was but a cub when father first brought her to me, so the house servants grew accustomed to her roaming about. At night she slept on the foot of my bed, and during the day she followed me about like my own shadow."

"You said she was gentle?"

Danaë took a bite of melon and found it delicious. "Very much so. Though I am not certain what she would do if she thought I was in danger." Her gaze met his. "She is not accustomed to being separated from me, and she must surely be lost without me."

Ramtat shifted uncomfortably, knowing this was still another anguish he had caused Danaë. "You have a hawk. Tell me about the bird."

"Tyi is a hunter. He has a very marked personality. He is actually jealous of Obsidian and pesters the poor cat." She smiled as if she were remembering. "You may not believe this, but Obsidian is a little afraid of him."

"How can that be?"

"Because Tyi is the dominant one of the two. He flies at poor Obsidian and makes her cower. Of course, Obsidian could injure or kill the hawk with one swipe of her paw, but she would never think of doing such a thing. I'm sure there is a lesson in that somewhere."

"The little can be mighty. It comes down to bravery, does it not?"

Danaë nodded. "My father said it was love for me that motivated the bird, and respect for Tyi that kept the cat from retaliating." She nodded her head. "Tyi is quite brilliant for a hawk. He seems to know that if I'm not wearing my leather glove, his claws will hurt me. Is that not amazing?"

Ramtat was staring at the way the lantern

light fell on her hair, making it shimmer. "Remarkable."

"My father thought so."

"I met Lord Mycerinus when I was younger but had no conversation with him. He was very respected by the royal family."

Danaë plucked at the green ribbon woven into the hem of her gown. "Everyone liked him — he was a man of honor and kindness. If you only knew about his kindness to me, you would understand —" She broke off. "He was an extraordinary man."

Ramtat poured her a cup of wine and handed it to her. "You are quite extraordinary yourself."

Looking into the depths of his eyes, she felt herself gravitating toward him. "Another compliment. This seems to be the night for them. No man other than you and my father have found anything exceptional in my looks."

He watched her raise the cup to her lips and take a sip. Unable to help himself, he took the cup from her and placed it on the table. His hand encircled her wrist, and he slowly brought her closer to him. "I need to hold you in my arms again. I don't know what you've done to me."

Danaë had no time to react as he tilted her head upward and whispered, "I have been in torment, able to think of little else but you since we swam together in the pool." His lips descended, and her eyes opened wide. At the first soft touch of his mouth against hers, her eyes closed. Her breathing seemed to follow the rhythm of the rise and fall of his chest. She heard him moan as he brought her across his lap so he could partake fully of her lips.

Danaë was lost to all reason. She never wanted to be parted from Ramtat — neither in this world nor the next. Shyly her arms stole around his broad shoulders.

Ramtat lifted her up, his mouth still on hers. Danaë made no protest when she realized he was taking her to his bed. Gently he placed her among the soft pillows and went down beside her, gathering her in his arms. Although Ramtat seemed to hold back, Danaë did not hesitate to press her body against his. She gasped with pleasure when she felt the swell of him between her thighs.

Ramtat sought the softness of her lips as if they were the sweetest nectar. Her skin was smoother than silk; her hair smelled of exotic flowers. This time he wanted all of her. "Give yourself to me," he murmured, his mouth following the valley between her breasts.

Danaë trembled with longing when his hand curved gently over her breast, gliding smoothly from one to the other. She ached inside, yearned, needed, and when he broke off the kiss, she felt bereft.

"Be mine, Danaë. Belong only to me."

She felt him pause as his fingers brushed against the pendant she had forgotten to remove.

For Danaë the spell was broken, and she froze. Her father's warning echoed in her mind. She had been careless. Already Ramtat lifted the pendant, holding it toward the light. The emerald sparkled like green fire, proclaiming its rarity.

Ramtat frowned. "What is this?"

In a panic, Danaë yanked it from his fingers and pushed it back beneath her robe. " 'Tis but a trinket that belonged to my mother."

"No, not a trinket," he said, his gaze sweeping across her face. "Unless I am mistaken, that is a royal pendant."

Danaë tried to think of something to say that would satisfy his curiosity — she could not tell him the truth. "My father was the Royal Animal Trainer," she reminded him. "He was the recipient of many fine gifts from the king," which was the truth, she reasoned, as far as it went. Of course, her father had never received a gift as rare as the pendant. She dropped her gaze, not wanting Ramtat to read deceit in her eyes.

"I'm sure your father received many gifts." He looked doubtful. "But a royal cobra — I think not." She was hiding something from him, and jealousy, an unfamiliar companion, slammed into him. "Did some man from the royal household give you this gift?"

"As I said, it was my mother's."

There was no lie in her eyes, but she was still deceiving him in some way he could not fathom. He pulled her into his arms, his lips touching the pulse beat in her throat. "Sweet, sweet Danaë, trust me —"

Danaë hadn't heard the footsteps of someone entering the tent, but Ramtat had. He quickly slipped through the netting and pulled it together tightly to keep Danaë hidden. "You'd better have a very good reason for coming here like this," he said angrily.

Danaë heard the other man's voice. "I ask your pardon, lord, but a messenger has just arrived from Caesar. He says he bring news of great import."

"Very well. Give him food and tell him I shall see him presently."

The netting parted, and Ramtat held out his hand with regret in his dark gaze. "Duty before love, my sweet."

"I should not have allowed —" she began.

He pulled her to him so fast, it left her breathless. "Yes, you should have. We already know we were meant for each other. Don't deny what the gods have ordained."

Danaë gazed into his eyes. "What is happening between us?"

He touched his lips to each eyelid and then stared down at her. "You are so young — not jaded like many of the ladies at court, and that is one of your most endearing qualities."

"I have had no experience with . . . love."

He held her to him, reluctant to leave her when she was feeling so uncertain. "Neither have I." He laid his cheek to hers. "Alas, we shall have to wait to end this conversation." He drew in a deep breath. "I shan't be long — wait for me here."

"Please tell me if you have a wife, or wives — even a harem."

He clasped both sides of her face and rested his forehead against hers. "I have no wife, no harem. Only you."

She felt his hard body against hers, and she wanted to melt into him. "If Caesar calls you to him, will you go?"

"Aye." His lips descended, and he kissed her hungrily. He pulled away regretfully, turned, and left.

Ramtat glanced at the messenger speculatively. "You say Queen Cleopatra has been found?"

"Yea, lord. She was brought to Caesar by her servant, the Sicilian, Apollodorus. It is said she was concealed in a rug so her enemies would not discover her."

Ramtat turned to one of his men. "Saddle my horse — I must leave immediately." With longing, he glanced back at the tent where he'd left Danaë. It was difficult to depart now that they were beginning to understand each other, but his first duty was to the queen.

Ramtat hurried to his aunt's tent, where he found her preparing for bed. "I would have you look after Lady Danaë until my return. I do not know when that will be. But whenever it is, I will want a wedding celebration."

"You will wed the animal trainer's daughter?"

He smiled. "Her and no other."

"She has bewitched you."

He did not deny it; he did not even want to. "In truth, that is so. I have been her slave since first I saw her."

Zarmah suddenly beamed. "At last, a woman to tempt my nephew into marriage. My sister, your mother, will be most pleased — she has despaired of your ever taking a wife and giving her grandchildren."

"Take care of my love, and let no harm befall her."

Zarmah looked her nephew over carefully. "No harm will come to her — this I swear." She was puzzled, remembering how eager Lady Danaë had been to escape. "Has she agreed to marry you?"

"I haven't asked her yet, but I'm hoping she will."

His aunt touched her lips to his cheek. "Your men speak of the lady's connection to the boy king. Be very sure before you commit yourself to her that she is not in the enemy's camp."

"I don't believe she ever was. I just have to convince Caesar."

When Ramtat returned to his tent, he pulled aside the netting around the bed. Danaë was there waiting for him. He saw the questioning in her eyes and shook his head. "I must leave you for a time. I am needed in Alexandria."

Danaë could tell that his mind was already on other matters.

"Take me home."

That was the one thing he could not do until he knew she would be safe. "Unfortunately, that will not be possible — not yet."

"I understand." She was disappointed, but Ramtat was a man who would always put duty above his personal life.

"I am loath to leave you at this time. There is so much left unsaid between us. There are things I want to tell you about myself, and I want to know all about you. While I am gone," he said, taking her hand and raising it to his lips, "sleep here in my bed. Let me think of you here waiting for me." He looked inquiringly at her. "You will be waiting for me, will you not?"

She touched his cheek, and he turned his head so his mouth would touch her fingers. "I shall wait for as long as it takes."

He gave her an agonized smile and turned away. His robe billowed out around him as he left the tent, disappearing into the night.

Danaë said a quick prayer to the gods to keep him safe on his journey. And she prayed he would soon return. She was still trembling inside, hungering for the touch of his hands on her body.

How would she exist while he was away?

She slid past the curtains and sank down onto his bed. Tears were trickling down her cheeks, but she wasn't quite sure why she was crying. She touched her lips, where the feel of his kiss still lingered. She loved him, and she would wait for him until the day she left this life.

CHAPTER SEVENTEEN

When Ramtat arrived in Alexandria, it was the middle of the night, certainly too late to call on Caesar. He rode to his own villa, deciding to wait until sunrise to go the palace. In total exhaustion, he fell across his bed without removing his clothing or boots.

An hour before dawn, Ramtat snapped awake, his senses aware that someone had entered his room. He lunged forward and grasped the sword that lay on the floor beside his bed.

"So it's a fight you want, is it?" a female voice asked. "Be warned, I have been taught swordplay by the best."

His hand dropped away from his sword, and he smiled in the near darkness. "So you think I am the best, do you? A considerate sister would permit her weary brother to sleep, Adhaniá."

She giggled and threw herself into his arms. "I thought you'd forgotten you had a sister, and our mother is sure she is naught but a faded memory in your mind."

He hugged her to him. "I could never forget a pest like you."

Adhaniá drew back and studied his face in the near dawn. "We hear the queen has been found. Is it true?"

He sat up, swung his legs over the side of the bed, and stood. "Aye. It is true."

She slid off the bed and went into his arms. "Then the war will only grow worse."

His sister, Adhaniá, was tall for a female. Her hair hung to her waist and was as black as cinder. Her Bedouin heritage had given her honey-gold skin, and eyes of deep amber. He had tried to be a father to her since their father's death, but war had taken him away from Egypt just when she most needed his guidance. He held her out from him. "You seem to grow more beautiful every day. I'll have to set someone to guard you to keep the men from swarming around."

She pursed her lips. "That will not be necessary. Our mother sees that I am watched at all times." He could hear the pout in her voice. "She says I'm too young for male company. Do you think that's right? Many of my friends are already married."

"I would never dispute anything our mother says."

"You didn't answer my first question," she said, pulling the filmy curtains aside to find it was still dark outside. "Will the war grow more intense now that the queen is back in Alexandria?"

"I fear so." He moved to the door. "Accompany me to see our mother. I have something to say to both of you."

They had only reached the end of the hallway when their mother met them. "I just discovered you came home during the night. Why did you not awaken me?"

"I assumed you needed your sleep, Mother," he said, pulling her into his arms. "As did I."

"It is good to know you are safe — we hear such stories about fighting in the streets of Alexandria."

"The stories are true. That is why I want you to pack up the household and move to the country villa, leaving only those necessary to the running of the house."

"I'm not afraid of war," his mother said with a touch of irritation.

Ramtat's mother was still a handsome woman, and in appearance seemed no more than half her age. Her dark hair was barely dusted by gray at the temples, and her face was unlined. He motioned toward his sister. "I know you do not fear war, but you must think of my sister."

His mother nodded in understanding. "I will do as you say. We should be able to leave in three days' time."

"Then my mind is at ease, and I can attend to my duties without worrying about the two of you."

"Send word to me when it is safe to come home," his mother told him.

"Do not expect it to be soon," he said sadly.

"Come," his mother told him, linking her arm through Ramtat's. "I will see you fed before you leave this house."

It was an hour later when the messenger from Caesar arrived, informing Ramtat that he was to be in attendance in the throne room within the hour.

He hurriedly dressed in his court finery, impatient while his servant applied kohl to his eyes and set his braided wig upon his head. Since it was the swiftest conveyance, he chose to take his chariot. It had been hitched and was waiting for him when he hurried out the front door. He cracked his whip and urged his matching grays into a fast pace. There was an eerie silence as he raced through the nearly empty streets of

Alexandria. It was market day, yet there were no stalls set up and hardly anyone about. Something untoward had happened, and he was afraid to guess what it could be.

The guards at the arched entrance recognized Ramtat and must have been told to expect him, because they waved him through without question. When he reached the palace steps, he tossed the reins of his chariot to the waiting attendant. Ramtat hurried inside and down a long corridor toward the throne room.

He feared the worst — he was afraid Caesar had sent for him because Cleopatra was dead.

He was almost overcome with relief when he entered the room and saw that Queen Cleopatra was very much alive. With the stature and bearing of a mighty ruler, she sat on her throne in all her glory, holding the scepter and flail, Egypt's symbols of power, crisscrossed over her breasts, and wearing the Hawk Crown of Isis on her head.

But something was not right.

Ramtat quickly glanced about, searching the faces of the others in the throne room. King Ptolemy's tutor, Theodotus, was standing on the dais, looking disgruntled, while Cleopatra's adviser, Antinanious, stood at her right hand. A scribe sat cross-legged near the queen, taking down everything that was said. Several of Caesar's guards stood near the doors, but King Ptolemy was nowhere to be seen.

Caesar was pacing in front of the throne, waving his arms in frustration. "I ordered your brother to be here — where is he? Why has he not come?"

"You can hardly expect His Glorious Majesty to sit beside his sister, who tried to kill him on several occasions," the sullen-faced tutor remarked viciously. "The king is not himself lately. His prized cheetah, Jabatus, has become unmanageable and has to be kept in its cage. The boy suffers mightily because the animal turned on him. He lives only because I was there to help control the cat."

"Of what are you babbling?" Caesar demanded. "If you can't talk sense, remain silent."

Theodotus glanced from Caesar to Cleopatra with a malevolent glare. "It is our opinion that Cleopatra, by her rebellion against the rightful king, has forfeited her right to the throne of Egypt."

Caesar held up his hand for silence. "Theodotus, what you think doesn't interest anyone here. If memory serves me, and it usually does, you were not invited to attend this morning's council, so keep your opinions to yourself."

If anything, the tutor looked even more sullen, but he compressed his lips and fell silent.

"This bickering," Caesar continued, "will cease immediately. My wish — nay, my command, is that Cleopatra and Ptolemy rule jointly. In this, there will be no debate."

"You must allow me to speak, Caesar," Theodotus insisted. "Surely you must know that I speak with the voice of the king."

The Roman glared at the tutor. "If you say one more word, you will be escorted out!"

Caesar's gaze settled on Queen Cleopatra, and an intimate smile curved his lips.

The queen's own anger was barely concealed as she stared at the evil man who held her brother in his grip. "The tutor has it wrong. It was my brother who tried to have *me* killed. I have no desire to share my throne with a young boy who is so easily controlled by others."

"Nonetheless, you shall do precisely that," Caesar demanded as he glanced toward the door. That was when he noticed Ramtat. "Rome was made executor of your father's will, Queen Cleopatra, and I'm here to see that his wishes are carried out. Does anyone object?"

No one spoke. Caesar acknowledged Ramtat with the merest nod of his head. "Well, you certainly took your time getting here," he said in annoyance. "What kept you?"

Ramtat had ridden two days and nights with very little sleep to arrive as quickly as he could, but he said naught to Caesar of this. The proconsul knew how long it took to make the journey to Alexandria from his encampment. Ramtat had learned over the years that much of what Caesar said was spoken only to impress those within the sound of his voice.

"I beg your pardon for my tardiness, Caesar," Ramtat said. "It was unavoidable."

"Come forward," Caesar said, still irritated. "I have business to conduct elsewhere. It is my wish that you remain beside Queen Cleopatra until I return." Caesar glowered pointedly at Theodotus while he spoke to Ramtat. "I leave ten of my guards with you to ensure peace."

Ramtat bowed. "I am always willing to serve."

Caesar arched a brow. "Yes, yes, we know all about that. Stay beside the queen to provide advice — and keep your sword handy at all times."

What Caesar left unsaid, but plainly implied, was that Ramtat's appointed task was to keep the queen safe. Caesar's retreating footsteps echoed down the marble floors, but Ramtat's attention was focused on the queen. He swept her a deep bow.

"I have been informed of your loyalty, Lord Ramtat. You may approach me and speak," the queen said, a mischievous light in her green eyes.

Cleopatra had been but a child when last they had met — now she was a young woman with the confidence of a queen. On close inspection, Ramtat noticed that Cleopatra was no great beauty, but one would hardly notice because there was something about her that cast all other women in the shade of her glory. Her voice was hypnotic, her eyes reflected intelligence, and every move she made displayed a practiced grace. When he studied more closely, he almost stopped breathing. With subtle differences, Danaë could almost be the queen's twin! The queen had a larger nose than Danaë's, and she was a little taller, but they had the same green eyes. Their features were almost identical, though the queen seemed softer, a bit heavier, and her skin was somewhat darker.

The resemblance was astonishing.

"Your Majesty, it has been some years since last we met. It does my heart good to see you."

"I remember you well, Lord Ramtat. I also remember you were a favorite of my father's."

Theodotus glared at the queen, still not aware of the dangerous ground he was treading. "Lord Ramtat and his legions are loyal to King Ptolemy. Both you and Caesar would do well to remember that."

"Silence!" the queen commanded, and the tutor immediately closed his mouth, compressing his lips in anger.

Looking past Theodotus, Cleopatra plainly dismissed him from her mind and turned her attention to Ramtat. When she smiled, Ramtat saw a faint resemblance to the young girl he'd known so many years ago.

"I am told how faithfully you serve Egypt, Lord Ramtat."

He bowed. "You are rightly informed, my queen."

"But —" the tutor started to protest.

Holding a hand up to silence him, Cleopatra stated, "Enough time has been wasted on triviality. There are people with real problems waiting for an audience. Lord Ramtat, it is my wish that you stand beside me during the proceedings."

She had just bestowed a high honor on Ramtat. At her right hand stood her trusted adviser, Antinanious, so Ramtat moved to stand at her left. Cleopatra's adviser looked Ramtat over carefully and, at last, nodded his approval.

Ramtat planted his body between the queen and the tutor, and Theodotus was forced to give ground and move behind Ptolemy's empty throne, an insult Ramtat knew he would not soon forget or forgive.

After an hour, the proceedings became mundane: One man wanted the return of sheep he swore had been stolen by his neighbor, while a woman wanted her husband to send his second wife away because she was barren and caused upheaval in their home. The queen artfully settled a squabble between the governors of two of her provinces, a diplomatic feat her brother could never have accomplished.

Ramtat became alert when he heard the chamberlain announce a new petitioner: "Lord Harique, of the House of Sahure, seeks Her Majesty's justice."

Ramtat watched the man cross the marble floor, remembering that Sahure was Danaë's family name.

"Approach, Harique, of the House of

Sahure," Antinanious said. "State your grievance before the queen."

"Great Majesty," Harique began, dropping to his knees and lowering his head. "I have been greatly wronged. One of my slaves has not only run away but is pretending to be someone she is not — she is plotting and scheming with persons who would harm Egypt."

"You dare bring such a matter before this throne?" Theodotus injected in an attempt to have his voice heard. "There are more important matters to attend to than a runaway slave. Go to the local authorities with this matter."

"But, Illustrious Majesty," Harique continued in a trembling voice, "this slave involved the king in her deception. She tricked him into believing she is the daughter of my uncle, Lord Mycerinus, who has recently passed to the other world. I was also told she presented the king with the gift of a rare cheetah that was not hers to give."

"What is this?" Queen Cleopatra asked, rising to her feet. "Of what are you speaking, fool?"

Theodotus stared at Harique with rising fear. It would not be wise to let the man elaborate on the gift of the cheetah. The queen would surely pounce on the fact that her brother might have erred in his judgment, and that they had all been tricked by a slave. "I know the lady of whom this man speaks of. He should be punished for defaming her good name. Do not listen to this man's ramblings."

Cleopatra was studying Harique with suspicion. "Would you say the slave in question is a friend of my brother's?"

Although Harique had fought on the king's side, he had decided to switch loyalties before he entered the throne chamber. If the mighty Caesar was supporting the queen and sharing her bed, as was rumored, it would behoove him to be on the side of the queen. "I speak only the truth when I say she favors your brother. Who knows what plots and intrigues she is involved in? For a slave to reach so high, she must have coaching from someone."

"Speak her name, fool!"

"She is my slave, Danaë."

Cleopatra shook her head. "A slave would have nothing to gain by taking part in such an intrigue. Where is your proof?"

Harique ducked his head, wondering if he'd made a mistake in bringing this issue before the queen. "Danaë is sly and manipulative — I know she is scheming with persons who would do you harm."

The tutor moved quickly down the steps to peer into Harique's face. Sliding the hilt of his dagger beneath Harique's chin, he forced the frightened man's head upward so his face was more visible. "Admit it! Your story is false!"

Cleopatra pointed her finger. "Leave the man alone, tutor. This matter does not concern you. I am the one who sits in judgment in this chamber, not you."

Ramtat felt his stomach knot. Here could be the mystery Danaë had been hiding from him. Certainly not that she would harm the queen, but that she was a slave. Nay! He could not believe it.

The tutor reluctantly stepped back. "Great Majesty, I would not trust this man."

"Still," Cleopatra injected, "serious charges have been lodged against this Danaë. I want to know the truth of this matter."

Ramtat watched Harique carefully. The fool's life hung by a thin thread, and yet he did not change his story. Ramtat felt something inside him wither — the man could be speaking the truth. If so, Danaë had deceived more than just the king — she had deceived him as well.

"Majesty," Ramtat stated, watching beads

of sweat pop out on the face of the accuser. "I have it within my power to discover whether this man lies or not. If you will but give me a week, I shall lay the truth of the matter before you."

"How so, Lord Ramtat?" the queen asked. "Do you know of whom he speaks."

"I do know her. I stood beside your brother the day the gift of the cheetah was presented to him."

Cleopatra looked steadily at Ramtat. "You shall bring this woman before me, and I shall judge her for myself."

"She is at present some distance from Alexandria. It will take time to reach her and bring her here."

"Do it." Cleopatra smiled, her gaze going to Harique, who had turned pale and kept his head lowered. "While you are seeking the truth, Lord Ramtat, this man will linger in my prison. If I learn he speaks false, he will never leave it."

Anger burned inside Ramtat as he waved one of Caesar's guards forward. "Stand beside the queen, and do not leave her for any reason." He motioned to a second guard and nodded at Lord Harique. "Take that man away and confine him — he is to speak to no one. And when you have imprisoned him, go directly to Caesar and tell him that I am on the queen's mission."

"It shall be done as you say, Lord Ramtat." The Roman guard prodded Harique forward with the hilt of his sword.

Ramtat was battling anger, but he was not sure at whom he should aim it. If Danaë was involved in some kind of plot against the queen, he would find out when he questioned her.

"With your permission, Majesty, I should leave immediately."

"Yes, go, my good Lord Ramtat. Ride swiftly, for there are many plots afoot." Cleopatra looked pointedly at the tutor. "If this is another of my brother's schemes, I need to know of it."

Ramtat saw the sickly color of the tutor's face and tried to remember everything that had happened the day Danaë had presented the cheetah to the king. He had been in the chamber the entire time, and the king was not a good enough dissembler to fool him. The king had not known Danaë before that day; he was sure of it.

He bowed to the queen and backed toward the door. When he was outside the throne chamber, he stalked down the marble corridor; his mind was already racing ahead of him. There had been something mysterious about Danaë from the very beginning, and she was definitely keeping secrets from him. But she was too educated and refined to be a slave.

He suddenly felt sick inside. The royal pendant — who had given it to Danaë? The king? Or someone close to him? And what had she promised in return?

His questions led back to Harique — why would the man lie when he knew it would mean his death?

Ramtat rode into the night, stopping often to change horses. Once, at an oasis, he was so weary he lay on the hard ground, his eyes closing in an exhausted but troubled sleep.

His dreams were of green eyes and a laughing mouth — a mouth that formed lies and practiced deceit.

Nay. His heart told him Danaë was not the deceiver Harique accused her of being. She would confirm his trust in her. She had to be Lord Mycerinus's true daughter.

CHAPTER EIGHTEEN

Danaë had fought against loving Lord Ramtat, but once she'd yielded to him, her surrender was complete. She was lying in his bed, where she had slept each night since he went away. He had asked her to wait for him, and that was just what she would do. She opened her mind, trying to imagine him lying beside her, just as she had every night.

No one had ever explained to her that love could be so all-consuming. Everything about her life had changed because of love. She no longer thought of herself as Ramtat's prisoner, but rather the woman who awaited his return. Since realizing she loved Ramtat, everything was sweeter — the food she tasted, the air she breathed.

How was that possible?

The waiting was the most difficult part of all. She needed Ramtat beside her for the rest of her life. A deep longing tore through her like a devouring beast. He loved her; she knew he did — that was what made the waiting bearable.

Danaë imagined being wrapped in his strong arms. He would chase all the shadows from her mind and take away her loneliness. She would belong to him and never again feel alone as she had since her father's death.

She closed her eyes and smiled. Ramtat had overpowering strength, and yet he was capable of such gentleness. She wanted to be everything to him, his love, his wife, the one who walked beside him in this world and followed him into the afterlife.

It was the middle of the night when Ramtat reached the encampment. Despite the lateness of the hour, one of his tribe was there to lead his horse away for a rubdown.

On the ride home, there had been a lot of time to think, and he had come to the decision that Danaë always seemed honest and open with him. She was so guileless, she would not know how to be deceitful. That meant the man who claimed to be Lord Mycerinus's nephew must be lying, no doubt for some treacherous reason of his own — or perhaps his lie was part of a plot hatched by King Ptolemy's entourage.

Perhaps the man wanted to steal Danaë's inheritance, and that was why he was attempting to besmirch her honor.

Ramtat's footsteps were hurried and noiseless when he entered his tent. He had hoped he would find Danaë asleep in his bed, and he was not disappointed. As he quietly pulled the curtain aside, there was just enough light coming from the single lantern to allow him to see her face. Her breathing was deep and even; she was asleep.

Shimmering light flickered across her smooth shoulders and reflected on her dark hair. Passion tore through Ramtat like a knife — he had been denied her body for too long.

But he dropped the curtain back in place and closed his eyes.

What if Danaë had lied to him? If only he could know for certain.

His mind swung first one way and then the other. One moment he wanted to thrash Danaë; the next he wanted to kiss her senseless. Was she a traitor or a pawn, a temptress or an innocent? He could not rest until he heard the truth from her own lips.

As quietly as possible, he stripped off his dusty clothing and washed the sand from his body before slipping into a clean robe.

Once more he stood beside his bed, his heart thundering inside him. Never before had he allowed his desires to overcome his strict attention to duty. But at this time, and in this place, Ramtat the man was battling with Ramtat the queen's general. Whether Danaë was honest or deceitful mattered not to him. There was only one question that filled his mind.

If he took her in his arms, would she come to him willingly?

He eased his weight onto the bed and felt her stir. "Do not be afraid — it is only I."

He felt her hand on his arm as she raised herself up, and he was taken by surprise when she moved closer and laid her head on his shoulder. Passion smoldered inside him; it would take very little for his desire to burst into a roaring flame that he could not control.

She pressed a kiss on his shoulder. "I feared you might not come back."

"I told you I would. I will always keep my word to you if I'm able."

She pressed her lips against his cheek, her hand on his chest, and his body trembled with need.

"Do you know what you're doing to me?" he asked in a voice thick with passion.

"I know I am in danger from you. I know

you are like stone, and if I give myself to you, you could shatter me into pieces." She rose up on her knees and pressed her body fully against his. "And even knowing this, I am willing to take the risk," she whispered. "I cannot seem to help myself."

Ramtat was close to losing control. He had intended to keep a clear head and question her about her past, but he was unable to fight the need that almost consumed him. He stared at her sultry lips, and he lost the battle. It didn't matter if she was who she claimed to be; he didn't care if she had deceived him from the very beginning.

He only knew she was offering herself to him, and he would have her.

Danaë was overjoyed at Ramtat's return. Happiness such as she'd never known made her light-headed. She did not know if she was behaving as a proper maiden should, but she had to touch him, to press against him, to feel his skin and know he was really there.

"I missed you," she admitted, almost shyly.

His breath hissed through his teeth as he laid her down on her back and gathered her close, swelling against her. "And I, you," he admitted. "Surely you can feel how much I need you."

She touched her lips to his briefly and then gazed into his glorious eyes. "I feel it."

Ramtat dropped passionate kisses onto her face while his hands deftly found all the right places to make her moan with pleasure. His hands drifted across her shapely hips, and he pulled her against him. "I want you more than I have ever wanted anything in my life."

"I know," she whispered, nibbling at his lips. "It's the same with me."

He gasped in pleasure when she bit his lip. He was certain she had never been with a man before, yet her feminine instincts were driving him wild. His mouth skimmed hers, and she leaned into him to deepen the kiss. In the back of Ramtat's mind was the question of her deceit, but it was pushed aside by the feel of her trembling lips beneath his.

He had no control over his hands; they roved over her body at will, pressing her tighter against the swell of him. When he pulled back to catch his breath, her hand drifted up his arm to clamp on hard muscle.

Danaë thought she would die if he didn't do something to relieve the longing building up inside her. She moved her lower body to accommodate his, and lost her breath when he raised her robe and gently caressed her, making her hips rise off the bed. Even knowing she was behaving provocatively, Danaë could not stop herself. She ached with a hunger that rocked her body.

"Please," she pleaded.

He needed no further invitation; he could take no more torture. Gently he parted her legs and paused. "You're sure?" he asked gruffly.

She raised her hips, taking him into her warmth. "I am sure," she managed to say. But she could not have uttered another word when he eased farther inside her. She gasped and twisted when he drove deeper.

"Sweet green-eyes, you have stolen my heart," he said, sliding halfway out of her and lunging forward once more. Ramtat brushed his mouth across her ear. "I knew you were made for me alone when first I saw you."

Danaë took his face between her hands and brought his lips to hers. Plunging into her, Ramtat knew their joining was like nothing he could have imagined. His life-giving seed poured into her, and still he wanted more. Surprised he was still hard, he took her again, and yet again, until they both lay back in exhaustion.

He brushed his knuckles down the side of

her cheek. "From this night forward, you're mine."

"I believe we both know that." Danaë snuggled closer to him, her body still throbbing from his lovemaking. She had the feeling that every part of her belonged to him.

He moved her head to rest against his chest. He had been right about her being chaste — no man had touched her before him. Ramtat was even more sure she was not guilty of what Harique had accused her of. With Danaë's help, he would expose the man as a fraud. He wished he did not have to subject her to the ordeal of condemning the man. But he must put the questions to her so he could assure the queen of Danaë's innocence.

He touched his lips to her cheek. "I saw Queen Cleopatra while I was in Alexandria. I attended her audience."

She could hear his words rumbling through his chest. "Then she is safe — I know that makes you happy. Have she and her brother forgiven each other?"

His fingers drifted down her arm. "Nay. That will never happen."

" 'Tis a pity."

He chose his words carefully. "And you? How do you feel about the queen returning?"

Having been taught to speak her mind by her father and Uriah, Danaë took a moment to ponder the situation. Now that the queen had been brought back to Alexandria, it would surely cause more unrest and bloodshed. "I believe we will pay a terrible cost for her return."

"You speak of the war escalating?"

"I do. If the brother and sister do not get along, war cannot be avoided. If it were within my power, I would send Cleopatra away."

Ramtat felt a tightening in his chest. "Perhaps to her death?"

"That would not be my choice. But for the peace of Egypt, either she or her brother must die — surely you can see that. And if one of them must die, I prefer it to be her."

"I have never heard you speak so. 'Tis treason."

"And you would have the brother die? Which of us speaks treason?"

"It is a thin line you walk. That is why I must ask you some questions that may offend you." He tilted her chin up so he could see her eyes. "Do not speak false, or I shall know it."

Danaë was confused; where he had been warm and loving moments before, Ramtat was now cold, with a dangerous glint in his eyes. It was as if they had not just made love and exchanged sweet words afterward. "I have always told you the truth, except for the times I held back from saying anything at all."

"I remember you once spoke to me about a man named Harique . . ." He watched the color drain from her face, and her bottom lip trembled. "Tell me all you know about him. Is he Lord Mycerinus's nephew? Is he the heir to everything your father possessed?"

Danaë hesitated for only a moment. "Yes, he is the nephew, and he inherited most of my father's land." She clutched Ramtat's arm. "Why do you ask me such a question? Have you seen him?"

Ramtat watched her eyes darken with fear, and then they became secretive — or was it his imagination? He watched her even more carefully before he asked: "Are you Lord Mycerinus's true daughter?"

Danaë was quiet for so long, he thought she might not answer. He waited, hoping his growing suspicions were unfounded. He gave her a shake. "Answer me — are you Lord Mycerinus's blood daughter?"

Danaë saw his jaw settle in a firm line while he stared at her with growing mistrust. Her father had warned her that Harique would attempt to discredit her as his daughter. She imagined that had already happened, since Ramtat was asking these questions. She had proof that her father had adopted her legally. It stung a little that she had to defend herself against whatever accusations Harique had lodged against her. Danaë watched Ramtat's eyes suddenly grow dull with mistrust. "You have spoken to Harique, have you not?"

"Let us say I heard him speak. He made some very damaging accusations against you."

Her chest was so tight, it was difficult for her to breathe. "What kind of accusations?"

"That you are not who you claim to be." He watched her closely as he spoke the next words. "He told the queen you were his slave, and implied you might be a threat to her. You, yourself, just admitted that you wished Queen Cleopatra dead."

Danaë shook her head in disbelief. Clutching the coverlet about her, she slid off the bed and fumbled with the netting until she found the opening. She was devastated that Ramtat suspected her of contriving to do harm to the queen. She could only guess at what Harique had said about her.

"So," Danaë said in a pained voice, "you have it all worked out in your mind. You think I'm involved in some devious plan to slay Queen Cleopatra?" She shook her head. "Did you come to me tonight with the intention of awakening my passion, prompting me to confess all my dire plots?"

He slid off the bed and stood beside her. "Nay. That was not my hope. Just tell me that Harique lied about you. Say you are innocent, and I shall believe you."

Tears burned behind her eyes, and she refused to look at him lest she cry. If he could believe she was capable of such evil, if he was willing to take Harique's word against hers, she would say naught to defend herself. "You can believe what you want. I will say no more."

He gripped her arms and turned her to him. "If your cousin speaks a lie, confess it now, and I will believe you!"

"He is not my cousin, and that is the truth."

Ramtat looked puzzled. "But he is blood kin to Lord Mycerinus, is he not?"

"Aye." She was so angry, she wanted to push him away. "Harique is blood kin to the House of Sahure, while I have not a drop of that bloodline in me."

He felt betrayed. Her grief for Lord Mycerinus had seemed genuine, and she had drawn him in with her stories of growing up as the Royal Animal Trainer's daughter. He flung her away from him, and she stumbled, falling onto the couch. Burying her face in the soft leather, she wanted to weep, but she would not allow herself to give in to that weakness. She was disappointed in Ramtat — he seemed on the verge of believing Harique's vile lies. If he had only asked her the right questions, she would have gladly told him the truth of being her father's adopted daughter.

"Give me something, anything, to take back to the queen. Were you forced to fall in with someone's plot against Cleopatra because you feared for your life? Did someone threaten you? Was King Ptolemy in on the plot all along?" He watched her raise her head, and he saw the angry glow shimmering in the green depths of her eyes. "You don't understand the danger you are facing. Tell me everything so I can help you."

Danaë was furious. With every word out of Ramtat's mouth, her resolve grew stronger. "I will not tell you anything."

The couch shifted when he sat down beside her, and she stiffened when he pulled her into his arms. "You cannot know what they will do to you if you have been involved in plotting against the queen."

Danaë wriggled out of his arms and stood.

Without a word, she marched through the tapestry into the connecting room. Slumping onto the sofa there, she hung her head in despair. If Ramtat suspected her of dishonesty and treachery, she would not lower herself by begging him to believe the truth. No doubt he would be taking her to Alexandria, and that was what she wanted to happen. She would ask that Uriah be summoned to speak on her behalf; he could produce the documents to prove Harique's claim was false.

Danaë had been through the grief of her father's death, had been forced to flee from both her father's house and her home in Alexandria. She had been kidnapped and imprisoned by the man who was now hurling accusations at her. The fact that she had come to love him and he had merely used her only compounded her grief.

She raised her head as everything fell into place. Ramtat must have suspected her from the very beginning when she'd presented the cheetah to King Ptolemy as a gift. It all made sense now — that was the real reason he had taken her captive.

Danaë picked up a cushion and threw it across the room. She could see it all now: When nothing else worked to wring a confession from her, Ramtat had wooed her and professed to love her, hoping he could make her talk.

She laid her head back and stared as the wind rippled the top of the tent. It had all been a game to him.

And she had been the fool who walked into his trap.

Hearing footsteps, Danaë realized Ramtat had come after her. She raised her head, fighting back tears, and saw the determined look on his face. "You can do what you will to me," she declared, turning her back on him. "I will say no more."

He seemed coldly detached when he said, "If you are part of a plot to slay the queen, I will find out — never fear."

"I remember that day at the palace when you warned me to keep silent about your identity — even then you suspected me for some reason." Danaë stared past him. "Leave me alone."

"I will leave you to consider what will happen to you if you don't speak in your own defense. If there is anything you want to tell me, I'll await you in my quarters. It would be better if you confess all to me and name those who plot against the queen."

Oh, how that hurt.

He thought her devoid of decency and honor.

As Danaë heard his retreating footsteps, she bent almost double and silently cried. Ramtat could wait until the sands of time ran out for them both; she would never again go to him.

CHAPTER NINETEEN

Danaë remained huddled on the couch for the rest of the night, wondering what manner of death the queen would devise for her if Uriah was not allowed to present the proof that she was innocent of the claims against her. She still had not closed her eyes in sleep as she watched the fingers of light creep across the patterned rug announcing sunup.

This time when the tapestry parted, it was Ramtat's aunt who entered.

"You are to dress for a journey," Zarmah told her, laying a robe and veil beside Danaë and placing a pair of soft leather boots on the rug. "My nephew says to dress with haste. You will barely have time to eat and bathe before he is ready to leave."

Danaë stripped off her robe and obediently washed herself. "I'm not hungry."

Zarmah handed Danaë a jar of scented oil and met her defiant gaze. "My nephew suspected you would take that attitude. I am to warn you that if you don't eat, he will have you force-fed."

Danaë nodded, wondering why Ramtat did not kill her and bury her in the desert where no one would be the wiser. After dressing in the robes of a Bedouin woman, Danaë did manage to eat some of the meat and a bite of cheese. A subdued Danaë pulled the veil securely over her face.

"You will find a horse saddled and waiting for you."

"I understand."

Zarmah reached out and placed her hand on Danaë's arm. "I don't understand. If you know something that will prove your innocence, tell it now. I fear what might happen to you if you don't break your silence."

"I balk at anyone's' attempt to intimidate me, especially your nephew."

"I believe in you. Have I not seen your goodness and witnessed your kindness to those who served you?"

"Am I to go to my death?" Danaë asked with the weight of her hurt crushing down on her.

"This I do not know." Zarmah's eyes filled with sympathy. "But I feel I should tell you I have never seen my nephew as angry as he is at the moment. Be warned, Ramtat is not a forgiving man. He has always had a steadfast devotion to duty and has never been swayed by sentiment."

Danaë knew she had done nothing wrong, and she was not going to defend herself, not even to Zarmah. "I feel like a small boat on a turbulent ocean being tossed about by swamping waves. Your nephew should know I have no power to harm the queen, and wouldn't even if I had the opportunity."

"Tell him that."

"Nay. I will not." Danaë stepped to the tapestry. "Will Lord Ramtat be accompanying me to Alexandria?"

"I am told he will be leading your escort. You must hurry — he is impatient to be away."

Danaë felt her heart turn to stone. "I thank you for your kindness. You are the only one I shall miss when I leave here."

Zarmah sighed. "I had such hopes for you and my nephew. If out of pride you remain silent, Ramtat will have no recourse other than to . . ." She could not finish. "Follow me: I will take you to him."

Danaë attempted to close herself off from thinking and feeling. She knew not what awaited her when she reached Alexandria.

Her death?

Probably.

And if she did die, and Ramtat later discovered the truth, would he even feel regret for his actions?

The first day's journey passed without incident. A hot desert wind was blowing, and Danaë kept her veil in place to prevent her skin from blistering. Her gaze would often go to Ramtat, who rode at the head of his Bedouin tribesmen and paid scant attention to her. She was positioned between two fierce-looking tribesmen, one of whom she recognized as the man who had questioned her when she was traveling with the caravan. She'd thought at the time he was a spy, and now it seemed she'd been right.

None of the men looked in her direction, and Ramtat paid no attention to her. It was as if they were strangers, as if he'd forgotten the intimacy they had shared, and the soft words that had passed between them.

It was a silent group that snaked its way across the desert, and as far as Danaë could tell, Ramtat spoke to no one. His followers dared not speak to him. Since she rode several horses behind Ramtat, she studied him without his knowledge. With his black robe flowing out about him and his head held at a proud angle, he seemed unapproachable. She could feel his barely suppressed anger, and it drove through her like a knife.

When evening fell, a small tent was erected for Danaë's comfort while the men bedded down on the ground. In the dark of night she lay curled up on a soft goatskin mat, too weary to dwell on what would happen to her when they reached Alexandria.

She really did not care.

At the end of the second day, a brilliant sunset lingered, washing the sand dunes in red, reminding Danaë of an ocean of blood. When night fell, the darkness was total, for a thin layer of clouds covered the moon and stars.

Inside the tent, staring out through the tiny opening at the top, she cried.

And cried.

When she had no more tears left, she fell asleep and slept the night through.

The next day passed, much the same as the first two. Danaë was thankful that they were not making a frantic dash across the desert like the one they'd made when she'd been abducted from the caravan. If she had not known better, she would have thought Ramtat was purposely delaying their arrival in Alexandria.

Could he be reluctant to part with her? She shook her head — he wanted nothing more than to be rid of her.

It was mid-afternoon when Danaë noticed an enormous dark cloud rolling toward them from the east. Having grown up near the desert and spending much of her time there, she knew at once they were about to be hit by a sandstorm. She also knew it was perilous to be caught in such a storm.

As the wind grew stronger, Danaë's horse seemed to sense danger and reared up on its hind legs. When she tried to control the animal, it shied sideways, trying to jerk the reins out of her hand.

Suddenly Ramtat was beside her, lifting her onto his horse so that she was seated in front of him. He had to yell to be heard above the howl of the wind. "Find protection for yourselves and the animals! This storm will soon be upon us. Take shelter quickly!"

To Danaë's surprise, Ramtat gathered her close and raced toward the storm, rather than trying to outrun it as the others were doing. To her, it didn't seem like a wise choice until she saw the outline of a steep rock formation jutting out of the sand. Of course, he knew this part of the desert, and he would know where to find refuge.

The storm was almost upon them — already Danaë's face was stinging from the grains of sand that pelted her. Her eyes stung, and she closed them, pressing her face against Ramtat's shoulder.

He slid off the horse with her in his arms and raced for the formation. He placed her on her feet and pushed her against the rocks, then covered her with his body. Gently he turned her face into his shoulder and pulled her to him.

She was puzzled when he drew back and removed her veil until she watched him lift his waterskin and dampen the filmy material.

"Are you frightened?" he asked.

She could have said that naught could frighten her while she was in his arms, and it would have been the truth. But instead she replied, "I have been in sandstorms before and have always been a little afraid."

"With good reason." He draped the wet veil over her face and tightened his grip on her. The wind howled, the dust swirled and stung those parts of their bodies that were not protected by clothing. It was stifling and difficult to breath, but Danaë was in Ramtat's arms, and that was all that mattered.

It was difficult to hear anything but the screaming of the wind. Despite Ramtat's efforts to protect her, Danaë felt as if she'd swallowed half the desert. Even with danger all about them, she became aware of the muscled body pressed against her. He was heavy, but she gloried in the feel of him. She turned her head, her lips touching his cheek.

"So," he whispered near her ear, "it's a distraction you seek. I can help you with that." His mouth sought and found hers, moving softly, caressingly, stealing what little breath she had left. Danaë felt the swell of him against her thigh, and she knew he was as affected by her as she was by him. He ground his body against hers and deepened the kiss.

"Since I partook of the forbidden fruit of your body, I find I have a lasting hunger to taste it again." He pressed his rough cheek against hers. "I will never have my fill of you."

"I feel the same," she said, pressing her face against his neck.

"Even with death at our side, you fire my blood. I cannot resist you," he told her, placing his lips against her ear so she would hear his words. "But if I must die, let it be with your kiss on my lips."

The kiss seemed to go on forever, and it certainly blocked out any thought Danaë might have of danger. All she could think about was the feel of Ramtat's mouth, and his body moving sensuously against hers. She vaguely wondered how he could kiss her with such feeling if he believed her devoid of honor.

"You have captured me in your web like a spider," he said, tearing his lips from hers. "I don't seem to have an antidote against you."

She could not see his face, but his lips descended once more in a kiss so consuming, she had to fight to breathe. His hand slid down her thigh, and he pushed her robe up to her waist. She was aware that the worst of the storm had struck, and the wind sounded very like the wail of a woman. But the storm did not matter — nothing did except what Ramtat was doing to her. He slid his finger inside her, and she was lost to everything but the pleasure he gave her.

"You like me to touch you like this."

"Yes," she managed to whisper.

"And I cannot keep from touching you. I need you like a man dying of thirst needs water."

"It is the same with me."

He pushed her robe farther up her thigh and drove into her, stealing what sanity she had left. His hardness filled her aching body, and she rode the waves of passion with him. She felt him stiffen, and his body tremble, but he stayed inside her, and after a long, drugging kiss, he hardened and took her again.

"To lose you will leave my life without purpose," he growled into her ear. "I despise the need in me that hungers for you."

Danaë could make no reply because her body trembled, and she held onto him, taking his quakes into her body.

For a long moment neither of them spoke. She noticed the storm had lessened, and night had fallen. In the distance she heard the cry of a jackal, but other than that, they were surrounded by an eerie silence.

"What will I do with you?" he asked, raising her chin so he could see into her eyes in the dusty light.

"I know not."

"You are a traitor."

"To whom?"

He sat up and rearranged her robe. She watched him stare into the gathering night, deeply troubled. "Our horses have run away," he said at last. "My men will find them; then they will be searching for us. It will be difficult for them to locate us in the dark."

"What will we do?"

He turned back to her. "I know what I

would like to do — but each time I possess your body, I lose more of myself."

She placed her hand on his shoulder. "I take only what you give. You could always let me go and put an end to this torture for both our sakes."

He rolled to his feet. "It's too late to save me."

"What do you mean?" she asked in desperation.

"I hear my men coming," Ramtat told her. He grasped her hand and helped her to her feet.

She shook her head, trying to dislodge the sand that clung to her scalp. "What will we do now?"

"Ride through the night so we can reach Alexandria by morning."

"What will happen to me?"

He refused to look at her as he said in an unfeeling tone, "That will be for the queen to decide."

By now the Bedouin horsemen had dismounted, one of them leading both their horses forward. Ramtat lifted Danaë onto her horse and spoke in a low tone so none of the others could hear. "What happened between us was a mistake, and we both know it. It will not happen again."

The faint smile she gave him was bittersweet. "Your aunt said you would never choose love over duty. I almost pity you, Lord Ramtat. You are destined to be a very lonely man."

Helplessly Danaë watched Ramtat turn away from her and mount his horse. She knew he was ashamed of the feelings he had for her, and she wanted to hate him for that. Even though his rejection of her was causing her pain, she could never regret what had happened between them.

Silently the column galloped through the desert with Ramtat riding at its head.

Danaë's pride was all she had to sustain her as she faced an uncertain future.

She was innocent, and there were many who could testify to that — but most of them were under Harique's control at the villa, and he had probably threatened them if they spoke in her support.

She thought of Uriah and Minuhe, who would not be moved by Harique's threats. What if he had done something to them to keep them silent?

One thing she knew for certain. She would rather face a quick death as a traitor than fall under Harique's evil power.

The descending night seemed a little darker, and she shivered, though not from the cold.

CHAPTER TWENTY

When they entered Alexandria just past the noon hour, their horses' hooves echoed through nearly empty streets. Danaë glanced about, wondering where all the people were. As they galloped past a silversmith's shop, the hammers were silent. A leather shop that was usually bustling with clients was closed and barred.

There was no one about. No one.

When Danaë looked questioningly at the Bedouin who rode beside her, he frowned and fastened his gaze on the roadway ahead.

The Bedouin knew that if he spoke to the sheik's woman without permission, he would be severely punished, so he remained silent.

As they continued on toward the center of the city, Danaë heard the sound of clashing swords, and her eyes widened with fright. The fighting seemed to be advancing from street to street, and it sounded as if it was coming in their direction.

Ramtat raised his arm to halt his cavalcade. Danaë assumed he told his men to leave, because they dispersed, and Ramtat grabbed the reins of Danaë's horse, leading her back in the direction they had just come. As they wound through streets and backtracked several times, the sound of fighting became distant and more muted.

Ramtat kept one hand on the hilt of his sword, held the reins of Danaë's horse with the other, and controlled his horse with the sheer power of his leg muscles.

"Have no fear — you're in no danger," he told her. "We'll soon be out of the city. Be assured, the fighting has not yet spread to the rural area."

Until now, the war had not seemed quite real to Danaë. Her gaze skimmed along the horizon, and she now realized that what appeared to be clouds was actually smoke. Refusing to admit she was frightened, Danaë pulled her veil across her face and turned her head away from Ramtat. The heaviest fighting seemed to come from the direction of the palace, and she realized the war between the different factions must have escalated.

As they rode down a long, tree-lined street, everything suddenly seemed familiar to Danaë. She yanked the reins out of Ramtat's hand and spun her horse around. Just a few paces away was her very own house!

Ramtat reached over and jerked the reins out of her hand. His eyes were smoldering, and his jaw was clamped in an angry line.

"Don't try that again," he said abruptly. "I'm not letting you go to your home."

She searched his features, then turned away to watch a man in a white robe rush across the almost deserted streets, hoping it would be Uriah. But of course it wasn't him at all — the man was too short, and his girth too round.

She removed her veil, fully exposing her face and hair, hoping some of her own servants might be about and recognize her. That hope was dashed when they left the city behind and galloped across open country.

They rode for some time in silence, and Danaë wondered where Ramtat could be taking her. They slowed to a canter when they came to a curving road lined with cypress trees, and she saw they were entering a great estate.

"What is this place?"

Ramtat merely glanced at her, making no reply.

"I thought you were taking me to the queen."

Again he said nothing, but she saw the muscles tighten in his jaw.

Never one to give up easily, Danaë moved her horse closer to Ramtat's and pressed on with her questions. "Who is fighting in Alexandria?"

Ramtat glanced into the distance. "I would assume it's King Ptolemy's troops taking on Caesar's legions."

She paled. "If only they would reach a truce, this war would end."

He looked at her in irritation. "A truce can't settle what lies between Ptolemy and Cleopatra."

"A war isn't the answer either; it leaves us vulnerable to an outsider like Caesar, who will only cause more devastation for our people."

"It's Ptolemy who cares little that his people and nation are being destroyed," Ramtat accused.

"It's like the end of the world," Danaë said sadly.

Ramtat glanced sideways at her. "It is only the death of folly." He turned his full attention to her. "Even now you defend this king. Surely you can see he must die."

She shook her head. "I do *not* see it."

He nudged his horse to a gallop, and since he still held the reins of her horse, she was forced to hold on tightly to remain in the saddle.

The roadway wound past several small outer houses, vineyards, and wheat field — in the distance she noticed thick walls of an outer courtyard. When they neared the gate, Ramtat rapped with his fist.

"Open — 'tis I."

Ramtat nodded at the gatekeeper as they rode beneath the arches. He had intended to take Danaë directly to the palace and ask for a private audience with the queen, but the fighting in the streets made him decide on an alternative plan. At least that was what he told himself. In truth, he did not want to release her into anyone's care — not even the queen's. Not until he discovered what Danaë was hiding from him.

He helped Danaë from her horse and led her toward the house.

"Who lives here?" she asked.

"I do."

"But I thought you lived at a villa near the waterfall."

"I have several residences. You will be expected to remain here until I decide what to do with you."

Danaë stopped and waited until he turned

to face her. "Why do you think you're entitled to such control over my life? Are you going to keep me your prisoner forever?"

He let out an impatient breath and ran his hand through his hair. He had no answer for her, so he just took her by the arm and led her forward.

Danaë was miserable as Ramtat guided her through a beautifully landscaped garden filled with fountains and flowering fruit trees. The gravel on the walkway crunched beneath her sandals as she walked toward the steps that led to the sprawling white villa.

When they reached the huge double doors, she was reluctant to go in, fearing she would never be allowed to leave. She turned her attention to Ramtat and did the one thing she thought she would never do: She pleaded with him: "Please let me go home. Can't you see I'm a danger to no one? You can't believe I would harm the queen, or anyone, for that matter. There is fighting, men dying in the streets. You no longer need to keep your allegiance to Rome secret; how can I be a threat to you anymore?"

Ramtat frowned, and she saw him hesitate. He knew Danaë was not a woman who pleaded for anything. In that moment, he would have liked nothing better than to take her to her own home. But the queen had commanded him to bring Danaë to the palace, and when the fighting in the city was over, he would do just that.

"You will remain here."

"So I am to continue to be your prisoner?"

His mouth settled in a hard line. "Look at it any way you like. You will be treated with the same courtesy you received at my encampment."

Her head sagged. "Not knowing what is going to happen to me is the hardest part. Why don't you trust me?"

"Why don't *you* trust *me?* Tell me the secrets you are hiding."

Danaë looked into his dark eyes and saw no yielding in their depths. "Lock me away, then. It is the kind of life I have grown accustomed to since coming to know you."

He turned and led her inside, through halls with polished white marble floors and walls. They progressed through a room that was graced by a waterfall and colorful mosaics. If Danaë had not been so miserable, she would have appreciated the tall columns inset with carvings of lotus blossoms brushed with gold.

"Master!" a woman cried, hurrying into the room and bowing low. "Had I known you would be arriving today, I would have had everything ready for you."

"Do not speak of that, Neva," he said briskly. He pulled Danaë forward. "This woman is to be my guest for a time. Her name is Danaë. She is to be confined, and not allowed to walk about on her own. But see that she is shown every courtesy and provided with every comfort."

Again the woman bowed. "Is she to be a prisoner?"

"Aye. Until I say otherwise. Put her in the blue bedchamber."

The servant looked shocked. The master had never before brought a woman to the house. "The room next to yours?"

"Just do it," Ramtat said in an irritated voice.

Danaë's face reddened under the woman's close scrutiny.

"I will make certain that she is well tended," the servant said.

"Send Hafa to me and have him lay out my armor."

"It will be as you say, master."

Danaë raised her gaze to Ramtat. "Why not make me your slave? I could work in your stables tending the animals — or would you rather I was assigned kitchen duty?"

He looked at her through lowered eyelids. "As you know, your fate is not in my hands."

Danaë watched him move across the room and disappear through an arched doorway at the end of the corridor. The man who had held her in his arms and introduced her to the joys of the flesh now treated her like a criminal. She turned to the servant and found her still staring at her.

"What did you do to the master that he should want to imprison you?" the woman asked.

Neva was wide of girth, and her gray hair was pulled back and styled in the Grecian manner. Her dark eyes held no spark of compassion, and Danaë knew it would do no good to try to gain her freedom with this woman's help. Ramtat surrounded himself with loyal servants, or perhaps they were just too afraid of him to disobey. "If you find out what I have done to deserve captivity, I wish you would tell me, for I do not know."

"Come with me," Neva said sternly. She motioned for the guard who was stationed at the door to follow them. "Don't attempt to escape from this place — it isn't possible."

The guard, a tall, handsome man with dark hair and eyes, regarded Danaë with suspicion. "Neva is right," he said briskly. "Someone will be outside your door to prevent you from leaving."

It felt to Danaë as if the walls were closing in on her. She could not guess what fate awaited her, but she doubted it would be a happy one. When she was led into a large bedchamber, Danaë was too dejected to notice her surroundings. While she stood in the middle of the room, the servant and guard departed, and Danaë heard the grinding of a key in the lock.

She hung her head as sorrow washed over her.

"Oh, Father, if only you were here to advise me," she cried, sitting on the edge of the bed and then laying her head against its softness.

"Surely I will never leave this place alive."

As for Ramtat, he paced the length of his apartment, irritated with himself because his thoughts turned too often to the green-eyed beauty in the next room. Even now he thought of her graceful walk, the stubborn set of her chin, the creaminess of her throat.

He closed his eyes; what was the matter with him? He wanted to go to her, to do whatever it took to see a smile on her face.

He felt himself weakening, and he stiffened his resolve. The words she had flung at him just a few days ago haunted him still. To choose love over duty was a weakness he would not allow himself.

Angrily he removed his sword and tossed it onto his bed. He would cut her out of his heart, or he would never know a moment's peace.

CHAPTER
TWENTY-ONE

Ramtat tried to avoid the streets where the fighting was heaviest and found his way to the palace grounds through the secret passages. When he entered the main palace courtyard, which was heavily guarded, the Roman guard on duty immediately escorted him to Caesar's quarters.

When Ramtat stepped inside the door, his gaze went first to Cleopatra, who was having an intense argument with the proconsul of Rome, and then to Caesar, who seemed to be enjoying himself, if the smile on his face was any indication.

Not wanting to disturb the two of them, Ramtat waited to be noticed.

"By sending my brother to head his own army, you have given him leverage against us both. You are outnumbered, Great Caesar — you have made a tactical error."

Caesar seemed amused by the young queen. As Ramtat studied him closely, he decided the proconsul was more than amused by her — he was enchanted.

"Child, do you think I would be so foolish as to give myself the disadvantage? I have probably just made you undisputed Queen of Egypt, and you thank me by criticizing my methods of raising you to a solitary throne."

Cleopatra had a quick, intelligent mind, and it took her only a moment to grasp Caesar's meaning. She tossed her hair in a flirtatious manner and touched Caesar's arm, allowing her fingers to drift up to his shoulder. "You did not call me 'child' last night, or the night before that."

Caesar cleared his throat. "I believe we have a guest." He nodded at Ramtat. "Have you news for us?"

"Approach," Cleopatra said authoritatively. "Did you find the woman you spoke of?"

Ramtat bowed low. "I did, Majesty. She has been safely placed under guard at my villa."

"Why did you not bring her to me?" Cleopatra demanded.

"I tried, Majesty, but the fighting in the streets made it too dangerous."

"Yet you managed to arrive without harm," Caesar said speculatively. "Surely you knew I would have the palace well guarded?"

Cleopatra's eyes narrowed to green slits. "Lord Ramtat, you well know I expected you to bring the woman here. If she is part of some devious plan to cause me harm, I have men who can make her confess."

Ramtat's stomach knotted at the thought of placing Danaë in the hands of some ruthless jailer. "With your permission, I myself will discover the truth."

Caesar stepped near Ramtat, studying him closely. He smiled and turned to regard the queen. "I believe our Lord Ramtat is taken with this woman." He looked questioningly at the young lord. "What is her name?"

"Lady Danaë."

"Or her name may be 'assassin,' " Cleopatra said, looking Ramtat over carefully. "She's already accused of being a slave who passes herself off as a noblewoman."

Caesar laughed heartily and clapped Ramtat on the back. "At last you have found a woman who pleases you, and she may be a dangerous spy. I applaud your originality."

Cleopatra looked displeased as she stalked closer toward Ramtat. "Your heart's wishes do not take precedence over my life. Is this woman under lock and key?"

"Yes, Majesty."

"You will bring her to me tomorrow, no later than the noon hour."

Caesar clasped his hands behind him and walked around Ramtat, still smiling. "I believe you are reluctant to give the woman over to us. Have I got it right?"

Ramtat could feel his face redden. "I merely want to see justice done. If she is innocent, she should not be subjected to the indignities of being imprisoned with criminals."

Caesar spun around to look at Cleopatra. "I believe we can safely leave this woman in Lord Ramtat's custody until such time as we are ready to question her. If Lord Ramtat has her under guard, she can be no danger to you."

Cleopatra nodded reluctantly. "Guard her well," she warned petulantly. "Should she escape, I will hold you responsible."

Ramtat bowed.

"Now that that is settled, there is something I would have you do for me," the queen stated, tapping her finger on her chin.

Again Ramtat bowed. "I am yours to command."

"Never doubt that Lord Ramtat is your man," Caesar said, still amused as he glanced at the queen. "The scoundrel is loyal only to you and Egypt. He never allows me to forget that he serves me only because it is in your best interest."

The queen smiled, and Ramtat drew in his breath — in that moment her resemblance to Danaë was unmistakable. Danaë and the queen were even close to the same age. In truth, Danaë was the more beautiful of the two — but the fact that they were so alike had to be more than mere coincidence.

"I don't want my most loyal subject near the battle," Cleopatra stated. "I would have him near me as my personal bodyguard."

Ramtat bowed. Although he would much rather join the battle and protect Alexandria, he could not deny the queen's wishes. "It would be my honor."

"Nay," Caesar argued. "First, there is something I must have him do for me before I retire him from my service. He is the one man I can trust completely to perform this errand."

Cleopatra looked as though she might debate the point but gave in with a nod. "I give him over to you, but just for this one thing. Then I shall take him back." She looked curious. "What is it that requires my high lord's personal attention?"

"I would have him find out exactly where your brother is. You would like to know that, would you not? And who but Lord Ramtat would know his way around the battlefields and be able to slip in and out without notice? Certainly not one of my Romans."

" 'Tis too dangerous," the queen insisted.

"We live in dangerous times, my dear," Caesar reminded her, all the while watching Ramtat. Caesar knew the young lord well enough to see he was disturbed about something. "What troubles you, Ramtat?"

"I'm not exactly troubled. I was merely trying to solve a puzzle that worries my mind."

Caesar's voice held an undertone of curiosity. "Well, speak of it — by all means, let us know what you are thinking."

Ramtat nodded grimly while watching the queen. "It's just that Lady Danaë has an uncanny resemblance to you, Majesty — even to the color of her eyes. And there's another piece of the puzzle: Lady Danaë wears a pendant of great value, a pendant with royal significance. When I questioned her about it, she became secretive and said only that it had belonged to her mother."

Cleopatra's lips thinned in irritation. "Most probably the mother gave birth to one of my father's by-blows. She was probably a slave who caught my father's fancy."

"I have considered that possibility," Ramtat admitted.

"Describe the pendant to me," the queen said. "What does it look like?"

"I can do better than that if you will allow it, Majesty. I believe I can draw it for you."

The queen nodded to indicate a table stacked with papyrus and an ink pot. "Do so."

Ramtat dipped a prepared reed in ink and scribbled on the papyrus, then handed it to the queen. He watched her study the drawing, and saw her face whiten.

"Are you certain this is the exact design?"

"Yes, Majesty. It is crafted in gold in the shape of a coiled cobra. The eye is a very large emerald."

"I know this piece. My father had the royal goldsmith design and craft two pendants just alike. One for my mother, and the other for . . ." Her voice trailed off, and her face grew whiter still. She dropped down onto a padded stool and shook her head. "It has long been thought that the recipient of the second pendant was dead. If the woman still lives, or if this Danaë is her daughter, she may well be a danger to me in ways you cannot imagine."

"Nonsense! I have never been convinced this slave, if slave she is, could be a threat to you," Caesar stated skeptically.

Her face expressionless, the queen leaned

forward so she could look into Ramtat's eyes. "I must know if she is the daughter. I must now consider the possibility that she may be attempting to supplant me."

"Of whom do you speak?" Caesar insisted. "Who is the woman your father gave the jewel to?"

"Eilana was the daughter of my father's most trusted general, Commander Alekos. One of his early ancestors was among the men who accompanied the great Alexander when he conquered Egypt. It is even said that he was a relative of the great Alexander. I don't know all the details, but the general was from a highborn family, and I believe I heard my father say that Eilana's father was of pure Greek lineage, the same as we Ptolemies. I grew up on stories of his daughter's rare beauty, and how men couldn't help falling in love with her — my father being no exception. It was even whispered that my father married her, but if that is so, there is no documentation."

"What happened to her?" Caesar asked, drawn into the story.

"She disappeared not long before I was born." Cleopatra looked into Caesar's eyes. "It was said she was fleeing from one of my father's other wives who meant to do her harm. It is also whispered that she was carrying my father's child when she fled." The queen's eyes widened, and a small curve touched her bottom lip. "If this woman is Eilana's offspring, there could be those who would use her to take my throne."

Ramtat took a deep breath. "I cannot believe Danaë would become involved in a plot to steal your throne."

"Lord Ramtat, you are not thinking with your head but another part of your anatomy," the queen declared with disgust. "This woman has power over you — I can see that. You are allowing your love for her to interfere with your duty."

Ramtat was shocked.

The queen's green gaze never left Ramtat as she stated, "I will discover the truth about this woman. If it happens that she is Eilana's child, she must be eliminated."

"She may be naught but the daughter of a slave," Caesar suggested yet again, watching the strained emotion revealed in Ramtat's eyes.

Cleopatra shook her head. "Who can say? But I intend to find out." Her gaze locked with Ramtat's. "Accompany me — I would show you something."

The queen swept out of the room, and Ramtat followed while Caesar dismissed the matter and turned to study his maps and plan his strategy for the continuing battle.

The queen's footsteps were light as she led Ramtat through marble corridors decorated with tall Corinthian columns, past a room with ornate couches, and rooms housing irreplaceable treasures the Ptolemy family had collected over the years.

At last she stopped before double doors of hammered gold. "This was my father's bath and bedchambers," she told Ramtat. "No one uses the suite now."

Ramtat followed her past the massive bed with gossamer netting, past a dressing chamber that still held the late king's clothing. Passing through another set of double doors, Ramtat realized he was in the most elaborate bath he'd ever seen. Gold and marble was the theme that ran throughout. But what caught and held his attention were the figures depicted on the walls. One showed a battle with the great Alexander — there was no mistaking the image of the goddess Isis receiving the spirit of a Ptolemaic queen. He moved along a wall worked in turquoise that depicted a priest pouring a pitcher of sacred Nile water onto a king's head.

Queen Cleopatra nodded at the back wall, which was painted in bright colors — it appeared to be a painting of family life. "Look carefully at the women there, study their faces — see if you recognize any of them."

Ramtat moved down the wall, his gaze inspecting every face. There was a scene of Cleopatra's father on the throne, and one of him with his children on what seemed to be an outing. Ramtat did not recognize any of the other faces at first, but then his gaze fell on a woman dressed in blue, smiling up at the figure of the king.

Ramtat felt a cold hand move up his chest and squeeze his heart. The artist had artfully captured the young woman in a pensive moment. The face, the eyes, the delicate bone structure were almost the same as Danaë's.

Ramtat reached out and touched the woman's likeness. "Majesty, may I inquire about the identity of this woman?" he asked, although in his heart he already knew who it was.

"That is Eilana. Does she look familiar to you?"

"It is very strange, because Lady Danaë resembles you, and so does this woman." He turned to face her. "How can that be?"

"She was my father's cousin — and certainly of royal blood. Eilana's father married my father's younger sister. You can see why I have concerns."

Ramtat wondered if it was possible that Danaë and the queen shared a father. No wonder she refused to discuss her mother or anything about her identity. She was probably afraid it would mean her death. "Majesty, I have come to believe in Lady Danaë's innocence. I would trust her with my own life — and more importantly, with yours."

Cleopatra was momentarily troubled. "Take the best care of this woman, and bring her directly to me when you have completed your task for Caesar. I will want to question her myself, and the fewer people who know of her existence, the better."

Ramtat bowed. "I will do as you say, Majesty," but the usual conviction was missing from his voice.

"Meanwhile," Cleopatra went on, "I shall question those in the palace who knew Eilana. Perhaps someone can shed more light on this mystery."

Ramtat bowed low. "I hope the riddle will soon be unraveled and we shall know all, Majesty."

She nodded. "As do I." She waved a hand in dismissal, her gaze on Eilana's likeness, studying every feature. "You may leave now. Go directly to Caesar, for he's expecting you."

Again he bowed, this time taking a backward step before the sound of her voice stopped him.

"I would have you know this: Caesar holds the power in Egypt, and I admire him more than any man I know. I may even love him in my own way — but I will always do what is best for my people, and if you are loyal to me, so will you. You belong at my side, son of Egypt, not in Caesar's army."

The more he came to know Cleopatra, the more he knew she belonged on the throne of Egypt. "First and foremost, you have my loyalty."

She smiled slightly. "I am counting on that."

CHAPTER
TWENTY-TWO

Danaë was awakened by a stirring of the morning breeze that brought the sweet aroma of flowers from the garden. There were footsteps outside her chamber as someone unlocked the door. A servant entered with a tray of food, and Danaë forced herself to sound cheerful. "Has your lord returned?"

Although Danaë was certain the slave understood her, the woman silently shook her head and went about the task of unpacking a trunk that had been brought in the day before. Danaë had no interest in the beautiful clothing that had been provided for her or the richness of the bedchamber. Stoically she watched the young woman fold a fine silk garment and drape it across a wooden rack.

This time, Danaë was determined that if the opportunity presented itself, she would find a way to escape.

Later in the afternoon Danaë paced the chamber like a restless tiger. Since the women who attended her never spoke or answered her questions, she did not know when Ramtat would return.

Danaë could not rest, and at night she could not sleep. Even now plans could be going forth to accuse her of treason or remand her to Harique's custody. Lowering herself onto a stool, she buried her face in her hands and stared at her sandaled feet, feeling utter devastation.

Danaë did not hear the soft bootsteps as Ramtat entered the room, nor did she know he was there until he knelt down beside her.

"Can anything be so bad that it would cause this sadness I see in you?"

She jerked her head up and stared at him. She was unable to see his expression because his face was in shadow, so she could not tell if he was being critical or if he genuinely cared about her state of mind.

"If you have to ask, you cannot know what it feels like to be a prisoner. Do you think I should celebrate the fact that I may lose my life for reasons I don't understand?"

He eased himself onto the stool beside her. "Danaë, I need to know everything you can tell me about your mother. It's important."

What he really wanted to know was whether her mother was Lady Eilana — now he secretly hoped she was merely the daughter of some unimportant slave. "I leave it to you to convince me otherwise. Is your mother still alive?"

"A prisoner does not confess to her jailer. A slave has no right to a past life and no hope for the future."

He was stung by her words and ached for her sorrow, but he had to know the truth before he took her to Cleopatra. "I would like another look at the necklace you wear."

She hesitated. "The pendant is the one thing that belongs to me." Then she shook her head. "Nay, that is not right, is it? Since I'm your prisoner, the necklace is yours for the taking." She reached to the back of her neck, unclasped it, and dropped it into his hand. "Do with it what you will."

Ramtat studied the beautiful object carefully. It was the twin of the one worn by Lady Eilana in the drawing on the wall of the royal bath. He opened Danaë's hand, placed the pendant in her palm, and closed her fingers over it. " 'Tis yours, and no one will take it from you."

Her fist tightened. "You have taken everything else from me — why not this?"

He gazed in to the distance as he spoke.

"You accuse me when you seem to have built your life on lies? You claim a father who is not yours, and deny the mother who gave birth to you."

"What do you know that I don't know?" Danaë asked. "You speak to me in riddles."

He shook his head. "I am here to get answers, not to give them."

Danaë merely glared at him.

"The queen has commanded me to bring you to her."

"When? Today?"

"Not for a few days." He watched her for a moment while a plan formed in his mind. He was beginning to doubt he would be able to turn Danaë over to the queen after what he'd learned today. "Let me ask you something: Would you consider leaving Egypt with me?"

"I don't understand. Why would I want to do such a thing?"

"Would you . . ." He stood. "No matter — 'twas merely a passing thought."

She stared at him, puzzled.

"I will be away for a while. There's something I must do for Caesar. The war is over but for a few pockets of resistance scattered about the city and in the desert."

Silence fell heavy between them. Danaë flicked her tongue over her dry lips and turned away from Ramtat. Where once they had been as close as two people can be, they now had nothing to say to one another. She stood and brushed past him as if dismissing him.

Ramtat listened to the whisper of her footsteps as she walked away from him, fighting the impulse to go after her. What if she was the daughter of a king? Then she would be as far above him as he had thought her below him when he had believed her to be a slave.

Ramtat quietly left, locking Danaë's door behind him — there was nothing more to be said. When he reached his chamber, he looked at the bed, weary and wishing he could get just one good night's sleep. Danaë was in the next room, but he had to put her out of his mind. He would be leaving at first light, and the mission he was going on was the most important, and most dangerous, of his life.

Danaë clasped her pendant tightly, feeling a deep ache. Why had Ramtat prodded her to tell him about her mother, and why had he wanted to see the pendant? Her father had warned her that her mother had been terrified of someone. Had Danaë unwittingly become a part of whatever her mother had fled? Had she stepped back into her mother's past — was she now in the same danger?

A lovely young woman with large brown eyes and a willowy shape entered, carrying the evening meal. The woman had long ebony hair which hung loose about her shoulders. She wore reed sandals and a rough linen shift — clearly, she was a slave.

"Lady," the slave said, bowing low. "The master instructed the cook to make every delicacy to please you. Will you not eat?"

At last, here was someone she could talk with. "I will eat," she said, finding she was hungry.

"Shall I return to take you to the bath?"

"I think a bath would be very nice."

The young woman hesitated as if she had more to say. "My name is Vika," she said softly. "I have been chosen by the housekeeper as your personal servant." She looked doubtful for a moment. "Unless you would prefer someone else."

Danaë paused with a sugared date halfway to her mouth. Was a prisoner entitled to a personal servant? She could see that the young woman was anxiously awaiting her answer. "I'd be pleased to have you serve me, Vika."

A look of pure joy spread over the woman's face. "I will do everything I can to please you." The maid went about the room folding clothing and gathering sandals that she would later polish with oil of palm.

Danaë had been so lost in thought, she barely heard the woman move across the room and out the door, but she did hear the loud click as the key turned in the lock. When she returned to her meal, the food had grown cold, so she nibbled on a crust of bread.

There was a certain urgency in the air now that she had reached Alexandria. Something had changed. She was in more danger than she had imagined, and she still did not know why.

The bath was a huge room and luxurious beyond anything Danaë could have imagined. Brightly colored mosaics depicted veiled maidens dancing across the sand of a desert. The pool itself was deep, with wide steps on one side. The sweet scent of sandalwood wafted up from the water. It was pure delight for Danaë to sink into the water and feel it lap against her body.

Vika nodded, and two other women poured warm water over Danaë's skin. "This feels wonderful," Danaë exclaimed. She dunked her head under the water so she didn't see Vika and the two servants bow and back away from the pool, their eyes wide as Lord Ramtat entered.

When Danaë emerged from the water, she noticed a pair of bare feet standing at the edge of the pool. Raising her gaze higher, she saw Ramtat dressed only in a white tunic.

Ramtat quickly positioned his body so his manservant could not see Danaë's nakedness. "Leave us," he said, and the three women, along with Ramtat's male servant, hurried out of the room.

"I see you have come to bathe," Danaë said, moving toward the steps. "If you will allow me a moment to dress, I will leave you to your bath."

Ramtat's eyes were fastened on Danaë. Water streamed down her hair and across her lovely shoulders.

Danaë's face flushed as she glanced at the powerful man before her. "Had I known you wanted to bathe, I would have waited. I will just leave you now, and you can call your servant back."

He dropped down on the edge of the pool and slid his feet into the water. "Instead of leaving, why not allow me to be your attendant?"

"Nay!" She backed away. "I will not do that."

Before she could stop him, he had removed his tunic and slid into the pool, swimming in her direction. "I come to bathe and find an enchanting mermaid in my bath."

Danaë was grateful for the foaming oils that helped cover her nakedness. She remembered when she and Ramtat had swum in the waterfall pool, and she knew she had to escape before she ended up in his arms. "Turn your head. I'm leaving, or you can leave."

Slowly he shook his head. "I have neither the will nor the inclination to leave when I have such tempting beauty before my eyes."

Danaë took a step backward, blood pounding through her body. This time she was not going to give in to him — she couldn't bear to have him reject her again.

"I was determined to keep a distance between us, but with you in my house, it has proved impossible."

He took another step toward her, like a man in a trance, and she did not move away this time. His fingers slid through her wet hair, and he stared down into her face. He bent to rest his cheek against hers, and she felt him tremble.

"Do you truly want me to leave, Danaë?"

She tried to speak but couldn't find her

voice, so she shook her head. She felt him take a deep breath as he pulled her close, fitting her body against his. There were so many reasons she should not succumb to temptation, but she wanted to feel him inside her — she wanted to be held in his strong arms and to have him kiss her until she could no longer think.

"Little green-eyes, if only you and I were just ordinary citizens and had not become entangled in court intrigue, I could have you for my own and never let you go."

She raised her face to his. "You are not ordinary, but I am."

He smiled, his thumb brushing across her cheek. "There is naught ordinary about you. Perhaps you are keeping a secret from me. Is the secret that you are of royal blood, Danaë?"

Suddenly Danaë's head cleared enough for her to push his hand away. "Are you addled? What kind of lies has Harique been telling?"

Ramtat grabbed her by the arm and pulled her to him forcefully. "Who is this man Harique to you?"

"An enemy. Just as you are."

"I'm not your . . ." He broke off and stepped back. "It never occurred to me that you thought of me as your enemy."

"A blind man would have come to that conclusion days ago." She moved to the steps and without embarrassment climbed out of the water, reaching for her linen robe. After wrapping it about her, she turned back to Ramtat to find him watching her.

"I would ask a boon of you, if you do not mind," she said.

"Ask."

"I am accustomed to being outdoors. Being confined inside is very difficult for me. Would you give permission for me to walk about in the garden? Your walls are high, and you could set a guard on me if it would make you feel better. Just let me walk about for a portion of the day."

"You are very athletic. My wall may not hold you."

"I must be in the open air. I need to feel the sun on my face."

He could tell that she was distraught, almost frantic. When he had first met her, she was not easily intimidated by him or anyone. Now there were shadows beneath her eyes, she'd lost weight, and it had been many days since he'd heard her laugh. "I'll arrange it."

She bowed her head. "Thank you."

Ramtat watched her move to the door and disappear into the corridor. He closed his eyes and sank into the water to sit on the bottom step. He had been willing to take her out of Egypt. He still might have to if things went against her at the palace.

Considering their situation, he leaned back and stared at the ceiling, which was painted with blue and white cloud banks and bright sun rays. What if he took her back to the desert, where she would be safe and even Cleopatra would not be able to find her? His people would help protect her, for they could keep a secret better than anyone he knew.

He shook his head. Danaë was already too enmeshed in court intrigues. This thing must be followed to the end. If not, she would never be free, and neither would he.

CHAPTER
TWENTY-THREE

Ramtat had been gone for four days. Danaë had overheard two guards outside her room mention that their master had left on a dangerous mission, although neither knew what it was. All she knew was that Ramtat had to do something for Caesar, and it had probably plunged him into the heat of battle.

She sat brooding on her bed, waiting for the time when she could go into the garden. Ramtat had kept his promise, and each day she was allowed an outing in the morning and early evening. Unfortunately, there was always a guard nearby, which took much of the joy out of being outdoors.

At last, the guard came for her. She walked along a graveled path and paused by a huge marble fountain depicting three graceful maidens pouring water from onyx pitchers. Dropping onto a low bench, she dipped her hand into the water and watched it ripple to the sides.

Her head ached — it was too hot to be in the sun — but she was reluctant to give up one moment of freedom. Moving toward the back wall, she stood under the shade of a tree, knowing the guard would soon seek her out to remind her that she must go inside.

Danaë wished she could remain in the open until the sun went down and the stars filled the sky. She plucked a lotus blossom and breathed in the sweet scent. Her head jerked up when she heard the cry of a hawk circling above her. If only it was her Tyi — if only she could have something with her to remind her of her previous life, of freedom.

Danaë frowned. With each circle the hawk came lower to the ground. At first she thought the bird might be closing in on some luckless prey, but the closer it came to her, the faster her heart beat. She stood as if frozen and held out her arm.

Joy burst from her when the hawk landed on a branch above her and cocked its head, looking at her. She could tell by the distinct golden markings on his wingtips that it was her falcon!

Again she held her arm out to him, even knowing his claws would hurt — but Tyi had been too well trained to land on her arm unless she was wearing leather protection.

So he hopped to a lower branch and stared right into her eyes.

How had he ever managed to find her?

She glanced toward the house to make sure the guard wasn't watching her, and she spotted him just on the other side of the fountain, talking to someone she couldn't see. Cautiously she rose on her tiptoes and touched Tyi's wing. The falcon cocked his beautiful head and hopped onto a still lower branch so she could reach him.

"Tyi, my dear, wonderful Tyi. I don't know how you found me, but I'm so glad you did."

Amazingly, Tyi leaned his head forward and touched it to Danaë's cheek. Tears blinded her as she kissed the dark feathered head. "I have missed you so," she said softly.

Then her gaze dropped to the hawk's leg. "What is this —" She untied the leather strap and found a tiny strip of papyrus rolled up inside. It had to be from Uriah — he'd found her!

Again she glanced toward the guard. She couldn't see him, and that was unsettling. She would rather know where he was than have him come upon her unaware.

"Lady Danaë," the man called, moving down the walkway toward her. "It is time to leave."

"Can I not stay a few moments more?" she asked, tucking the small bit of papyrus inside her sash. "I have a longing to see the sunset."

The guard's name was Ma'sud, and he was one of Ramtat's Bedouins. The man treated Danaë with respect, but she would use him in any way she could if it meant her freedom. There were times when she thought she saw pity in his dark eyes as he looked at her. She watched him waver, and then he gave her a stiff nod.

"I see no harm in it."

He turned away, and she glanced up, disappointed that Tyi had taken to the air. She wanted to call him back, but that would be too dangerous, so she watched until the falcon was no more than a tiny speck against the darkening sky. Eager to read what was written on the papyrus, she stepped into the shadow of the cypress tree, where she would not be disturbed. The writing was small, and in the gathering shadows, it was difficult to decipher:

I will be here every day at this time.

It was unsigned, but she knew Uriah's hand. She tucked it back into her sash, her heart feeling light for the first time since she'd been imprisoned here. Here was her chance to escape!

She could not think how Uriah had managed to find her, but he had. She allowed her gaze to skim along the rock wall, and her heart stopped.

Uriah!

The high wall must have been a difficult climb for him. He had cleverly hidden himself in the branches of a cypress tree. He motioned for her to come closer, and she held up her hand and nodded.

Keeping her steps unhurried, Danaë walked around the fountain and found the guard talking to Vika. Apparently, the two of them were more than friends: He was holding her hand and looking lovingly into her eyes.

Their feelings for each other could work to Danaë's advantage. If they would linger a while longer, Danaë might manage to talk to Uriah.

She casually moved toward the wall, stopping only when she was even with the cypress tree.

"Can you hear me?" Uriah asked.

She nodded.

"I learned three days ago that Lord Ramtat had returned to Alexandria. On the slight chance that you might be with him, I have come here every day since. I saw you yesterday, but I had no way to draw your attention."

"So you thought of using Tyi."

"I will never again doubt that hawk's intelligence. When I tied the papyrus to his leg, he knew exactly what to do."

Danaë bent, giving the impression she was removing a pebble from her sandal. "Have a care. I would not want the guard to discover you."

"Are you in danger?"

"I am, Uriah. Real danger."

"Has Lord Ramtat hurt you in any way?"

Hurt her? He had ripped her heart to pieces. "No one has harmed me . . . yet."

"Then we must get you away as quickly as possible."

Excitement thrummed through her. "How will we do it?"

"The guard seems distracted by that woman," Uriah said. "Is theirs a relationship you can use to our advantage?"

Danaë looked pensive for a moment as she tried to think of a way she could trick the lovers. Feeling only a prickle of guilt, she said, "Perhaps I can."

"I will be here at the same time tomorrow. Try to find a way to make it to this wall."

She nodded, not daring to linger any longer lest the guard become suspicious.

"Until tomorrow."

Ramtat slipped over the side of the reed boat and waded ashore. The night was dark, and he could see nothing as he stood on dry land waiting for the appearance of the man he was supposed to meet.

Hearing movement, Ramtat spun around to face the man who came up behind him.

"Have you come from Caesar?" the man asked in a deep, gravelly voice.

"I have. Has there been a positive identification of the body?"

"I saw him for myself. I was told the boat capsized, and he drowned."

"You are certain?"

The man handed Ramtat a golden amulet. "This was on the body."

Ramtat clutched the object in his fist. "Then it's over."

"Not entirely." Another man appeared out of the darkness, and then another. "Your dead body will be a special message to that Roman you serve."

Ramtat's hand went to his sword. "What

is the meaning of this!"

"You are no son of Egypt if you serve that Roman cur."

Ramtat's sword swung through the air. "So you serve Ptolemy — a dead king."

"Proudly," stated the man who was obviously the leader. "We discovered your Roman spy among us, and if we didn't have to kill you, you could inform Caesar his spy told us everything we wanted to know before he died. I took his place and met you in his stead."

Ramtat's sword swung forward to clash with one of the other men's swords, but he wasn't quick enough to avoid a dagger thrust. At first he felt nothing, and then his side burned as if on fire. He gritted his teeth and bore the pain, knowing he must not show weakness. "I will tell Caesar I stood over your dead body."

Two of Ramtat's soldiers leaped out of the boat and rushed into the fray. Swords clashed, and three men fell dead — one of Ramtat's men and two of the enemy.

Ramtat grasped the handle of the dagger and yanked it out of his side, feeling the heat of blood running down his leg. He hit the only man still standing with his elbow, knocked him down, and placed the very same dagger at his throat. "Speak truth before you die — or would you rather I take you to Caesar and let him make you talk?" Although Ramtat could not see the man's face, he could sense his fear, and he would use it against him. "It would be better for you to talk to me." The man attempted to speak, but Ramtat had pressed the blade too tightly against his throat, so he nodded.

Ramtat eased off the dagger, but felt his strength draining away. "Speak truth."

"It does not matter. Everyone will soon know that Egypt's king is dead, and Caesar's harlot sits upon the throne."

Ramtat nicked the man's skin, and he shuddered before crying out, "It's as I told you — King Ptolemy is dead!"

Ramtat pressed his blade tighter. "How did he die?"

"Just as I said — he drowned."

"Do you speak true?"

"I swear on my loyalty to Egypt, and may the gods strike me dead if I lie."

Ramtat nodded. "There has already been too much Egyptian blood spilled this night. I shall give you a gift because you fought valiantly for your dead king. I give you your life. Leave before I change my mind."

The man did not remain to argue but scampered away, to be swallowed up by the night shadows. The blade in Ramtat's hand was slick with his own blood, and he dropped to his knees, then fell face forward onto the sand.

As blood gushed from Ramtat's wound, his men carried him to the boat. The rowers put oars to water, and the small craft shot forward in a race against time. They knew that if they did not get their commander to a physician in time, he would bleed to death.

Danaë watched Vika tidy the room, wondering how to explain that she had witnessed the scene between the slave girl and Ma'sud. "How long have you lived here at the villa, Vika?"

The dark-eyed young woman paused in picking up Danaë's sandals. "I was born here. My mother is personal maid to Lord Ramtat's mother. My father was the high gardener."

"You are not a slave, then?"

Vika looked puzzled. "I am a slave, as are my parents, but to have a master like Lord Ramtat makes us more fortunate than most of our kind."

"You are allowed to choose whom you love and marry?"

Vika's expression became guarded. "Not without the master's permission."

"Then Lord Ramtat approves of your

choosing Ma'sud for a husband?"

The young woman's face lost its color, and she dropped her gaze. "You saw us together."

"I confess I did."

"Ma'sud is not a slave. It would not be acceptable for me to . . . for us —"

"For you to be in love?"

Vika met Danaë's gaze. "Aye." She looked away. "We cannot help the way we feel about each other. We tried, but it's very hard." She looked up at Danaë. "Will you tell the master?"

"Of course not. I do not owe Ramtat any loyalty. As you know, I am a prisoner here, not a guest."

Vika took a hesitant step toward Danaë. "It is whispered among the servants that Lord Ramtat has a deep love for you."

"Who would say such a thing?"

"Everyone. The master is not the kind of man who uses his slaves for his own pleasure. He is an honorable man, and a handsome one. Many women have wanted to be his wife. Although he has been with some, he looked at none of them the way he looks at you."

The foolish girl apparently did not know that Danaë was soon to be turned over to the queen to await her justice. "What will you and Ma'sud do?"

"It is hopeless for us. Ma'sud is one of the master's most trusted guards — did not the master set Ma'sud to watch over you? If Lord Ramtat ever finds out we have . . . that we love each other, he will sell me and send Ma'sud away."

Danaë felt a pang of regret for what she was about to do, but it was the only way she could escape, and she was desperate. "Lord Ramtat will be returning soon. I see no harm in you and Ma'sud spending time together."

There was dejection in Vika's dark eyes. "How can we?"

"With my help. While we are in the garden, we are away from prying eyes. If I were to spend my time at the opposite end of the garden by the huge cypress tree, you and Ma'sud could be alone." Danaë watched hope spring to life in the young woman's eyes. "Do you think Ma'sud would approve?"

"He truly loves me and would do anything to be alone with me."

"It is settled, then. Get word to him that you will meet him in the garden tomorrow afternoon."

Vika beamed. "I shall not be able to sleep tonight for the happiness that fills my heart."

Danaë was sure she would not be able to sleep either; she was betraying this young woman's trust and turning it to her own advantage. But as it happened, she slept very well.

Danaë looked over her shoulder before she climbed up on the marble bench. She stood on tiptoes and reached for a nearby branch and hefted herself onto the wall. Uriah caught her arm to steady her.

"Catch the rope and lower yourself down. I have horses waiting for us. Hurry!"

Danaë could hardly believe her good fortune — everything had gone even better than she'd planned. Vika and Ma'sud were so taken by each other, they hardly noticed her at all. But time was against Danaë, and she must be far away before she was missed.

She slid down the rope, and Uriah came after her. He had brought her a cape, and she slipped it over her clothing and pulled the hood forward to cover her face.

In no time at all, she and Uriah were riding through open fields. Danaë did not feel safe until they left the villa behind and were headed toward the center of Alexandria.

Danaë heard no sounds of fighting, and she wondered if the war was over. If it was, had the brother and sister reunited, or was one of them dead?

"Uriah, is any place safe for me? Must I hide for the rest of my life?"

"I do not have that answer. It is best we take each day as it comes and not borrow tomorrow's troubles." He saw a worried frown crease her brow. "Child, I have asked myself why so many woes have dropped onto your shoulders, but I have no answer."

It was almost dark when they reached the docks.

"Where are we going?" she asked Uriah as he lifted her from her horse. She quickly glanced over her shoulder to make sure they hadn't been followed.

"I have a brother who is a free man, and he has a small farm by the Nile delta — you will be safe there, since no one knows of it. We will be sailing with the morning tide. Meantime, you will become reacquainted with an old friend."

She looked puzzled. "Who could that be?"

"The captain of the *Blue Scarab* awaits you."

Danaë beamed and took a deep breath of sea air — the first breath of freedom she'd had in many weeks. The first person she saw when she hurried up the gangplank was her faithful Faraji, but the smiling guard was shoved aside, and Minuhe come hurtling toward Danaë. The maid wept and hugged Danaë to her.

"I thought never to see you again."

"I thought the same," Danaë admitted, laying her head on Minuhe's shoulder. "I have missed you."

"What about me, Lady Danaë?" a gruff voice asked. "Did you spare any thought for me?"

Danaë was overjoyed to see the captain of the *Blue Scarab,* and she laughed delightedly, going into his outstretched arms. "Good Captain Narmeri, little did I know I would be sailing on your ship again so soon."

He bowed low to her, his careful gaze on Faraji, who was watching him closely. "Lady Danaë, Uriah has told me of your troubles, and I have agreed to take you away from Alexandria. It is a shame that a lady such as yourself should be treated with such disrespect."

"You are a good friend and will not find me ungenerous."

"Lady Danaë, your safety is enough reward for me. But quickly, come with me so you can be hidden until we get under way. No one must know you are on board."

He led Danaë down wooden steps into

the dimly lit hold of the ship. It took her eyes a moment to adjust to the darkness.

Suddenly she stepped back as she heard the sound of splintering wood, and saw Obsidian burst from her cage. Danaë did not have time to brace herself, so she and the cat tumbled downward with the captain looking on in horror, wondering if Danaë needed rescuing. He relaxed when he heard her laughter and saw the smile on Faraji's rugged face.

Obsidian licked Danaë and gently swatted her face with her claws retracted.

"You bad, bad cat," Danaë said, giggling, turning her head away to avoid the lapping tongue. She locked her arms around the leopard's neck, burying her fingers in obsidian's soft coat. "What will I do with you? You broke out of your cage again."

Later Danaë guided the cat back and forced her into the cage. Faraji shoved a heavy crate in front of the opening in the hope of keeping Obsidian contained. After Danaë had devoted equal attention to Tyi, she moved onto the deck, loving the feeling of freedom.

Minuhe stood silently beside her, and faithful Faraji was nearby. Uriah glanced down at Danaë's pale face as if looking for signs of suffering. "You have been through an ordeal. Do you wish to discuss it?"

"I have lived a lifetime in a few weeks."

"Lord Ramtat did not misuse you in any way?"

She pondered the question, trying to decide how to answer Uriah. "Only inasmuch as I was a captive and was not allowed to walk outside alone. And," she said, meeting his steady gaze, "I lost my heart to the man who held the keys to my prison."

"I am not much of an authority on matters of the heart," Uriah said.

"You have always been my teacher, and the one I went to for answers, but in this I must find my own solution."

"Why did Lord Ramtat bring you back to Alexandria?"

Danaë gathered her thoughts and told Uriah as much as she knew, and that she had been implicated in a plot to kill the queen.

He shook his head. "This is serious indeed. I see no way you can ever come out of hiding if the queen is looking for you."

"I've been thinking, and I have decided that I will not cower like a guilty person. Rather, I will gather my strength and walk into the lion's den."

"What does that mean?"

"When I feel the hour is right, I shall come

back to Alexandria and ask for an audience with the queen."

Uriah nodded. "It is said this queen is wise. Let us hope she listens to reason. But what about Lord Ramtat?"

Although Danaë was happy about her freedom, she felt a dull ache inside. Her spirit reached out for Ramtat's. "I shall always love him and wish him well — but there can never be anything lasting between us."

"Time passes and wounds heal."

"Perhaps. I hope that is so in this instance." She stared out into the night, wondering what Ramtat's reaction would be when he discovered she had escaped. She felt pity for Vika and Ma'sud. But if she had it to do over again, she would still make her dash for freedom.

CHAPTER
TWENTY-FOUR

The morning was overcast as the *Blue Scarab* sailed out of Alexandria's Great Harbor. Virtually unseen by those on board was the small reed boat that passed near the bow of the larger ship. Danaë, standing on deck shrouded in a hooded cape, paid no heed to the occupants of the small craft, nor did she see the man who lay pale and bleeding within it.

Her gaze was on the distant horizon and freedom!

Ramtat briefly opened his eyes as the captain of his guard tossed another blood-soaked rag over the side of the boat. "The bleeding is bad, General. I have not the skills to stop the flow."

"You must get me to Caesar," Ramtat muttered. "He needs to know Ptolemy is dead."

His captain shook his head. "In this

instance, I believe Caesar will need to come to you, General."

Danaë felt a blast of hot air on her face and sensed the first stirring of unrest. Something untoward had happened — she felt it within her spirit. She should be overjoyed to be leaving Alexandria, but it felt as if some invisible string were pulling her back. She fought against the overwhelming sadness that weighed on her. She had known naught but trouble since arriving in that city. Why could she not feel joy to be leaving it?

Ramtat was feverish, and he tossed on the bed, his throat parched and dry. "Water," he whispered through cracked lips. "So thirsty."

A golden cup was pressed to his lips, and he swallowed thirstily.

"That is enough for now. You must not take too much all at once."

Ramtat frowned. Was it Danaë's face that came to him out of a fog? Was it her hand that was cool on his forehead? Fever had dimmed his eyesight, but still the face looked like hers. Then his vision cleared a bit, and he painfully rolled his head. This woman's nose was not as small as Danaë's, but the eyes were the same.

Pain stabbed at his side, and he clearly heard Queen Cleopatra's voice. It was she who had given him water.

"Have a care, Physician — the man you treat is important to Egypt," the queen warned.

Was Ramtat dreaming, or was it Caesar's voice he heard coming to him out of the swirling darkness.

"Lord Ramtat is important to Rome as well as Egypt. He risked his life to bring us the information that your brother is dead."

After that, Ramtat felt darkness swallow him, and he heard no more.

Danaë stood beside Uriah, watching the waves lap against the boat. For an instant, she felt she was reliving an earlier moment in her life. Not so long ago she had stood on the deck of this ship looking toward an uncertain future. Now it was even more uncertain. Ramtat would be searching for her, and her fate at his hands would be harsh. Harique was probably looking for her as well, and from what Uriah said, he'd taken over all her holdings. And then there was the queen, the greatest danger to her of all.

"If, as you say, Harique burned my father's copies of the adoption papers, and also burned the one in your possession, then I have no proof to take before the king."

"It will not be the king you petition, but the queen. King Ptolemy has been driven out of Alexandria, and there are rumors that he might be dead. His sister now sits upon the throne unchallenged."

Danaë was utterly dejected as she remembered the king that everyone had used and then discarded. " 'Tis a pity such a young boy should have had to rule without proper guidance."

"He was not capable of ruling," Uriah said.

Danaë's head felt too heavy to hold up, and tears choked her throat. "I wonder if anyone mourns Ptolemy."

"You do."

She wiped her tears away. "I have no hope of reclaiming my good name if I have to face Queen Cleopatra."

Uriah suddenly smiled. "You have every reason to hope. Not all the copies of your adoption papers were destroyed. When I gave the High Priest of Isis the white tiger skin, I also placed in his keeping one of the documents of your legal adoption, as well as deeds to the properties your father left to you. The high priest was overjoyed with the gift, and he wore the tiger skin draped about his shoulders for all to see. He assured me he will stand beside you and plead your case to the royal court should the need arise."

Danaë felt overwhelming relief, but she also had concerns. "Have you any word of Lord Ramtat?"

"None. But as we both know, if he stays true to form, he'll soon be scouring the countryside for you. Even now he may be searching for you. But there we have him; the sea leaves no footprints."

Danaë felt the pain of loss. Never to see Ramtat again would be a punishment in itself. "When we reach our destination, we will plan our strategy. I believe I should request an audience with the queen as soon as possible. Do you not agree?"

Uriah nodded, his gaze locked with Danaë's. "Aye. It would not be wise to let too much time go by."

She stared into the distance. "He will come after me, Uriah — he won't stop until he finds me."

"Lord Ramtat?"

"Yes. He is relentless."

"That is another reason we must clear your name as soon as we can."

Even though Danaë was free, she still felt chained to Ramtat. She tried to imagine what he'd do when he returned home and found she'd escaped.

"Life has become difficult, Uriah. There was a time when I knew peace and contentment. Now I know neither."

He patted her hand. "I know. But it will change — you shall see."

She met his troubled gaze. "Thank you for all your loyal service and for never giving up on me."

He looked out to sea. "Child, you are the joy of my life. I will see you happy before I die."

He hadn't called her "child" in a long time, and she was warmed by the affection in his voice. "There will be no talk of death." She suddenly smiled, heartened by the loyalty of those around her. She would not feel sorry for herself — she had everything to live for. Danaë touched her stomach and felt warmth spread over her. Her monthly flow had not arrived. She was almost sure a child grew inside her — Ramtat's child. For the sake of this baby, she had to reclaim her life so she could prepare a safe home before the birth.

Later, she would tell Uriah and Minuhe that she had conceived, but for now, she wanted to keep her precious secret to herself.

She turned toward Alexandria, wondering

what Ramtat was doing at that moment. What would he think if he knew he was going to be a father?

What did it matter? With this baby, she would always have a part of Ramtat with her.

The sun was going down, and the evening breeze rippled through the branches of the trees. Low clouds drifted by, shadowing the land. Ramtat hobbled outside, feeling pain with each step he took. A servant had placed cushions on a bench so he could be more comfortable. He had not realized how near he had come to death until the queen's physician had told him of the blood loss and the infection that had raged through his bloodstream.

With each passing day, the pain lessened, but he was still weak. Today was his first full day out of bed, and he was restless to return home . . . and to Danaë.

"Well, it is about time you got out of bed." Caesar smiled, looking pleased. "I send you on a little errand, and you manage to turn it into a fiasco."

"Taking a dagger in the side was not in my plans."

The Roman sat down on a nearby bench. "I'll say this for you — you know how to

347

get everyone's attention. Even the queen waited upon you like a servant. I was starting to get jealous of all the attention she was showering on you."

"I thought I remembered Her Majesty in my delirium, but then I wasn't sure if it was she, or Danaë, who gave me water."

"Ah. Then no one has told you that your little bird has taken flight?"

Ramtat tensed. "What do you mean?"

"I mean your prisoner went over the garden wall and fled." Caesar leaned back and stared at the sky. "I can tell you Queen Cleopatra was not happy with that news."

"She knows about Ptolemy?"

"Aye. Despite your delirium, you delivered the message. Cleopatra is the power in Egypt these days. I have to confess, when you first told me that she was the right ruler for Egypt, I had my doubts."

"And now?"

"I have watched her myself, and I have to admit, Egypt will be blessed to have her on the throne."

Ramtat was only half listening to Caesar. "What can you tell me about Lady Danaë?"

"That there was a search made for her, but it turned up naught. She has disappeared, and I fear you will never see her again, unless there was a real plot afoot, and that I doubt."

Ramtat leaned back and closed his eyes. Never see Danaë again — what a cold and empty world it would be. He should be angry that she had escaped, but in truth he was relieved that she would not have to face Cleopatra's wrath. Wherever Danaë was, he hoped she was safe. As soon as possible, he would search for her.

"Lord Harique told Antinanious that if he could find the Jew, Uriah, he would find the young woman. A search was made for him, but he too has disappeared, as has the lady's childhood nurse, so at least we can conclude she's not alone. Cleopatra sees your prisoner's escape as proof that she is not Mycerinus's daughter."

Ramtat closed his eyes, and realized he could not search for Danaë. If he brought her back to Alexandria, it would undoubtedly mean her death. It was better if he let her go.

Uriah's brother, Zaphaniah, was every bit as kind as his older sibling. Against her wishes, Danaë was given the best room in the small house. Other than an elderly housekeeper, Anai, the brother had no servants or family, tended his flocks alone.

Obsidian was a shock to Zaphaniah, even

though he'd been told to expect the big cat and had built a sturdy shelter to contain her. Tyi was given the freedom to come and go as he liked. Faraji found the farm to his liking and spent much of his time tilling the soil.

Minuhe, however, proved more troublesome. She had hardly entered the house before she insulted Anai. She refused to allow the woman to cook for Danaë or even serve her food. Anai was pouting, and Minuhe was scoffing.

Danaë knew she had to remove her group from poor Zaphaniah's life so he could again know peace.

It was late on the third night that Danaë sat under the stars with the two brothers. "I have a plan," Uriah stated. "It would involve your going to Alexandria," he told his brother.

Zaphaniah nodded in agreement. "I'm the obvious one to go — no one will recognize me. What would you have me do, Brother?"

Danaë put her hand on Zaphaniah's. "You have done so much for us already. I hesitate to involve you in my troubles. Even now if Queen Cleopatra discovers you have helped me, you may be in danger."

He studied the young woman who meant so much to his brother. "I care not for that.

You and your father have treated my brother with dignity, and I know he loves you like a daughter. If not for your father's generosity, I would not have this farm."

"This is something I know nothing about."

Uriah leaned back and stared up at the stars. "Lord Mycerinus bought me from the slave market the same day he bought your mother. From the first, he showed me nothing but kindness. When he discovered I knew ciphers in several languages, he determined I would be your tutor when you were old enough for me to teach."

"My father was a kind man. He would not be happy about the stain on his good name. I wish I could have been a better daughter to him."

"Do not say that," Uriah protested. " 'Tis Harique who stains the name, not you."

"How did my father help you, Zaphaniah?"

"Lord Mycerinus loaned me the money to buy this farm. He gave me years to repay him and charged me no interest. He was a truly good man, and I am proud to have this opportunity to do something for his daughter."

Tears gathered in Danaë's eyes. "Thank you. Thank you both."

"Now —" Zaphaniah spoke in a gruff, but

gentle, tone. "Tell us your plan, Brother."

"Everything must be timed perfectly for it to work," Uriah said, huddling nearer to the others and lowering his voice although there was no one about to overhear them. "First, you must go to the High Priest of Isis and ask him if he will present the adoption documents to the queen on the day she grants us an audience. When she hears who asks for the audience, I think she will not keep us waiting too long."

Zaphaniah nodded. "Will the high priest see me?"

"All you have to do is tell his servant you come in the name of Lady Danaë."

Danaë's eyes widened. "And then what?"

Uriah rose up and walked to and fro, his rough garment slapping against his legs. "This is the way I see it . . ."

Theodotus stared into the starry night as the horse-drawn cart rattled over cobbled streets. He directed his slave onto a dusty road that led out of the city, his mind racing ahead to the task that awaited him. King Ptolemy was dead — drowned in his heavy armor, or so it was said. The rival Theodotus had hated above all others was also dead, killed by the queen's man, Apollodorus.

His heart burned with the need for revenge — not that he'd loved the king, or even liked him, but with the king's death, Theodotus's ambitions had died as well. Word had gone out that he was to be arrested on sight, and he'd guessed that his death was imminent. But before he died, he would take the true enemy of Egypt with him.

Queen Cleopatra!

It was said the queen had been impregnated by Caesar. Surely the gods would smile on him if he could send the queen and her unborn Roman whelp to their deaths!

They were now in open country, and the full moon illuminated the landscape. Theodotus wished it had been a darker night, but his task would not take long, and he hoped there would be no one to witness his task. But what did it matter? He was a dead man anyway.

He congratulated himself on how cleverly he had avoided being arrested thus far. He'd taken three of his slaves through a secret passageway that led directly to the dead king's chamber. The rooms had been dark and deserted, stripped of all wealth. Even the silken coverlet had been rolled up to be discarded. Queen Cleopatra had wasted no time in erasing every trace of her brother —

but luckily the cheetah was still in its cage. Theodotus had easily smuggled the animal out through the secret passages. He had taken up residence in a deserted house at the edge of Alexandria, where he had meticulously completed the cheetah's training. Until now, Jabatus had not killed a human. But tonight the cat was to be put to the test.

He'd instructed a frightened Nute to poke and prod the cat with sharp sticks wrapped in clothing that had belonged to Cleopatra, introducing Jabatus to the queen's scent, and identifying her as his tormentor. Yesterday he'd stopped feeding the animal so it would be hungry enough to kill — he hoped.

In the back of the cart he could hear the cheetah pacing and growling. It was making his slave Nute extremely nervous. Poor Nute had every reason to be apprehensive.

Tonight he would be the cat's prey.

The silly slave had been so grateful when Theodotus had presented him with a fine robe, and charged him to wear it tonight. Little did Nute know he wore a robe that belonged to a queen, and carried her scent.

When they reached a secluded valley hidden by hills on three sides, he motioned for Nute to halt. "I will need you to climb that small hill to the north," he instructed the slave. "Run. Do it quickly."

Theodotus could tell that Nute was confused, but the slave immediately obeyed.

When Nute was halfway up the hill, Theodotus released the cat. "Go Jabatus! Kill!"

Theodotus had an anxious moment when the cat turned in his direction with a growl deep in his throat. Theodotus waved one of the queen's scarves under the cat's nose and said once more, "Kill!"

To his relief, Jabatus leaped from the cart and raced after the luckless slave. Theodotus waited breathlessly as the animal swiftly caught up with Nute and took him screaming to the ground. Theodotus gripped his hands while the cheetah ripped the slave's throat open, and blood splattered all about. With his heart pounding, Theodotus watched the hungry cat devour its prey.

He smiled. Now Jabatus was ready to perform a duty for the gods.

CHAPTER
TWENTY-FIVE

Ramtat tied the leather lace of his knee-high sandals and stood. His servant settled a leather jerkin over Ramtat's blue tunic and fastened him into his bronze armor. Today he was to take up his position beside the queen, and it was not a task he relished. Not that he didn't love his queen, but he thought the duty should have gone to someone other than him — someone who wished to be heaped with honor.

He slid his helmet in place and hurried through the corridor and out the front door. Ramtat stared at the escort of honor the queen had sent him, and he frowned. This was a frivolous existence, and not to his liking. He was a man who loved to ride across the desert with his wild Bedouin tribesmen or run his estates himself. He was not a courtier; he preferred a simpler life.

But what did any of that matter now that Danaë was not at his side?

"General," one of the soldiers said, crossing his arm over his chest in a salute and handing Ramtat a scroll. "Her Majesty asked that I give you this. We are to ride directly to the palace."

Ramtat unrolled the papyrus and read it as he walked to his horse. A moment later he stopped short and stared toward the palace. Then he mounted his horse and raced through the streets, his guard of honor scrambling to catch up with him.

Many citizens knew who he was and bowed respectfully as he passed them by. But Ramtat paid no attention to anyone. Chickens squawked and scattered as his horse knocked over a cage. On he rode with just one thought in mind.

Danaë.

He would see her today. That she had asked for an audience with the queen puzzled him. What could it mean?

Danaë did not know how this day would end. She was nervous as a guard led her and Uriah down a long corridor.

When she stepped inside the chamber, she found it smaller than the elaborate throne room where she had first seen King Ptolemy. On the dais there was a single throne — Queen Cleopatra ruled alone. There were very few people in the room, but Danaë kept her gaze averted, not wanting to meet anyone's eyes.

She glanced up at the dais and saw the man she knew must be the High Priest of Isis because he wore the white tiger skin across his shoulder. He nodded at Danaë and smiled. Uriah stood on Danaë's right, and she was comforted by his solid strength. She almost stumbled when she saw Harique standing across the room with his arms folded over his chest, his hard gaze upon her.

Uriah caught her arm. "Courage. You are the one in the right, and it will be proven here today."

Two tall men entered and climbed to the dais to stand on opposite sides of the throne. One was foreign in appearance, and Danaë imagined he was the Sicilian, Apollodorus. And that would make the other man the queen's adviser, Antinanious.

A gong sounded near the door, and a man's voice announced the arrival of the queen. Danaë was so frightened, she was afraid she would faint. She had eaten no morning meal because the smell of food made her feel ill.

She bowed low, watching as a pair of small feet adorned with gold jeweled sandals swept by. She grasped Uriah's arm, fearing she could not stand on her own, and he looked at her in concern.

Slowly Danaë raised her head. Her gaze collided with the most beautiful kohl-lined green eyes she had ever seen. Queen Cleopatra was magnificent in a blue Grecian gown with gold trim. Her hair was covered with the golden Crown of Isis. Danaë's gaze fastened on the necklace Cleopatra wore, and her heart shuddered. Her necklace was identical to the one Danaë wore about her own neck.

Looking up into Queen Cleopatra's face, Danaë saw the flash of a smile — or had she? It was gone so quickly, she wasn't sure if she'd only imagined it.

Movement to the queen's right caught her eye, and Danaë stared into a face she had thought never to see again.

Ramtat could not take his eyes off Danaë. Her black hair shone like ebony; unadorned, it fell about her shoulders like fine silk. She was dressed simply in a white robe and leather sandals, but no woman in the room, not even the queen with all her jewels, could compare with Danaë.

The queen motioned Ramtat closer, and he bent his head to hear what she had to say. "All the players are here. I wonder how it will end."

"I know not, Majesty."

"So this is the young woman who has stolen the heart of my greatest general. I see nothing in her that would merit a stout heart like yours, Lord Ramtat. What is it that you see in her?"

Ramtat knew what she wanted to hear. "She is you, Majesty."

The queen's gaze bore into the young beauty. "I see that she is a Ptolemy. It could well be that she craves my throne."

Ramtat was swamped by fear for Danaë. "You must remember she left safety and came to you. Would a guilty person do such a thing?"

"You defend her!"

"I, like the others here, await your judgment."

"Then let it begin." She settled her gaze on the handsome man who had been languishing in her prison until today. He looked somewhat paler than the arrogant lord who had brought accusations weeks before. "Lord Harique, do you still hold to the story that this young woman is your slave, and that she pretended to be the daughter of Lord Mycerinus's house?"

Harique swept into a low bow. "It is as I

said, Gracious Majesty." He pointed to Danaë. "She is my slave, and so is the man who stands beside her."

Queen Cleopatra motioned for Danaë to approach. "Have you an answer to this man's charge, young woman?"

Danaë moved hesitatingly forward and made an elegant bow.

"Well, speak!"

"Your Majesty, it is true I was not born of Lord Mycerinus's blood, but this I did not know until the last day of his life. I grew up believing I was his daughter, and he legally adopted me before his death."

"Lies!" Harique shouted. "She was always a slave in my uncle's house."

Ramtat was watching Danaë, and he saw her flinch. But she made no reply.

"Will you not defend yourself?" the queen asked, leaning closer. In truth, she was enjoying herself while watching Lord Ramtat squirm. "What of your mother?" The queen watched the young woman raise a clear, honest gaze to her.

"I'm told my mother died on the day I was born. I know nothing of her but that she was a slave. My father . . . Lord Mycerinus bought her at a slave auction and later made her his wife. She was with child at that time — and she gave birth to me a few months later."

Queen Cleopatra watched Danaë closely, for she was good at distinguishing truth from lie. "Do you know who your real father was?"

"Nay. And neither did Lord Mycerinus. I was told that my mother was frightened of her past, and she kept her secret to her death."

The queen leaned back, knowing honesty when she heard it. "Then you would have no claim on your real father's estate should you learn his identity?"

"No one knows who he is, Your Majesty, and I care not. I could not have had a better father than the one I grew up with."

"What say you to all this, Lord Harique?"

"Lies — all lies."

The queen swung her head back to Danaë. "Do you have documents that will prove Lord Mycerinus made you his legal daughter?"

Harique looked smug, and Danaë had to turn her gaze away from him before she could answer. "I have, Majesty."

The chamber fell into silence until Harique spoke. "Impossible!"

"Why so, Lord Harique?" The queen's gaze was steady on him.

"No such document exists."

"My good Kheleel, do you have in your possession such a document?"

The high priest stepped forward and bowed low. "I do, Exalted One."

"Produce it for my inspection."

Danaë could not help glancing up at Ramtat. His expression was reserved and distant as his gaze brushed across her face. She wished she knew what he was thinking. He was not the man who had held her in his arms, the man who had made her love him — now he looked every inch the queen's general, stoic, hard, unfeeling. She resisted the urge to place her hand on her slightly rounded stomach where his baby lay.

Looking back at the queen, Danaë watched as she read the document and then asked the high priest how it had come into his possession.

" 'Twas given into my care by Uriah, the Jew."

"Impossible," Harique hissed.

"Lord Harique, do you accuse my high priest of speaking false?"

For the first time, Harique felt uncertain — he'd been sure that all the documents had been destroyed. He saw the folly of accusing an esteemed man like the high priest of being untruthful. It seemed that Lord

Mycerinus had won, even from his grave. But Harique thought of one more way to turn the tide in his favor. "I do not doubt that the high priest believes the document to be genuine. But for all we know, it could have been faked by Uriah, the Jew. It is known by all that he has always been partial to Danaë."

The queen knew she had the man now, and she was ready to move in for the final stab. Lord Harique was not the smartest of men. He was about to tumble into a trap she had set for him, and, foolish man, he didn't see it coming. "What do you propose we do, Lord Harique?"

"I do not ask for the woman's death. I merely wish to take my slave, Danaë, and bother Your Majesty no longer."

Ramtat watched the queen smile — she was up to something. She leaned back and fixed a cold stare on Lord Harique that would have chilled the dead. Ramtat's gaze moved to Danaë, who was looking pale and shaken. He longed to go to her, but he knew he must wait for this game to conclude. If it turned out that Danaë was a slave, he would buy her from Lord Harique, no matter how much it cost.

Queen Cleopatra was clearly enjoying herself. "Lord Harique, would you ask me to turn over to you as a slave, a princess of the royal house, and my half-sister?"

The room fell silent!

Harique had turned a sickly color and stepped quickly backward.

Danaë's eyes widened with disbelief.

Ramtat was stunned.

The high priest looked smug.

Queen Cleopatra smiled.

"You see, Lord Harique, Lady Danaë, who is in all actuality Princess Danaë, was my father's daughter. Does that not make her my sister?"

Danaë was in shock. Could it be true that the dead king was her real father? She looked into Uriah's eyes, and saw that he was as confused as she.

Shaken, Harique dropped to his knees and lowered his forehead to the floor. "Majesty, how could I have known? Spare my life, I beg you!"

The contempt on Queen Cleopatra's face was apparent to all. "I will do better than spare your life — I will allow another to pass judgment on you."

Harique glanced up with hope on his face. "Most Gracious Majesty, from this day forward I shall be your true and loyal servant."

Queen Cleopatra nodded to the guard

who stood by the door. "Bring forward the person who will pass final judgment on Lord Harique."

A slight woman moved hesitantly into the chamber, her frightened gaze going to her husband, Lord Harique, and then in bewilderment to the queen.

"Come forward, Lady Tila," Antinanious said in a booming voice. "Your queen would speak to you."

The woman fell down on her knees, trembling. "What have I done to displease you, Mighty Queen?" she asked in a quivering voice.

"Nay, 'tis not what you've done. I would ask you what I should do with your husband."

Lady Tila looked even more confused, and she rose shakily to her feet. "But surely it is not for me to judge."

"Tell the queen," Antinanious ordered, "if you know why Lord Harique lodged charges against Princess Danaë."

At first the woman could not find her voice, and then she spoke so softly she could hardly be heard. A stern glance from Antinanious made her blurt out her explanation. "My husband has always lusted after his uncle's daughter. He would have her even if it brought the world down around him. He is sick in the mind, and I care not what you do to him."

The queen continued questioning Lord Harique's wife. "You always thought of Lady Danaë as Lord Mycerinus's daughter?"

"Aye. She was his daughter in every way it counted. Beyond that I know naught."

Queen Cleopatra's voice was cold and deadly. "I have decided your punishment, Lord Harique. First, all titles shall be stripped from you. All the property and holdings that came to you from Lord Mycerinus shall be ceded to his adopted daughter. You shall be escorted to the border of Egypt and banished for all time." Her head swung to the cowering man's wife. "You have the opportunity to go with your husband if that is your wish, or you may proclaim yourself divorced from him and remain a loyal citizen of Egypt."

Lady Tila did not bother to look at the pitiful man kneeling before the queen. "I choose Egypt."

"Very well. Then you may leave." After Tila was led from the room, the queen motioned for a guard to come forward. "Take this man to the border and see him gone from my country."

It took two guards to lift the quivering

Harique to his feet, and they had to practically drag him from the chamber.

During the entire proceedings, Danaë had stood in dignified silence, but her heart was pounding inside her. Too much had happened. How could she be the daughter of a king? She didn't want to be — she wanted life to go back to the way it had been before she'd been caught in this whirlwind. She hardly noticed when the guards led Harique out of the room, or when his wife was led away. She was leaning heavily on Uriah now, and Danaë hoped she could remain strong when the queen passed judgment on her. She now understood why her mother had been so afraid. Anyone who stood close to the throne was in jeopardy.

Danaë's head suddenly jerked up, and she felt the air charged with danger. Some sixth sense warned her that something was terribly wrong. Her gaze swept across the chamber, and she was the first one to see the peril. Theodotus, King Ptolemy's tutor, emerged from a curtained area with a chained cheetah at his side. From its distinctive markings, she recognized it as Jabatus.

To her horror, she saw the tutor unleash the chain and urge the animal forward.

"Kill!" he screamed. "Kill!"

It was as if everyone in the room were

frozen. Since the guards had left to escort the luckless Harique and his wife out of the chamber, Ramtat was the first to react. His dagger sang through the air, slamming into the tutor's heart, and sending him to the floor. By the time Ramtat turned to take on the cheetah, he realized his mistake. The cat was already stalking the queen, and his dagger was buried in Theodotus!

Danaë saw at once that the cat's attention was focused on the queen. As Jabatus slunk lower across the floor, his glassy stare never wavered from Queen Cleopatra. Without thinking, Danaë rushed forward, hoping she could reach the cat before it attacked the queen. She leaped in the air just as the cheetah sprang. With a heavy crash, Danaë and the cat fell to the floor. With her arms locked around Jabatus's neck, she felt pain rip through her arm, and then the deadly claws raked across her shoulder.

Apollodorus stepped in front of the queen while Ramtat rushed toward Danaë, knowing he would not reach her in time. Danaë had sacrificed herself for the life of the queen. Already the cheetah was going for Danaë's throat.

Danaë grabbed the cheetah's head, yanking hard. "Jabatus, look at me!" She yanked again. "I said, look at me!"

The cat snarled, baring its teeth.

"Stop!" Danaë tried not to think of the pain that was almost overwhelming her, but to concentrate on stemming the cat's lust for blood. "Jabatus, you will look at me!"

The yellow eyes that stared into hers were the eyes of a killer, wild, unthinking, driven only by blood lust. She slammed her fist into the animal's nose, and the cat blinked. Danaë knew the very moment Jabatus recognized her. "You will hear me and obey!"

A rumble started deep in the cheetah's throat. Where moments before, the cat had been intent on killing, he now purred deep in his throat.

Danaë was in pain, and the cat's weight was crushing her. The world was spinning, and she feared she would lose consciousness before she could control the animal.

She ran her hands soothingly over the soft fur. "Gentle down. Cease. Hear my words and heed me."

Ramtat stood over them helplessly, his sword drawn, but he was afraid to strike lest he hit Danaë. He didn't know how badly she was hurt; he only knew the blood pooling on the marble floor was hers.

Danaë met Ramtat's gaze, and she nodded sorrowfully. "You must do it. Beautiful

Jabatus has been corrupted and will kill if he's allowed to live."

Ramtat saw the sadness in her eyes, and he watched her hand glide over the animal's fur. "Strike between the shoulder blades for a quick kill." She closed her eyes, and tears fell on the soft coat. She took the head of the beautiful cheetah and held it to her as gently as she would a baby. "Do it now."

Ramtat's strike was true. The cat gave a long sigh, then shuddered and died.

Ramtat yanked the lifeless animal off Danaë and tossed it aside. "Beloved," he said, going to his knees and pulling her into his arms. "What have you done?"

Danaë saw the queen kneel beside her and wrap her own silken scarf around her wounded shoulder.

"Little sister, you would have sacrificed your life for mine. No one has ever done half so much."

Faces swarmed about Danaë in a swirl of light. Uriah bent beside her, the queen, and Ramtat. "Your Majesty," Danaë said so faintly that the queen had to lean forward to hear her words. "Do not let me lose my baby."

An anguished cry escaped Ramtat's lips, and he drew her tightly against him.

"Take her to my quarters," the queen

commanded. She glanced at the dead Theodotus, then turned to the high priest.
"Perform the ceremony and recite the ritual
that will cleanse this room of all evil."

CHAPTER
TWENTY-SIX

Danaë opened her eyes and blinked. She hurt everywhere, but especially her left shoulder. She licked her dry lips and tried not to think about the pain. When her vision cleared, she found she was lying in an enormous bed with soft cushions, and the coverlet was like gossamer. The room was huge and luxurious, and there were steps that led to a wide terrace, beyond which she could see the blue of the Mediterranean.

Hearing the door open and the sound of soft sandaled feet, she watched Queen Cleopatra sweep toward her, her movements like poetry. Danaë tried to rise, but the queen placed a hand on her arm to stop her.

"Little sister, you have been injured. You must not move, or you could break open your wound."

"Will I recover?"

The queen smiled. "You have strength in you — you shall recover."

Danaë licked her lips and placed her hand on her stomach. "My baby?"

"The baby is fine. But my physician wants you to remain in bed for a while longer." Cleopatra looked at the young woman who had saved her life. Danaë was blood of her blood, and she needed family — she needed a loving sister at this time of her life. "I am also with child," she admitted.

Danaë's eyes widened. "You will bear Caesar's child?"

Cleopatra's laughter was magical; it had the quality of making those who heard it want to laugh as well. "Little sister, you and I have been impregnated by warriors and strong-headed men. The sons of Caesar and Ramtat could rule the world."

Danaë found herself feeling sisterly love toward the queen, and she felt the blood tie between them. "Can you tell me why you call me little sister?"

"It is really quite simple. Your mother, Lady Eilana, was descended from Ptolemaic lineage. She was a cousin to my father, and perhaps the one woman he truly loved. When you are well enough, I will show you your mother's likeness."

"I know nothing of her."

"I knew only palace rumors until I found my old nurse, and she enlightened me. I had this knowledge before you came to the palace yesterday, but I wanted to see what kind of person you were before I decided whether I should claim you as my sister."

Danaë's eyes widened. "I don't know what to say. How are we connected?"

"Your mother, Eilana, was the daughter of one of my father's generals. From what I was told, my father — our father — fell in love with Eilana, and she loved him as well. She was already carrying his child when the mother of my half-brother, Ptolemy, tried to have her slain. Perhaps she felt threatened by the child Eilana carried, I do not know." Cleopatra looked thoughtful. "As you probably know, this family too often turns on its own, but we won't dwell on that. When your mother disappeared, everyone thought she was dead — surely a rumor fostered by Ptolemy's mother. My old nurse told me my father was inconsolable for a long time afterward." Cleopatra touched Danaë's cheek. "So you see, you are my sister, and a princess royal."

Suddenly Cleopatra's gaze became hard. "But never make the mistake of thinking you have any claim on my throne."

"Majesty, I would not want your throne. I would rather be a pauper and forage for food than face what you face every day."

The tense moment passed. "I know you are telling the truth," Cleopatra said. "Had you wanted my throne, you would not have risked your life for mine. I will never doubt you."

Danaë smiled. "Of all the men I could imagine as my blood father, I would never have considered the king." She looked wistful. "One day perhaps you will tell me about our father."

"And when you are feeling up to it, you can talk to my old nurse about your mother. She can tell you more than I."

Danaë was having trouble keeping her eyes open. "This is your room, is it not?"

Cleopatra smiled. "It is. You will remain here until you are completely healed."

"Thank you for your care."

"Thank you for my life." Cleopatra frowned. "I saw the cat coming toward me, and I knew what it felt like to taste death. Then I watched you run at the cat and place yourself between us, and in that moment, I knew the true meaning of loyalty. The scars on your arm and shoulder will show your bravery to all, and I will make certain everyone honors you."

Danaë saw no reason to tell Cleopatra that she had once favored Ptolemy to rule Egypt. Ramtat had been right — here was a queen worthy of the title. "I wasn't brave, Your Majesty. I just acted on instinct."

"My good general, Ramtat, was acting on instinct as well when he rushed to you." Cleopatra arched her eyebrow. "He has been waiting in the garden all night for a chance to see you. Do you want to see him?"

"Nay."

"You carry his child."

"I will raise my child alone. I don't need him."

A sad smile touched Cleopatra's lips. "In that, as in so many other things, we are not unalike, little sister. Caesar will be leaving before my child is born, although I would wish it otherwise."

Ramtat buried his head in his hands. Danaë was dead — he knew it. She had been unconscious when he'd carried her to the queen's quarters. Although he had made inquires, no one seemed to know anything.

He got up and paced, then stared into the distant sunrise while guilt weighed heavily on his shoulders. Slumping down on the bench once more, he shook his head. When he thought of the way he had treated her, it made him ashamed.

He heard footsteps and rose expectantly, but it was only a servant extinguishing the torches along the path. Ramtat would never be able to forget the vision of Danaë running toward the cheetah, or the moment he'd realized he couldn't get there in time to save her.

Again his stomach tightened. He had accused her of wanting to kill the queen. How Danaë must despise him!

A thought came to him that he had pushed to the back of his mind because it was too painful to consider. Danaë was with child — his child. If death claimed her, it would also claim his unborn baby. He thought of the long weeks they had been apart when she'd needed him the most. She had fled from him, prepared to have his baby alone. Would she ever have told him he was the father? He did not think so.

This time the footsteps he heard were light — the tread of a queen. Ramtat jumped to his feet and bowed. "Majesty."

"Lord Ramtat, I see you are still here."

"She's dead, isn't she?"

Cleopatra shook her head. "Nay. She lives. Her wounds are deep but not life-threatening."

"And the child?"

"It's too soon to tell, but Danaë is a Ptolemy, and that gives her certain strength."

He bowed his head. "How could I have known? In trying to do the best, I did the worst."

"Take no blame for that. You were not the only one who thought ill of my little sister."

Ramtat let out a long breath. "Then she truly is of your blood?"

"Princess Danaë is my father's daughter. That is why you saw the resemblance between us."

"May I see her?"

Cleopatra smiled. She thought it would do no harm if this valiant warrior had to wait a while for what he wanted most in the world. "Nay. It seems that my little sister refuses to see you."

"That is my child in her belly," he said, feeling a sudden possessiveness. "I have every right to be there with her."

Cleopatra shrugged, and hid her smile. "As for the child, I have not quite decided who the father is; I am toying with the notion that Danaë's child is the offspring of a god — a lesser god, of course, seeing that Danaë will never be queen."

"Nay, the child is mine, as is the mother."

He looked so fierce, it was all Cleopatra could do not to laugh. "Do you dispute the word of your queen?"

"Aye, in this I do, Gracious Majesty. I will

not deny my own flesh."

"Try to understand, Lord Ramtat, you are but a lord, and Danaë is royal. She also bears a heritage even I cannot claim. She is a descendant of the great Alexander. Does that not place her far above you? How can I sanction a marriage between the two of you? For the good of Egypt, Danaë may have to marry the king of some country we need as an ally."

Ramtat felt Danaë slipping away from him. "In truth, I am unworthy of her. She is an extraordinary young woman."

The queen decided to stop teasing Lord Ramtat. "Like her, you are extraordinary. Did you not also spill your blood in my service? I have decided that if she marries you, it will be good for Egypt."

Ramtat was still uncertain, even with the queen's approval. "Will she have me?"

"That I do not know. You will have to do your own talking." She moved down the path in the direction of Caesar's quarters. "Come back tomorrow. You may see her then."

Ramtat moved out of the garden toward the front gate. When he was mounted on his horse, he saw the old man who had accompanied Danaë to the palace the day before. Reining in his horse, he nodded. "If you want news of Lady Danaë, she is recovering."

Uriah looked at the man long and hard. "*Princess* Danaë has asked to see me. She can tell me how she is faring herself."

Ramtat watched the man walk away, light of step and with pride in his stance. She would see her servant, but she did not want to see him, Ramtat. Perhaps she would even refuse to see him tomorrow, or ever, for that matter.

Ramtat could not blame her after all that had passed between them.

Uriah stood beside Danaë's bed, staring at the scroll she had given him.

"You are free, my loyal Uriah. You can go anywhere you want, and you have enough gold to buy whatever you desire."

He lowered his gaze to her. "It should make a difference in how I feel, but it doesn't. I have always been treated as a valuable member of the House of Sahure. I have no home other than where you are."

Danaë could hardly contain her happiness, and she laid her hand on his blue-veined one. "I was hoping you would wish to stay. I need you in my life." She touched her stomach fleetingly. "I want this child to know and love you as much as I do."

Uriah sat down on the edge of the bed and smiled. "So, is this child going to give me the trouble you have?"

Her hand slipped into his. "Most probably."

"Then let it be. For you have brought me joy, even though at times you broke my heart."

"My dear, Uriah. What would I have done without you?"

"You would have survived — those with your courage always do."

CHAPTER
TWENTY-SEVEN

Ramtat had decided that if Danaë refused to see him, he'd bust down the door. But much to his surprise, when he reached the palace, he was met on the steps by a maid-servant who bowed to him.

"Lord Ramtat, if you please, will you follow me?"

He nodded, not knowing where she was taking him. When she swung open the doors to a huge bedchamber, he saw Danaë looking pale, her arm and shoulder bandaged and propped on cushions.

The doors closed behind him, and he was alone with her.

"I asked to see you, Lord Ramtat. I hope you don't mind." She watched him move slowly toward her, his eyes shimmering, a soft expression on his face, and she steeled herself not to let down her guard. There were matters she wanted to discuss with him. She needed to make him understand he had no obligation to her or her child.

She knew him so well, she could tell he had suffered. "I heard of your wound, and I understand it was serious. I am happy to see you have recovered."

He said nothing until he drew even with her, and then he seated himself on a stool. "Can you ever forgive me?"

She saw the pulse in his throat and knew he was having a hard time facing her. "I understand why you did what you did. Egypt needs Cleopatra."

"I'm not here to talk about Egypt. Why didn't you tell me you were with child?"

Danaë raised her chin, reminding him very much of her exalted half-sister. "I don't owe you any explanation — this baby is mine."

"I'm the father. No matter that the queen toys with the notion it was sired by a god."

Danaë could not keep from laughing. "Cleopatra likes to tease. I am finding her delightful, and I can see why Caesar is fascinated by her."

Ramtat leaned back and folded his arms. "So, all along you were a princess of Egypt."

"I would rather be known as Lord Mycerinus's daughter. He is the father of my heart."

"Your loyalty does you justice. I should

have recognized that quality in you from the first."

Her gaze fell to his lips, and she wanted more than anything for him to kiss her.

He stood and walked to the steps that led to the garden. "Danaë," he said, turning back to her. "I have so much to say to you, I hardly know where to start."

She plucked at the fine sheeting. "Start at the beginning."

He walked back toward her. She wasn't going to make it easy for him. "I want this child. By rights it's mine."

"This child comes with a mother."

He didn't know he was going to go to her — he didn't know how he found himself on his knees — he didn't know at first that the wetness on his face was tears, because he'd never cried before. "I want the mother. I love you. I have been in torment without you. I know you will have a far different future now that Cleopatra has recognized you as her sister. You have a portion of your father's wealth, and the queen will probably heap even more honors and riches on you. There is no reason you should want to be with me, save one: No one will ever love you as deeply as I do. When I saw you fall under the cheetah, I knew that if you died, my life would be over."

He waited to be rejected — he expected to be.

Danaë touched his face. "I have loved you almost from the beginning. The one thing that kept me from falling into total despair these last days was knowing I carried a part of you with me."

Ramtat wanted to crush her in his arms, but seeing her bandages, he eased his weight onto the bed and pulled her head onto his shoulder. "Suppose I was a high lord of the land and you were a princess royal — would you consent to be my wife?" He tilted her chin, staring into her eyes. "My only wife?"

She smiled. "But you know I have a temper, and you know I am not an easy woman to get along with because I always have my own opinions, and I can't help voicing them."

His lips touched the top of her head. "I do know that."

Danaë tilted her head to look up at him. "If this baby is a son, he will need you to guide and teach him the ways of Egypt, and also of his Bedouin people."

Ramtat's heart was so full, he could hardly speak.

"And if it is a daughter?" he finally asked.

"Ah," she said with a laugh, "then she will teach you."

He dipped his head and lightly touched her lips, unable to stop the passion that burned in him. "I will spend the rest of my life proving myself to you."

She felt tears in her eyes. "There's nothing to prove. I know of your honor, your steadfastness. I now realize what you suffered when you thought you would have to choose between me and Egypt. I love you, Ramtat."

His breathing stopped. He had done nothing to deserve her love, but he would accept it. "When will you be my wife?"

"I want to be completely healed before I come to you."

He wanted to protest. There was no need to wait. He wanted her under his protection now. Besides, he was afraid she might change her mind if he did not tie her to him immediately. But he was not in a bargaining position.

"If you're sure that's what you want."

"Is this a new Ramtat I see?" she asked teasingly.

For his answer, he bent forward, his mouth touching hers gently. When he raised his head, his eyes were glowing, and she snuggled against him.

"There is something I would ask of you for a wedding present," she said.

"Ask anything and it's yours."

"You have a slave named Vika; I would like you to free her."

"I do seem to recall her. She may have her freedom."

"I would also have you settle coins on her so she will never know want."

He nodded. "Agreed."

"And only one more thing. I would like her to marry the man she loves and for him to be honored by you."

He smiled happily, not realizing she was about to strike with the same cunning as her famous sister. "I gladly agree, Danaë. Who is the man? Do I know him?"

"Indeed you do. Ma'sud was your Bedouin guard at the villa here in Alexandria. Fearing he would be blamed after I escaped, I had Uriah inquire into his whereabouts. I was told you sent him to the desert in disgrace. I tricked him — he really didn't deserve that."

She watched Ramtat's eyes narrow with anger; then he looked puzzled, and presently he laughed. "So that's the way you escaped."

"I feel guilty about what I did to the two of them. I encouraged their love for one another so I could slip over the wall."

Ramtat eased her into his arms. "She can

have her freedom and I will settle coins on her; they can marry, and I will honor Ma'sud."

She sighed, her eyes drifting shut. Now that everything was settled, she was so tired she fell asleep.

And Ramtat held her.

Much later, when she awoke she was still in his arms.

It was Danaë's wedding night. The celebration had been going on all day, the wild Bedouins mingling with Egyptian nobility to honor Lord Ramtat and Princess Danaë.

She had met Ramtat's mother and sister, and they had graciously welcomed her into the family. His mother was overjoyed about the baby and was very attentive to Danaë, seeing to her comfort. Minuhe had been in her element, giving orders to everyone, Bedouin and Egyptian alike, and Uriah had stood at Danaë's side until Ramtat claimed her as his wife.

She could hardly wait until the guests retired to their tents so Ramtat would come to her. Instead of being married in Alexandria, they had both decided that as soon as she was well enough to travel, she would go to him in the desert.

Cleopatra had not wanted either of them

to leave her, but grudgingly gave in to Danaë's demand that her husband must be free of palace life or he would not be truly happy.

It had been a sad day when Caesar had sailed away from Alexandria. Danaë had stood beside her half-sister and given her what comfort she could.

Danaë heard scratching on the tapestry at the entrance of the tent. With an impatient growl, Obsidian slashed the delicate weave and came ambling in, hopping on the bed.

"Bad cat," Danaë scolded. "You broke out of your cage again."

Ramtat chose that moment to enter. He glanced down at the shredded tapestry, and then his eyes went to the huge leopard on his bed.

"I don't intend to spend my wedding night with that animal."

Danaë giggled. "Then you remove her. She's being stubborn."

Ramtat went to the bed and glared down at the cat, who merely looked up at him and yawned, swishing her tail.

"Down!" he commanded.

Obsidian rolled onto her back and pawed the air.

Ramtat shoved her, and she licked his hand.

He stabbed his hand toward the cat and

frowned. "Do something."

Danaë slithered toward Ramtat, her eyes half closed. "That cat isn't going anywhere." She rubbed her body against him, and he forgot about the animal on his bed. Lifting Danaë into his arms, he carried her to the inner room and placed her on the bed there. "I have been without you for too long."

Danaë opened her arms to him, and he came to her. "I never thought to be this happy," she said, touching her lips to his.

"You are my life," he whispered.

"I wish we could be at our waterfall."

His voice was gruff. "Tomorrow we'll go there if you like. I have a surprise for you."

Danaë's eyes widened. "Tell me."

"You once planted a thought in my mind, and it was something I knew you would like — can you guess?"

"I said you should build a house there!" She looked at him expectantly. "Can that be it?"

He nodded. "I can deny you nothing."

With joy, she threw her arms around his neck and slid her tongue across his lips, smiling to herself when she heard his quick intake of breath. She was glad she could move this powerful man.

His mouth rested against her forehead. "We will not be taking that pesky cat with us tomorrow."

His hand swept down her thigh. "Or the hawk."

He tugged at her green robe. "Or Uriah."

Then he turned her to face him. "And certainly not Minuhe."

Danaë put her hands on either side of his face. "It will just be the two of us, like the first time we were there."

The sweet scent she wore was going to his head. "Something like that."

She brushed a dark lock of hair off his forehead and looked into the eyes she loved so much. Parting her lips, she offered them to him, and he pulled her closer.

"It is hard to think that I once looked upon you as my enemy," she said.

"I can hardly bear to think about how I treated you then."

"Even while you held me captive, I loved you."

"I had never met a woman as stubborn as you. At first you amused me, and then . . ."

She cocked her head to see his face. "What?"

"And then I became slave and you became master."

She rubbed her lower body against his and smiled. "Although I am a princess royal, I consider you my equal."

His laughter was deep and filled her heart.

"Do not torture me any longer," he said, drawing off his tunic.

She snuggled close to him while he caressed her naked body, looking at the changes in it. His hand moved over her breasts. "These are fuller," he said in wonder.

"Yes. That happens when a woman is with child."

His hand moved over her slightly rounded stomach. He bent and touched his lips to the gentle swell. "I never thought about children until I met you."

Her arms went around him. "We shall have many."

He touched his lips to hers and nudged her legs apart. When he slid into her warmth, he trembled over and over.

She smiled, as only a woman can when she is sure of the man she loves.

ABOUT THE AUTHOR

Constance O'Banyon, a *USA Today* best-selling author, has more than forty books to her credit. A third-generation Texan, she lives in San Antonio with her husband, Jim. You can contact her at obanyon@texas.net.

We hope you have enjoyed this Large Print book. Other Thorndike, Wheeler, and Chivers Press Large Print books are available at your library or directly from the publishers.

For information about current and upcoming titles, please call or write, without obligation, to:

Publisher
Thorndike Press
295 Kennedy Memorial Drive
Waterville, ME 04901
Tel. (800) 223-1244

or visit our Web site at:

www.gale.com/thorndike
www.gale.com/wheeler

OR

Chivers Large Print
published by BBC Audiobooks Ltd
St James House, The Square
Lower Bristol Road
Bath BA2 3SB
England
Tel. +44(0) 800 136919
email: bbcaudiobooks@bbc.co.uk
www.bbcaudiobooks.co.uk

All our Large Print titles are designed for easy reading, and all our books are made to last.